A Masterpiece of Corruption

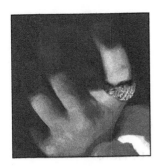

A Masterpiece
of Corruption

L. C. Tyler

FELONY & MAYHEM PRESS • NEW YORK

A MASTERPIECE OF CORRUPTION

A Felony & Mayhem mystery

PRINTING HISTORY
First edition (Constable): 2015
Felony & Mayhem edition (First US edition): 2018

ISBN: 978-1-63194-139-9

Manufactured in the United States of America

Library of Congress Cataloging-in-Publication Data

Names: Tyler, L. C., author.
Title: A masterpiece of corruption / L.C. Tyler.
Description: Felony & Mayhem edition. | New York : Felony & Mayhem Press,
  2018. | "A Felony & Mayhem mystery." | A reissue of the first edition
  published by Constable, 2015.
Identifiers: LCCN 2018006846| ISBN 9781631941399 (pbk.) | ISBN
9781631941573 (ebook)
Subjects: LCSH: Attempted assassination--Fiction. | Mistaken
  identity--Fiction | Great Britain--History--Commonwealth and Protectorate,
  1649-1660--Fiction. | London (England)--History--17th century--Fiction. |
  GSAFD: Mystery fiction. | Legal stories.
Classification: LCC PR6120.Y545 M37 2018 | DDC 823/.92--dc23
LC record available at https://lccn.loc.gov/2018006846

To Tom and Rachel

The icon above says you're holding a copy of a book in the Felony & Mayhem "Historical" category, which ranges from the ancient world up through the 1940s. If you enjoy this book, you may well like other "Historical" titles from Felony & Mayhem Press.

———————————

For more about these books, and other Felony & Mayhem titles, or to place an order, please visit our website at:

www.FelonyAndMayhem.com

Other "Historical" titles from

FELONY&MAYHEM

ANNAMARIA ALFIERI
City of Silver
Strange Gods
The Idol of Mombasa
The Blasphemers

FIDELIS MORGAN
Unnatural Fire
The Rival Queens

KATE ROSS
Cut to the Quick
A Broken Vessel
Whom the Gods Love
The Devil in Music

CATHERINE SHAW
The Library Paradox
The Riddle of the River

LC TYLER
A Cruel Necessity

LAURA WILSON
The Lover
The Innocent Spy
An Empty Death
The Wrong Man
A Willing Victim
The Riot

OLGA WOJTAS
Miss Blaine's Prefect and the
Golden Samovar

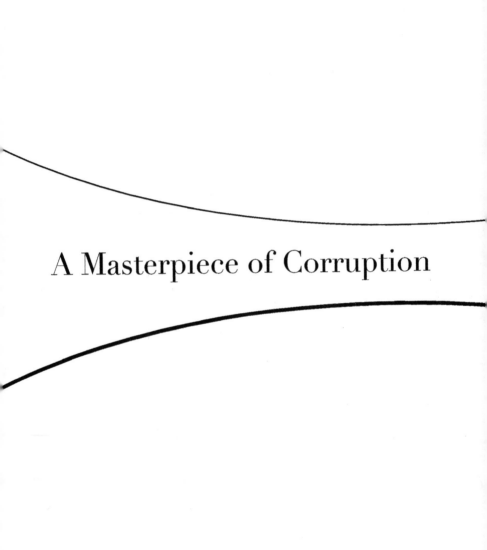

A Masterpiece of Corruption

Shoreham Beach, October 1651

It both deafens and soothes. The thunderclap as the pebbles are flung landward in a cloud of salt spray, then the long, hollow sucking-back as the dark water rushes home. The sea has inched itself almost to the ragged line of bleached driftwood left by the last high tide. There is no point in delaying further, watching one foam-flecked wave follow another. Cromwell's troops are out there somewhere in the black circle of the Downs.

The King does, however, delay further. It is still his right. His Divine Right, you might say. He is looking at some far point on the deserted beach, pale gold in the moonlight. He stands, wrapped tightly in his rough woollen cloak, on the last precious sliver of his kingdom.

'The boat, Your Majesty,' says the taller and older of his two companions, a nervous man it would seem and made more nervous by having to repeat himself. 'A passage at last— France...safety. Would it please Your Majesty to embark?'

'Would it *please* me?' The King cannot help laughing, even now. Laughter. He'll always be known for it. Even during the many long, bleak years to come.

'It would be best to board now, sir,' says the shorter of his companions. He's young, little more than a boy, but he has the sort of aristocratic confidence that new money will never buy you. He's a baronet, having already inherited the title from a father who died contentedly in the old King's service. The young baronet would be willing to die in the new King's service if he had to, but preferably not tonight under this bright moon. They need to get the King into the boat before they are all spotted dithering in a knot on the shoreline.

Time, which was once so plentiful, has run out.

'It will be at least another hour until the tide is high enough,' says the King.

'In an hour's time, Captain Tattersall may have sobered up,' the young baronet points out. 'He may then remember that Your Majesty has a price of one thousand Pounds on his head. It would be more convenient if you and he were both on board when that happens. It would certainly be better that he should not remember it while still within shouting distance of some meddlesome officer of the Republic.'

'Tattersall says he is loyal to the Crown.'

'The whole country was loyal to the Crown once. Men's loyalties change nowadays almost without their noticing. Tattersall is a greasy fellow and smells of fish, but for the moment he sincerely believes he is a Royalist. He has a fine and noble role to play if we can but keep him drunk. And there may yet be men in England whose support for you does not depend on strong ale. Once this night's work is complete, we begin the task of finding them and rallying them.'

'You won't cross to France with me?'

'Wilmot will go with you. We two shall stay.'

The King—for so he can call himself, having been crowned in Scotland at least—laughs again. 'Faith! That will be an uneven contest, Sir Michael: Cromwell's Ironsides on the one hand and any sober Cavaliers you can sweep up on the other. Parliament will outnumber you a hundred to one.'

'They merely have the numbers. We have the cunning. There's more than one way to fight a war.'

The King nods. He has fought the war several ways since Cromwell executed his father, and none of them have been good. That's how he has ended up on Shoreham beach, waiting for the turn of the tide. If they know another way, let them try it by all means.

'Where's Tattersall now?' he asks.

'I can see the good captain making his way down from the tavern. Very slowly.'

'Still loyal to the Crown?'

'Any more loyal and he would pass out.'

'France it is, then,' says the King benignly. 'God pox it.'

He sits motionless in the bows as the sails unfurl, flap wildly, then fill. He does not look back at the lumpy pebble beach nor at the dark mass of the South Downs gathered behind it. His eyes are on the future. The past has proved a disappointing place to be.

The small boat's outline is visible in the moonlight for some time as it tacks backwards and forwards. A Royalist tide is with them, but the wind is fickle and Parliamentary—and the captain's commands are sometimes slurred and difficult to understand. With a slow reluctance, the masts and canvas dwindle into nothing. The moon shines down on a floating image of itself in an otherwise empty world of flickering water.

'That's the end, then,' says the taller man. 'We've just watched the last King of England creep away in a coal barge, leaving his country to rot as it pleases. You, Sir Michael, may do as you see best, but when the Roundheads arrive, I intend to assure them of my undying loyalty to Parliament.'

'You won't help me carry on the fight? You won't help me rally some good-hearted gentlemen to the cause?'

'What fight? What cause? The King is gone. And, just in case you were going to say it, I have to point out that if God ever was on our side, He defected to Cromwell in '45 or '46. The war is lost. For all your brave words, only a fool would now take up arms for the Stuarts. Cromwell has the best army in Europe after the King of Spain. We have nothing.'

'We have our wits,' says Sir Michael. 'And God will see the error of His ways in due course. In the meantime, we must hide our allegiances. We must dissemble. We must plot and scheme. We must wait in the shadows, gather information and write letters. Perhaps with our eyes and our pens we can gain what we have lost with our fists and our swords.'

'Our pens? I doubt you will undo many Roundheads with your pen, however much you sharpen it.'

Sir Michael smiles. 'Really? I'll wager I can write a letter that will kill any man who reads it.'

CHAPTER 1

Six Years Later

London, December 1657

The letter is a single sheet of paper, folded in two and unsealed. It would have been easy for my landlady to have read the contents, which means that she has.

'It was shoved under the door,' she says, making a little pushing motion with her hand, illustrative of the method of delivery. Her face gives nothing away. A plaster saint could not bear a countenance more innocent.

'So you didn't see who left it?' I ask.

'Of course I saw who left it. What do you take me for? I spied him through the small window.'

I wait for her to continue, but information of this sort is not to be had without a little begging.

'And, pray, what did you see, Mistress Reynolds?'

'I saw a fine gentleman, velvet cloak, silk breeches, beaver hat. And lace. Such a lot of lace.' She sighs. There is too little lace in this world today. Too little lace, too much black fustian. Too many sermons, too little laughter. Too much Puritanism, too many prohibitions. Too many fast days and no Christmas ever again. That is her complaint. Disappointingly for her, I own no lace at all and do not regret the lack of a tyrant King. I am not the lodger she hoped for when her husband died and left her so much useful space in the house.

'You saw his face?' I ask.

'He was already walking away.'

'You didn't speak to him then—you didn't ask who the letter was for?'

'I told you—he was walking away.'

'So this may not even be intended for me?' I turn the paper over again in my hand. It does not bear my name, though, equally, it does not bear anyone else's name. 'I mean, if he didn't say it was for John Grey... He might have meant it for you, Mistress Reynolds.'

'Why should anyone write to me like that?'

'Like what?'

'Like in the letter.'

So, she has read it then. But plaster saints are mere Popish idols and only a fool would trust them not to intercept mail.

'Nobody except my mother knows that I am here,' I say.

This is not quite true. My tutor at Lincoln's Inn knows where to find me and I believe that my tailor has discovered my address as a precautionary measure. But I am a new arrival in London and am on letter-writing terms with few. Anyway, as I too read my letter, I see that I have many good reasons for suspecting my mother in this.

Mr S. K. presents his compliments to one newly arrived and begs your presence at his chambers at Gray's Inn. He wishes to be better acquainted with you. Have no fears— he is an honourable man and wishes you no hurt. Tonight at seven o'clock would be agreeable. Ask the porter for directions. The one-eyed porter, not the other one.

'I don't know anyone called Mr S. K.,' she says. 'Do you?'

'Yes,' I say.

'Then it clearly is for you, Mr Grey.'

'I must assume so.'

'He is a friend of yours?'

'Mr S. K.? A friend of my mother's.' I had hoped he was merely a former friend, but it would seem not.

'You have never met him yourself?'

'After a fashion, but we are not well acquainted.'

'And that is why he wishes to set your mind at rest that he intends you no harm?' She purses her lips, as she so often does. It is one of the few things she does really well.

'I agree that the wording is odd in a social invitation, but it is like him to give such an assurance. It is superfluous, which is also much like him. I have no fears for my safety.'

'He is a *gentleman*?'

I notice that my landlady stresses the word 'gentleman'. A person of breeding and taste. A person with gold in his purse. A person with no need to toil for his bread nor to present his bill with compliments and respectfully request prompt payment of the same. Mistress Reynolds has a daughter of slightly more than marriageable age. It is rare for a day to pass without her expressing the fervent hope that I may invite one of my unattached gentleman friends to my chamber, where her daughter may serve us with wine and display such charms as she possesses, which are fewer than her mother imagines. But only a real gentleman will pass muster. She has never encouraged her daughter to linger in my chamber when I am alone there, nor has she encouraged me to consider myself a suitor in any way.

'You could say Mr S. K. was a gentleman,' I concede.

'Not a lawyer like you then?' The Gray's Inn address worries her.

'Some lawyers might be considered gentlemen,' I say. She shakes her head. She has met lawyers before. Like surgeons, we are merely amongst the better sort of tradesmen in her eyes. 'Your friend is a soldier, perhaps?' she suggests. An army officer (at least, a Royalist one) may be impoverished, drunk or illiterate, but nobody would question his gentility.

'He has certainly seen a great deal of fighting,' I say.

'He is of good family?'

'He is related to many of the greatest families in the land.'

'Does he possess much land himself?' She asks the question as though neither she nor her daughter could have any personal financial interest.

'Enough land to satisfy most men, and indeed women, though some of it is forfeit to the State because of his support for the late tyrant Charles Stuart.'

She nods. For her this is no impediment. Like my mother, she still clings to the notion that the Stuarts may one day return and we shall have a King and all will be well. Ancestral castles and abbeys will slip effortlessly back into the hands of impoverished and exiled Cavaliers. Young girls, garlanded in spring flowers, will dance around maypoles. Husbands, handsome and tractable, will be in plentiful supply for maids and widows alike.

'He has a title perhaps?' she asks.

'He possesses many an ancient title.'

She nods again. Not merely a gentleman then, but a nobleman. And the multiplicity of titles points to an ancient Earldom, if not a Marquisate. 'And your good friend...he clearly lives in London?'

'He is no friend, but he lives in London, Brussels, Paris, Yorkshire, Wales, Antwerp, Devon, Calais... He has the ability to be in many places at once, and nowhere at all.'

My landlady frowns. She is no fool and knows when I am mocking her. But she does not yet know what the joke is.

'But he has not been banished for his loyalty to the true King.'

'We have no King, Mistress Reynolds, true or otherwise. Only the threadbare Pretender named Charles Stuart living in the Spanish Netherlands. As for Mr S. K., he travels freely enough by all accounts.'

This last mollifies her a little, but she is still suspicious. Perhaps I am grinning more than I think. She makes one last sally.

'Then, Mr Grey, I hope you will bring him here and take wine with us?'

'That is impossible.'

'Why?'

'Because,' I say, 'he is scarcely six years old.'

'But you said he is a soldier!'

'I assure you he is not a day older.'

My landlady glares at me. 'If you were a proper gentleman yourself, you would not make fun of a poor widow woman so. Indeed you would not.'

'I beg pardon, Mistress,' I begin, but she has turned with a great swish of skirts and petticoats, and is gone back down to her kitchen before I can explain the joke. For everything I have said about Mr S. K. is true. He is scarce six and may not live to be seven. But I have no intention of befriending him in any way and I intend to go and tell him so to his bearded face.

For this is my mother's doing. Oh yes, there can be no mistake about that. She knew Mr S. K. very well indeed. My fear is that she has not abandoned that connection as she promised me she would.

'I hope that you are no longer in correspondence with Mr S. K.,' I said to her not long ago.

'Of course not, dear,' she said, carefully threading a needle. 'I gave all that up, just as you proposed. I am, after all, the wife of a Justice of the Peace.'

'It would be dangerous if you hadn't,' I said.

'You must trust me that I have,' she said, breaking off the crimson thread. 'Though your father, of course, still knows the gentleman concerned.'

'My late father,' I said.

She looked up from her sewing, frowning, head on one side.

'My *late* father may have known him,' I said.

'But of course. Your poor lamented father,' she said, pushing back a wayward curl and resuming her work. 'Whom we miss greatly.'

'Precisely,' I said. 'My dead father. Whom we miss. Let us not forget that. Speaking as a lawyer, my advice to you is that you should not forget that my father is sadly no longer with us.'

My Mother

My mother's difficulty in recalling that my father is dead is due in no small measure to the fact that he is alive and living in Brussels with a Flemish whore.

It is, however, a convenient fiction and one that she would do well to continue, if only for the benefit of her second husband. Since my stepfather is the local magistrate moreover, and would thus have the unfortunate duty of prosecuting his own wife for bigamy, it would certainly be kinder to him that my mother should harbour no lingering doubts about my father's death. Hence her unblushing references, whenever she remembers, to 'your late father' and her occasional but very sincere prayers that he should rest in peace. She is understandably vague about which battle he died at—Naseby and Marston Moor have both been proposed at different times. But she has said nothing to my stepfather about the possibility, however remote, of his living quite comfortably with a young woman of easy virtue in the Low Countries.

At least, she has said nothing in my presence. If it amused my mother to tell my stepfather in private, however... It is perfectly possible that at two or three o'clock in the morning, when a man is most off his guard, she may have chosen to raise it as a topic of conversation. A man without his breeches is a feeble opponent for most women and especially for a woman like my mother. She may well have reasoned that, should he choose to take no immediate action (and my stepfather never takes immediate action on any matter), then he would quickly become an accessory rather than a prosecutor. Indeed, now I think of it, it is very likely that she has done precisely that. Of course, she also possesses information about his own treasonous correspondence with friends of Charles Stuart. That too might weigh with him if he considered denouncing her. The ability to have each other hanged may be the secret of a happy and peaceful marriage.

But I am certain that my mother has told my stepfather no more about her past dealings with Mr S. K. than he needs to know. She has, she says, broken her connections with Mr S. K.— broken them utterly. It would not do for a lady in her position to know him. What puzzles me therefore is why my mother believes that I (who, uniquely in my family, engage in no treasonous correspondence) should now wish to risk my own neck in making the acquaintance of the gentleman she claims to have forsworn.

Outside I hear a bell strike the half-hour. If I leave in ten minutes, I shall be able to meet Mr S. K. at the appointed time and inform him that I am not the fool that my mother takes me for. For this indulgence I hope I may be forgiven. I have little enough money while I study law at Lincoln's Inn and my amusements are few. I have no shillings to pay for the theatre, even if the theatres had not been closed (with good cause) by the State. I have few enough pennies to pay for ale, even if drunkenness had not been proscribed (very wisely) by the Lord Protector's ordinances. Of course, I could go and listen to a learned sermon, which, as for all citizens of the Republic, really ought to count amongst my greatest pleasures. But this evening I can also go and have a little innocent fun at the expense of some of my mother's Royalist acquaintances—foolish young men of distinguished ancestry, with a taste for Brussels lace and ineffectual plotting.

Providing Mr S. K. with a mirror in which he may see himself will afford both pleasure and instruction for us both.

I carry my law books up to my chamber and leave them on one of my two chairs. I would change my suit of clothes if I had another to change into; but I do not, for my tailor has calculated to the last inch of ribbon how much credit it is safe to give me.

As I set off, I pause briefly and wonder why Mr S. K. feels the need to be so obscure if he really does wish to be my friend. But I reassure myself with this thought: What harm can possibly come to me at Gray's Inn?

CHAPTER

3

Mr S. K.

It has grown cold of late. This evening, a low, chill mist has crept in from the distant banks of the Thames, wheedling a passage, narrow lane by narrow lane, until it has reached Theobalds Road. Above and through it, a blood-red sun inflames the sky, giving fire to west-facing windows. It is an hour for mean and glorious deeds.

At Gray's Inn I pause at the porter's lodge. A man sits inside the little wooden hut, a patch over one eye. He wears a rough, mended woollen cloak over what seems to be a good velvet suit with lace cuffs. From time to time he tugs at the eye-patch as if unused to wearing it. Perhaps the loss of that eye is very recent. He looks at me suspiciously with his one uncovered organ of vision, though he must have seen many lawyers pass this way before. Indeed, at Gray's Inn he must see little else.

'I am seeking Mr S. K.,' I say, rubbing two cold hands together. 'I am told that you may be able to direct me to him.'

'Who says I may?' His accent is somewhat of Devon, but only somewhat. I show him the letter. Strangely, for such a lowly minion, he has no difficulty in reading it. He thrusts it back at me.

'And who might you be?' he asks.

'That's none of your business, as you know well.'

He nods. This is the sort of answer he expects from any friend of Mr S. K., who would damn his remaining eye as soon as glance in his direction. 'First building on the left, third floor right.' His accent is now somewhat of London though it is also somewhat of Suffolk. He seems not to have fixed firmly on his county of birth.

'Thank you,' I say.

'It is my pleasure to assist you,' he says. 'But I'd go quickly if I were you. I suspect they are already on their second bottle.' He looks at his threadbare cloak with undisguised distaste, then pulls it around him.

He solicits no money for the information provided, which I regard as far more suspicious than his shifting place of origin or the lace cuffs that must be so inconvenient in his chosen trade of portering.

I follow his directions and climb the broad oak staircase to the top floor of the building, where Mr S. K. is apparently to be found. Close by the chamber door is a small wooden sign, which has been hastily covered with a piece of sacking. I lift the sacking without difficulty and read: *Sir Richard Willys*. I replace the sacking and knock on a panel to alert Mr S. K. of my presence. There is no response, but I am not expecting one. I push the door and it swings open easily as if lately oiled to prevent it drawing attention to itself. There are two gentlemen seated by a blazing fire; though there is still a chill in the room, as if the conflagration has not yet had time to heat more than a narrow arc round the hearth. Each man holds a glass of wine. There is a bottle, still almost one third full, and a fairly clean glass on a table nearby. I am expected, it would seem. It is time for the fun to begin.

'I seek Mr S. K.,' I say with a smile.

There is a long and awkward hiatus as the gentlemen look at each other. Then they look at me again. The shorter man strokes a blond moustache. But neither says a word. This is not what I expected. Nor, I realise, is this what *they* expected. Something about me puzzles them.

'He's not here,' says the owner of the blond moustache. He is dressed in a suit of crimson silk with much lace about neck and wrists; it is not, you would have thought, an outfit for one who wished to pass through the streets unnoticed. Not in these times of decent sobriety. He takes a sip of wine, but his bright eyes don't leave mine for a moment. There is, I now observe, a pistol on the table as well as a bottle. The game is afoot, but the stakes are slightly higher than I had imagined. I find that I need to swallow hard.

'Nevertheless, you are his representatives,' I suggest.

'Why should you think that?' The older, taller one has untidy, dark hair. There is black stubble on his chin. He is dressed in a plain suit of dark blue stuff and lacks somewhat the ostentation of his friend. I think the porter was right that this is not the first bottle they have opened. This man is drunk and a little dangerous.

'Your temporarily one-eyed friend at the gate told me to come to this chamber. See—I have a letter of invitation to meet Mr S. K. It seems correct in all particulars—I am indeed lately arrived here. And it was delivered to my landlady's door. But if you gentlemen truly do not know Mr S. K...'

My words hang in the air. I do not, on reflection, think that these people will stand the gentle chaffing that I had planned— the drunk one in particular looks as if he has a poor sense of humour. But I shall still make it clear to them, very politely, that I am no Royalist and that they need trouble me no further, whatever my mother may have told them. I wish Charles Stuart no ill, but I do not desire to see him on the throne of any of these three kingdoms. I shall say that. Then I shall go quickly before the conversation turns to pistols.

'Stay!' commands the dark-haired man, perhaps sensing that my thoughts are tending towards an early departure.

'I apologise,' says the man in the red silk, as if sensing my disquiet. 'I apologise for my colleague's brusque tones. But since you have chosen to join us, we cannot allow you to leave so abruptly. That would be neither hospitable of us nor polite of you. You will come to no harm if indeed you are here with good intent.'

For some reason, this does not make me feel any better. I begin to wish I had spent the evening reading my law books. I swallow hard once more and remain where I am, watching the pistol.

They glance at the letter, which I think they have seen before, and then their puzzled gaze reverts to me. No, I am not what they had expected. But, on reflection, this is no surprise. My mother will have told them to expect a soldier—the man of daring and resolution that she so much wishes me to be. What they see is a young lawyer, country-bred but rapidly gaining a good London pallor, the dust of the library of Lincoln's Inn still upon his shoulders, his arm still crooked as if holding a large leather-bound tome. I do not look as if I laugh in the face of danger. I do not look as if I regularly run men through with a sword for my own amusement but, on reflection, I suspect that these two may do so. Mr S. K.'s written promise that no harm will come to me begins to ring hollow. Or perhaps, bearing in mind their puzzlement that I am here at all, it was a promise made to somebody else entirely—somebody with whom I have been confused. I have misjudged things in a way that I do not yet understand.

'Nevertheless, if I were to leave now...' I say. 'After all, no hurt has been done.'

'A moment longer, sir, if you please,' says the younger man. 'We shall detain you no more than we have to.' He half-turns and has a whispered conversation with his companion. It goes on for some time. Midway through, they both pause and stare at me again. They utter no word of rebuke, but they are greatly disappointed with what they see before them.

'You expected somebody else?' I say.

'To be perfectly honest with you, yes,' says the dark-haired man. 'There has been a mistake of some sort. The man who informed us of your coming is a fool. But you say you have just arrived from Brussels?'

'Brussels?'

'We were warned to expect your arrival from Brussels.' He seems to feel I should know this, if that's where I've come from.

Then suddenly, all becomes clear. Only one of my family resides in Brussels. It is not my mother's meddling hand that I should have seen in this, but my father's. They were not expecting me at all—but him! If my father too has recently come to London—and he would have had no reason to inform me if he had—then it is not too difficult to see how a letter intended for him might find its way to me, also newly arrived, albeit from Essex. My hosts are understandably surprised to find me so youthful. I had thought that my mother was mistakenly trying to introduce me to some convivial but ineffectual Royalist sympathisers—that far from abandoning her links with the Stuarts she wished to influence me in that direction. As a result of disbelieving her many assurances, I now find myself impersonating my other parent, whose purpose in coming to London is utterly unknown to me but unlikely to be lawful.

'I think you were expecting another member of my family,' I say.

The younger one nods. His nimble mind has been running beside my own. 'Then the message we received was correct except in one minor but important detail. We were, as you see, not expecting the *son*. Indeed, we were unaware of your existence. You are…?'

My father has clearly chosen not to tell anyone that he has a son in England—and why should he? Our paths have diverged in so many ways. In Brussels I doubt that he feels a need to mention that he has a family here, any more than my mother feels it necessary to talk about a redundant husband overseas.

'I'm John,' I say. 'I think you were expecting my father, who is currently exiled in Brussels and—'

He holds up his hand. 'Of course. I see what has happened. I must apologise if we appeared bemused. Now we understand. We knew your family was in Brussels. We didn't know that you were too. Now we do know, and all is well.'

By 'family' he doubtless means my father and his whore. But are things well *only* if I am living in Brussels? That would seem to be the case. I must take great care what I say until I am more certain of my facts. Whatever my father's reasons for visiting London, they must be important. As a known, if not particularly distinguished, Royalist, he would be taking a great risk in coming here.

The dark-haired man takes another mouthful of wine and pulls a face. I do not think he regards me as a friend. 'You are too trusting, Sir Michael. How do we know this John is who he claims to be? He could be any man's son. I sense an unease on his part. He shuffles his feet and looks towards the door. You clearly know his father. Does the young man resemble him in any way? If not, then he may be an agent of the Republic come hither to undo us utterly. He seems disinclined to take wine with us, as a gentleman should. No Royalist, and no son of a Royalist, would refuse a glass of good Canary. Consider, Sir Michael: if he is an imposter then we are all undone. I say we shoot him now and make an end on it.'

Well, perhaps they have already told me more than is safe for any of us. If they do not shoot me, I shall certainly now be able to report to the authorities that one of them is called Sir Michael. But will they shoot me? It seems to be Sir Michael's decision. I look yet again at the pistol on the table and wonder if it is loaded. I have never thought I was much like my father in character, but hopefully there is at least a small similitude in the flesh.

'There is some resemblance,' says Sir Michael. To this I make no objection. I begin to like Sir Michael better than the other man, who eyes me as if he might yet see through me and my Republican ways.

'Even so...' The dark-haired man pauses. He is not convinced by my appearance alone. 'I think, Sir Michael, that we should question him a little.'

'As you wish.' Sir Michael waves his hand in my direction. His companion has leave to ask whatever he likes. I try not to shuffle my feet or look towards the door. I hope none of the questions are about Brussels, a place I have never visited.

'Where do you come from, John?' he demands. He rubs his face as if to aid thought. 'I mean what is your place of birth?'

'Clavershall West,' I say with relief. 'In the county of Essex.'

Sir Michael turns to his companion with a smug expression on his face. He clearly knows where my father came from. But this telling poof of my loyalties is insufficient for his friend.

'To which saint is the parish church there dedicated?'

'St Peter,' I say.

Sir Michael shrugs. I doubt if either of them know if I have told the truth. My father rarely set foot in the place.

'Who now owns the manor?' the other man persists.

'Colonel Payne,' I say. I do not add that Colonel Payne is my stepfather. If they know my father even a little, then the one thing they will certainly be aware of is that he is living. It might be difficult to explain how I come to have a stepfather.

'Who owned the manor before that?'

Well, he knows about my family then.

'We did,' I say. 'My family owned it. But not any more.'

That my mother has recently repossessed it by marrying my stepfather is again a detail that I would be wise to omit.

'Enough,' says Sir Michael. 'This young man comes from a family loyal to the King. And I assume he therefore knows who we are?'

'I am familiar with the Sealed Knot,' I say. 'Mr S. K., as you have called it in your letter. For the past six years you have worked secretly for the restoration of...' I pause. The words are like ashes in my Republican mouth but it may be as well not to upset the gentleman with the pistol. '...the restoration of the rightful King. You answer to Sir Edward Hyde at His Majesty's court in Brussels.'

'Just so,' says Sir Michael. 'We answer to Sir Edward Hyde.' He sees my eyes on the pistol and adds: 'Had you not been who you say you are—had you not been sent from Brussels—we would have been obliged to shoot you as my friend so devoutly wished. I would have regretted it almost as much as you, and for slightly longer, but it would not have been safe to let you leave Gray's Inn alive. I mean, if you had been some low Republican who had accidentally stumbled on our invitation.'

'Of course,' I say. I am a Republican but, I would argue, not a low one. Even so, the smallest slip might still be the end of me.

'Since we are friends,' he continues, 'and we are all friends of Mr S. K., let me introduce myself. I, as you will already have gathered, am called Sir Michael. Sir Michael de Ripley. Baronet. My indiscreet companion here is Mr Allen Brodrick, gentleman, wine-drinker, womaniser and Secretary of the Sealed Knot.'

Neither then is Sir Richard Willys, who may or may not know that his chamber is being used in this way. Unless Ripley is lying, which is quite possible. He looks like a man who holds truth and falsehood in equal respect.

For the next few minutes I have to remember that, if I wish to live to see tomorrow's dawn, I am a Royalist, newly come from Brussels for a purpose that I have no way of knowing. For as long as it takes, I must play my part. Then I must leave quickly.

'So, why did you summon me here?' I ask.

'Why did we summon you?' says Ripley, the merest hint of surprise in his voice. 'We know that you have come to London on business that concerns us. After all, Hyde would scarcely send you all this way and tell you to avoid talking to his agents in London—or would he?'

There is menace in his words. Either he doesn't like Hyde or he doesn't like me. One or the other. Or both.

'Why should I have been instructed to avoid you?' I ask.

Ripley looks at Brodrick and shrugs.

'Hyde is losing confidence in us,' says Brodrick. 'We'd like to know why. And we'd like to know what you are doing here. Why has he sent you and not told us?'

In some ways these are more difficult questions to answer than the name of my parish church, but in other ways it is not. I do, as I say, know something of the Sealed Knot and it is hard to think of anything that it has achieved in the six years of its existence. Many of its members have secretly gone over to Cromwell and are providing him with valuable intelligence. That Hyde has finally despaired of them is not to be wondered at. He does not want my father's mission, whatever it is, endangered. My father has been told to avoid the King's loyal supporters in London and get on with the job. By accepting Ripley's invitation I have fallen into a trap that he would have side-stepped. This may not, however, be the right time to tell Ripley all of these things. I am caught in some Royalist squabble of which I know only a little.

'Hyde has never said anything of the sort to me,' I say truthfully.

'You were overheard,' says Brodrick. 'We know what Hyde said to you before you left. You were told to avoid contact with the Sealed Knot in England.'

Ripley gives him a sharp look. He was not supposed to reveal that.

'If you overheard us,' I say, 'you have no need to question me on the purpose of my visit.'

Ripley says nothing. Either Brodrick is bluffing or their informant overheard at best only a little of what Hyde said to my father. None of us, then, has the first idea why I am here. It is helpful to know that.

Brodrick looks daggers at me. I have made an enemy in a very short time. 'We know exactly what your mission is,' he says. 'Don't we, Sir Michael? And it would be well for you, John, that you tell us.'

Ripley considers. 'Reluctant though I am to contradict my good friend here, let me confess that I do not know why you are here. I think it is a matter we may need to return to. But perhaps, since you have spoken to Hyde, I could enquire whether he has considered the proposal that we put to him?'

'Your proposal?'

'You can scarcely be unaware what it is.'

Is this another test? Have they put some new plan to Hyde that my father would know about?

'Of course,' I say. 'And the answer that you were hoping for was…?'

'Yes or no.'

Dare I now ask what the question is? I think not. I have already said I know. I am drowning in my own duplicity. Perhaps very soon I can flee from this place, change my lodgings and remain in the library of Lincoln's Inn for the next year, other than when I need to go out and piss. But Yes or No? Which is the safest? Yes may require further information that I do not have. But No implies the refusal of some reasonable request, which may go ill for me. They might ask: 'Why not?' And I do not know why not.

I draw myself up to my full height, which is greater than Ripley's, though less than Brodrick's by several inches. I suddenly remember, years ago, standing on a bluff, about to dive into a fast-flowing river of unknown depth. The dark water swirled beneath me. This is what it felt like then. I took a deep breath, closed my eyes and launched myself into the unknown.

'Yes,' I say. 'Hyde's answer to you is Yes.'

For a while I seem to hang in mid-air. Then Ripley speaks. 'And we should proceed with our plan, or some variant of Hyde's own devising? If it is our own plan then I shall need you to clarify one or two things.'

Clarify? I can't do that. Hyde's plan it is then.

'Hyde has a plan, but I cannot tell you any more than that,' I say cautiously.

'How then do we take it forward?'

'You don't. There is no need to trouble yourself further.'

Ripley nods again. For him this is a very good answer. I only wish I knew why. Unfortunately, Brodrick still wants further information.

'So, you are saying we can leave all that to you?' says Brodrick. 'Our offer was unnecessary because Hyde already has a plan of his own?' He seems relieved.

'Most assuredly. That is what I said. You may leave it to me.' I half-turn towards the door. Perhaps if I go now?

'We thought we would need to arrange the thing ourselves,' adds Ripley. 'We have spoken to one who is willing, as Hyde is aware. So that is the true purpose of your visit?'

'Precisely,' I hear myself say. 'That is why I am here.'

'But...' says Brodrick.

I feign, quite well I think, justified indignation. 'Are you questioning Hyde's instructions, gentlemen? I hope not.' The door is close but not quite close enough to make a run for it. My mouth is dry and I am not being offered any wine.

'Question Hyde's instructions?' says Ripley. 'Why should we wish to do that? If Hyde thinks you can do the business better than the man we recommended… Do you also have the ability to gain admission to the Protector's household?'

Even I can guess the right answer this time.

'That can be arranged.'

Ripley says slowly, 'Very well. I think I can see why you were reluctant at first to tell of your mission. I can even see why Hyde may have told you to avoid contact with known Royalists. The authorities may be watching us all—even me. What you have to do must be done with all secrecy.' He looks at Brodrick, who in turn is regarding me with greater respect than anyone has ever shown me before.

'You're a brave man,' says Brodrick. 'I would not take such a risk myself. Not for the world. Even if my conscience allowed me to do such a thing, which it does not.'

'No braver than you, I'm sure.'

'If you are caught, it will be a terrible death that you are condemned to.' The mere thought of what I am to do makes Brodrick pour himself another drink.

'I do not fear the hangman's noose,' I say. Though as a matter of fact, I do fear the hangman's noose as much as any other does. Perhaps a little more, for I have seen a man hanged. It is not a good death nor a quick one.

Brodrick laughs. 'A merry jest,' he says, 'not to fear the hangman's noose. Ha! No, it's what will happen after they cut you down, still conscious and able to feel pain, that would worry me. And the torture that you will need to endure before. After all, they will not believe you when you say that you acted alone, and they will want names that you will, of course, refuse to give them. It will be a slow and painful end, I'm thinking. A slow and painful dying over many days and nights. And Cromwell is guarded all the time. Even if you succeed in stabbing him, you cannot possibly escape.'

So that is what I have just agreed to? The assassination of the Lord Protector? For a moment I forget that I am not a low Republican. 'I cannot stab Cromwell!'

'Of course not,' says Ripley. 'They say Cromwell wears steel under his coat. I am sure that you have more subtle methods. Perhaps ones that may even give you a slim chance of getting away unscathed.'

'This other person that you mentioned...' I say.

'He will be disappointed. He had been looking forward to it. He hates Cromwell. But do not worry. He will not grudge you the first attempt. And, if you fail, he will have his chance then.'

'I would not wish to inconvenience anybody. Perhaps if you offered the task to him after all? As you say, I may fail.'

Ripley shakes his head. 'Sir Edward's wishes are clear. As you point out, it is not for us to question them. Nor shall I. I am sure he will have selected you for your skill and bravery. And, if you need help, the Knot will be with you.'

'Will it?' I ask.

'Do not fear. We shall not compromise you. But we have agents all over London. We will be watching you every hour of the day. Whatever you do, wherever you go, you may depend on it that our eyes will be upon you.'

I wonder if that includes the pissing place behind Lincoln's Inn library. I fear that it may.

'That is a great comfort,' I say. 'That is a very great comfort indeed.'

'It will be our honour, John, to assist you. You are a brave man. In future years, though sadly it will probably be after your death, your name will be honoured by all those true to His Majesty. But we shall not use that name from now on. That would be too dangerous even for you. If you wish to contact us, then write as Mr Cardinal.'

'Cardinal?'

'Unless you prefer some other name.'

'Cardinal is good,' I say, sitting down in one of the vacant chairs.

'Pour Mr Cardinal a glass of wine at once,' says Ripley. 'For I see he has gone quite pale with the cold.'

I am running through the dark streets of London. Sleet is lashing my face but I scarcely notice it. Occasionally I slip and slide in the dark, wet streets, but I wish to place some distance between myself and Gray's Inn. I have just promised to assassinate the Lord Protector of England, in exchange for which I have not been shot as a low Republican. I am free to go. But to go where? I have bought myself a day or two at the most before I am grabbed by some ruffian who wishes to resume the same conversation in a dark alleyway.

First, if they were indeed expecting my father, then (unless happily delayed) he is doubtless already in London and may still—depending on exactly what his partly-overheard instructions were—make contact with the Knot himself. He may then also give them Hyde's answer and they will be bemused why his son has already given them the same answer or perhaps a completely different one. If Ripley and Brodrick explain clearly what has happened before my father has a chance to open his mouth, then I am sure that he will not intentionally betray me. But since he is unaware of my plight, it would take little to trap him into admitting that his son was not a loyal adherent of the Stuarts but rather a dull and dutiful citizen of the Republic, who is likely to denounce them to the relevant officers. And I have no way of contacting my father to warn him how he should reply to casual questions about a family that he has evidently not admitted to having.

Second, even if my father has been delayed in his journey and however long I can remain undetected, I cannot even make a pretence of doing what I have promised. I have, for example, no friends at the Lord Protector's court who could offer me employment or any other way of getting close to him. My imposture will soon be clear to all.

Third, even if I do denounce Ripley and Brodrick to the authorities, as I could, I am sure that others in the Knot will swiftly take their revenge. They know exactly where I live. And my landlady would doubtless be very helpful to any aristocratic young man who enquired about my movements.

And last—what exactly is my father's role in all of this? He may simply bear a harmless message from Hyde. But unless Brodrick and Ripley have been wholly misinformed, it would seem that he *has* been told not to make contact with the Sealed Knot—perhaps for exactly the reason that Ripley has wrongly attributed to me: that my father is himself the chosen assassin. After all, if Hyde wants Cromwell dead, would he really trust the Sealed Knot with the task? Or would he send somebody from Brussels to do the job properly—a surgeon perhaps, like my father, skilled in the use of the knife and not unfamiliar with poisons? Though he deserted his family, I have no wish to see him caught and executed. And though my mother would be quite happy to have him hanged quietly and discreetly, the public execution of a man she had long claimed was dead might prove problematic for her.

If I had not begged my mother to repudiate utterly all her Royalist connections, then she might have advised me. And she is in any case far away in north Essex. I can think of only one person in London who can solve this riddle. I knew him well once. His name is Probert and, if he has not got himself killed in the meantime, he still works for John Thurloe, spymaster to the Lord Protector—a man I once worked for myself. I must get a message to him tomorrow morning.

If I am still alive tomorrow morning.

Probert

It is early on Tuesday and I am not yet dead.

I have given a letter to Will Atkins, Mistress Reynolds's boy, and told him to run to Westminster and deliver it to Mr George Probert at an address I have provided. If the Sealed Knot really are watching my every move, then it would be certain death for me to be seen in that vicinity, but it should, I hope, be less dangerous for Will.

In fact, he does better than I could have dreamed. He returns with a message to say that Mr Probert would be delighted to talk with me in the gardens of Lincoln's Inn, as I have proposed, at *nona hora*. Will repeats these last two words to me dubiously, not having come across this o'clock until now. I assure him that I understand, and I accordingly set out for a noon meeting with Mr Probert.

'*Salve,* Grey,' he says in greeting. '*Quid agis?* We meet some way from where we first met and under a weaker sun. Behold!

Fumum et opes strepitumque Londinii! But within this noisy and smoky city, you have picked a cold and dismal place for our meeting. These garden walks of yours are pleasant in the summer, but a warm tavern is more to my taste in December.'

He pulls a cloak more tightly around his large frame. Probert was never dainty in appearance. He has eaten well, I think, and shaved only occasionally, since I last saw him.

'The more congenial the place, the more people there will be to overhear us,' I say.

'True, but we could have met in your lodgings.'

'There above all.'

'The walls have ears?'

'No, my landlady has ears. The walls are merely impediments to her hearing. Let us stroll a little, Mr Probert, and see if anyone follows us.'

Probert looks up at the sky. He does not need to point out, in either English or Latin, that the scudding clouds threaten a drenching. We go out nevertheless through the wicket gate into Lincoln's Inn Fields and shelter for a moment under one of the great elms. Above us the branches thrash and hiss their warning of a coming storm. The wide expanse of lank, overgrown meadow stretches away on all sides, like an old tapestry faded to browns and greys. It is bleak and windswept to be sure, but here I can be certain we are alone. I watch the gateway to Lincoln's Inn to see who leaves in our wake, but there is nobody. This damp coldness tempts none from their chambers.

'From whom are we hiding, Grey? I am not one to skulk in the shadows, as you know. *Audentis fortuna iuvat.* Anyway, I am too large to escape notice except on the very blackest of nights. Whom had you expected to see emerging from yonder gate?'

'A member of the Sealed Knot,' I say. 'Do you know Mr Allen Brodrick or Sir Michael de Ripley?'

'Brodrick is the Secretary of the Sealed Knot and one of Hyde's couriers. He drinks too much and talks when he would do better to hold his tongue, especially to young women who may be happy to oblige him in one way or another; but he has managed to stay one step ahead of us for some time. I should greatly like to meet him, though he perhaps would not like to meet me. But Ripley... No, that name is unknown to me, which may mean he is harmless or perhaps merely that he is cleverer than Brodrick. But whoever he is, the Knot presents no menace to one such as yourself. *Bruta fulmina!* Their threats are as empty as their purses! Let them try to kill you! Ha!'

Probert does of course laugh in the face of danger and has a deep scar in his shoulder as evidence of this. He rubs that shoulder now through his thick cloak, as if the damp still troubles it. The wind is growing ever more bitter. There is now just a hint in the air of snow, a sharpness that pricks at the lips and cheeks.

'I think,' I say, 'that they will kill me if I do not do as they request.'

'And what do they request?'

'They wish me to murder the Lord Protector.'

'Murder His Highness? Why should they think that you would like to do that? It would be a strange deed, for a lawyer with good Republican principles such as yourself. They have made a poor choice.'

'I have been mistaken for...another,' I say. Better that my father's name is not mentioned at all, if that is possible—whatever the nature of his mission. 'They think I am also a member of the Sealed Knot or at least a sympathiser, lately come from Brussels. Once I had met the two gentlemen, I could not undeceive them; in short, they had already told me more than was fit for me to be told. They are aware that I know their identities—Brodrick told me Ripley's name almost at once. And they are also aware I know of the existence of a plot to kill the Lord Protector—one that will apparently proceed with me or without me. We must act—and swiftly.'

Probert is less impressed than he might be.

'Do you think, Grey, that we do not know that there are people who wish His Highness dead? *Experto credite*—that is to say you may trust my own judgement here. They are myriad. And not just the fools of the Sealed Knot. There are religious fanatics of all persuasions who would do the same deed; there are Diggers, there are Levellers, there are Adamites, there are Muggletonians. There are Ranters, there are Anabaptists, there are Fifth Monarchy Men. All mad. So would many of His Highness's closest and dearest companions wish him dead. His Highness has enemies in Parliament. He has enemies in the Army. And so far, I have listed only those on his own side who would kill him: we have not as yet even begun to consider the Royalists and the Papists.

'The State has fined many men to their ruin, and some of them would risk all to kill the man who has undone them and their families. There are those who feel, I could not say precisely why, that it was wrong to execute the tyrant Charles Stuart and that vengeance should be exacted on somebody. And there are those, of no particular persuasion, who would be happy to kill anyone in exchange for a purse full of gold. It may be only you and me and Mr Thurloe who truly wish His Highness well. That is why my Lord Cromwell will never tarry in a room with only one door to it. That is why nobody knows the route his coach will take until he steps into it. That is why he wears armour when he travels from place to place. That is why there are two loaded pistols in his carriage. We are prepared.'

Almost without our noticing, the dampness in the air has made up its mind to become rain and the wind has made up its mind to throw the rain in our faces. I pull my own cloak about me before replying.

'But these are general dangers,' I say. 'There is some very specific plot that the Sealed Knot is hatching and that Hyde has been asked to approve. If I fail to kill Cromwell, and I assure you I mean to fail, there is another already in place and eager to take up the cause: a man with a hatred for His Highness. I think it may be somebody close to him. Ripley said: "You *also* have access to the Lord Protector's household". So this other assassin, whoever it is, would seem to be able to enter the court freely. He may be somebody you know and trust.'

Probert considers this, while the cold rain drips down my neck. Lincoln's Inn has dissolved into a shadow of itself. He rubs his shoulder again and sighs. 'I must ask for further instructions. It may chance that you have discovered nothing we do not already know. Or it may chance otherwise. I must speak to Mr Secretary Thurloe or his assistant, Mr Morland.'

'Not Morland,' I say.

Probert looks at me oddly. Morland is, after all, a senior official. I saw him often when I worked for Mr Thurloe. Why should he not know of something that touches the Lord Protector in this way? Probert clearly suspects that I have not told him everything. But he lives in a world in which the whole tale is rarely offered up without the immediate prospect of torture. He does not press me.

'I shall speak only to Mr Thurloe if you wish,' he says, rubbing the rain from his face with a large palm, then wiping his hand on his cloak. 'Meet me here tomorrow, under this elm, at the same hour.'

'And if Ripley finds me and asks me what progress I have made?'

'Say that the cousin who was to give you a post at court is sick and that it will take longer than you thought to find employment there—or any other reason for delay that you choose to give him. Say that you will write to him when you are able to gain admission, but do not say there is no hope. While he has expectation of your victory, he will not unleash his reserve divisions—whoever the man is.'

'I have no cousin,' I say.

Probert slaps me a little too heartily on the arm. 'You must learn to lie a little, Mr Grey. There are times when too much truth can kill a man stone dead!'

Morland might have made much the same observation—if he and I were on speaking terms. I have, as I say, worked for Mr Thurloe, and indeed for Mr Morland himself. Morland is a clever man who places a high value on cleverness. He is a good-looking man who places a high value on good looks. He places little value, if any, on loyalty. I know him better than I would like. I cannot prove he is a secret Royalist, but if anyone within Mr Thurloe's office might betray me, it is Morland. He will betray me, however, only if it is to his advantage, and he will take his time to decide if that is so. In that sense he is less dangerous than my father, who may betray me out of ignorance, or my landlady, who may betray me out of love of ancient titles and Brussels lace. Perhaps it is my landlady whom I should fear most.

❁ ❁ ❁

'Will says you made him run an errand for you this morning. He says it was snowing. His shoes and hose are still wet.'

My landlady is less than pleased. Will was supposed to be laying fires and cleaning pots. I am sorry for the state of his footwear, but his alacrity to accept my commission is now explained.

'Rain mixed with a little sleet,' I reply. 'There is no snow as yet. I needed to send a message to Mr S. K.'

I have already discovered that Mr S. K. may take liberties that I may not. Mistress Reynolds readily cleaned my muddy boots when I returned from Gray's Inn, for example. She hopes that my Royalist friend Mr S. K.—to whom she sometimes refers hopefully as His Lordship—will visit me soon. She hopes I will apprise him of the merits of her daughter.

'Well,' she simpers, 'just this once. But next time, please ask me before you give orders to the servants.'

She speaks as if she had armies of footmen to command. The only other servant is in fact a witless girl, whose duties are vaguely specified but always onerous. She lives in the darkest recesses of the kitchen and is rarely allowed anywhere else in the house. I fear that if I gave *her* a message to carry, she would drop it and break it, as is her custom with most useful things that come her way.

'The gentleman with much lace about him who delivered the letter to me the other day—you have not seen him since?' I ask.

'No. You were expecting him to return?'

'I hope not—I mean, I'm not sure. Please inform me at once, however, if you do see him. And if he asks where I am, say that you do not know.'

'You are very mysterious, Mr Grey.' She prods me playfully in the chest, something she never did before I made the acquaintance of nobility.

I try to smile but do not succeed. I hope that, after tomorrow, I can stop being mysterious in any way whatsoever. Thurloe will arrest Ripley and Brodrick, without my name entering the conversation, and all will be well again.

My landlady's report of snow was premature but prescient. A thin layer of white now lies on Lincoln's Inn Fields, slowly melting as the day wears on and the sun takes the sharpness off the early chill. The air is damp and opaque. The antick turrets and crenellations of Lincoln's Inn are just an outline against the fog, with here and there a smudge of candlelight brightening the daytime dark. All around me is the noise of London—the voices, the grinding of iron-shod wheels on the cobblestones—but muffled and far away. *Strepitum Londinii,* as Probert would doubtless remind me. A solitary, bedraggled leaf spins slowly downwards to join the snow-covered drifts that have gathered beneath the London plane trees. Then for a while nothing happens at all. I think I am under the right elm, but Probert is late and my cloak is becoming as water-logged as everything else.

A shape emerges slowly and a dim shadow becomes a living person. But it is not Probert. A beggar approaches me with more optimism than is justified.

'A penny, kind sir, to buy bread on a raw day?'

I look him up and down. His clothes are as damp as mine but worn and patched. The brim of his hat is torn. But his beard is well-trimmed, as if he has a little pride remaining. I look over his shoulder in case I can catch a glimpse of Probert. Whoever this man is, I do not want him to see us together.

'I have nothing for you,' I say. 'Be on your way, my good fellow.'

'Just a penny, sir. Those who *give* also *receive.*'

'That is good theology but poor accounting.'

'You may receive sooner than you imagine, good sir. You might even receive something from *me*. For a penny.'

'You have nothing I could possibly want.'

The man edges closer to me. 'If you are too mean to give a penny to a starving beggar, just put your hand in your pocket, Mr Grey, and pretend to pass me a coin. Even you must be able to feign charity.'

I feel in my pocket and seize upon the first coin I can find, which I pass to him, almost dropping it in my haste. As I withdraw my hand I realise that he has placed a small wad of paper in mine.

'Thank you, sir,' he says. 'That was most generous of you. Most generous. May God bless you and all your family.'

I wonder what coin I gave him. By its weight, I fear it may have been half a crown. A penny, given freely and timeously, would have saved me two shillings and fivepence.

He shuffles off into the gloom, a little richer than before. I look around me again to ascertain who may have seen this exchange, but he has chosen his moment well. The fog has closed in and such shapes as I see may be men or may be phantoms. I slip my hand into my pocket and wait while I count to a hundred. Two figures pass by, hurrying towards Lincoln's Inn, but they do not even glance at me. They are thinking doubtless of the blazing fires and perhaps mulled cider in their chambers. I wait while the splash of wet leather soles on slushy snow recedes, then I take my hand from my pocket very casually, as if I had had the paper there all the time. I open it and read it.

Mr Probert sends his greetings to Mr Grey and asks that he attend upon him in Mr Thurloe's office presently. There is more to this matter than meets the eye.

He may be right. I stare into the mist. Nothing now meets my eye but the swirling vapour.

Mr Secretary Thurloe

There is no mist in Thurloe's office, but he too stares ahead of him. It is as if he has not noticed we are there, though in fact we are, and have been for some time. I am allowed to examine his profile, the flowing black hair, the straight nose, the full lips. His linen collar is broad, falling over the glossy black stuff of which his doublet is made. My landlady, observing his clothes, would feel he had spent much money to little effect. Beyond him, through the window, I notice that the sun has finally broken through the morning mist. I can see Westminster Abbey, its roof covered in melting snow. Its towers are fragmented by the many angles of the small panes of glass in Thurloe's window and by the lead strips between them. But everything, seen from this office, is of a slightly different shape than when viewed in the street below. This is where secrets are lodged, to be cherished or shattered, to be discarded or glued back together.

Thurloe has not asked us to sit. It may be that we are not to be here long, or it may be that he has forgotten. Either is possible, for I know Thurloe of old. It was my mother, who has friends in the office of Cromwell's spymaster as well as in the Sealed Knot, who once found me employment here and caused me to meet Morland. But my stay was brief. I am not a natural secret agent, for all that my mother considered it a safe and gentlemanly profession.

Thurloe has greeted me as politely as I might expect. He now pushes a pile of secrets to one side of his desk as if to clear his mind.

'Ripley and Brodrick?'

'Yes,' I say.

'Brodrick we are aware of,' says Probert, though whether for my benefit or Thurloe's is unclear. 'He is the Sealed Knot's Secretary and an accomplished traitor. We do not, however, know anything about Mr Ripley.'

'Sir Michael de Ripley,' I say. 'He claims to be a baronet.'

'And you think he is one?'

'He wore a great deal of lace. My landlady would have no doubt that he was a baronet at least—and she is a good judge of these matters.'

Thurloe looks at me to see if I am joking. Thurloe never makes jokes. I'm not sure he understands what purpose they serve. His mouth smiles.

'Many men wear lace,' he says. 'As for his antecedents…there was a Sir Everard de Ripley, who was in the King's army during the late war. Prince Rupert led him into a hail of musket balls but did not lead him out again. We thought that his son had died at the Battle of Worcester. Apparently not. I wonder where he has been since?'

I nod. A good friend of mine, Marius Clifford, also died at Worcester, the last throw of the dice for the Royalist party before the ignominious flight of Charles Stuart. My mother has never suggested Worcester as the place of my father's death. I do not know why. For many it was a perfectly good place to die. As for Ripley, I suspect that, like many Royalists, he slips backwards and forwards across the Channel as he needs to.

'And who is Sir Richard Willys?' I ask. 'We met in his chamber at Gray's Inn.'

Probert glances quickly at Thurloe. Thurloe frowns before speaking.

'A former Royalist officer,' he says. 'Like many Cavaliers, he has given his word that he has abandoned his old allegiances and is now loyal to the Republic. He attends to the law, just as you do, but perhaps a little more profitably. He practises at Gray's Inn. No harm in that. We—how shall I put this?—observe Sir Richard from time to time. And since he knows we observe him, he would not take the risk of using his chamber thus. Indeed, Mr Probert has recently informed me that Sir Richard is out of town at present. The porters at Gray's Inn are easily bribed. They possess keys to all rooms. They would have known that one was empty and made it available to Brodrick for a small fee. That is all there is to be said on the matter. It is the identity of these other two persons that interests us—I mean the man they have mistaken you for, and the man whom the Sealed Knot had intended should murder His Highness.'

'They have mistaken me for...' again I pause before my tongue runs away and accuses my father of treason '...for an agent of Hyde's, whose reasons for visiting England are unknown.'

Thurloe looks at me, as if he thinks I have not told him something, as if I should clarify that statement. But I think my father would prefer it if I did not.

'As to the man who will take over my task if I fail,' I continue, 'I have even less idea, but it would seem to be somebody now in London. Somebody close to His Highness. But he has been instructed to stay his hand until Hyde gives his approval.'

'I wonder if he has received that instruction,' says Thurloe. 'An attempt was made on the Lord Protector's life yesterday. Somebody cut through his saddle girth, intending that it should break while he was riding.'

'His Highness is not hurt?'

'No, God be praised. This person cut a little too far. Perhaps he does not ride horses himself—or perhaps he worked in haste, for the girth snapped as the groom tightened it. Of course, it may not be either of the men that Ripley spoke of. Or, then again, perhaps it is. This other courier or agent that you were mistaken for—you think he could be an assassin?'

I think of my father, out there somewhere, plodding along the Dover Road on a tired, mud-caked horse, cloak pulled up around his face. Or perhaps striding through the streets of London, making for Whitehall or Gray's Inn.

'It was merely Ripley's assumption,' I say. 'No more than that.'

'Perhaps then it is the second man on whom we should concentrate,' says Thurloe.

'I agree,' I say, with a certain amount of relief. 'I'm sure you will find him out.'

'No, Mr Grey, *you* will find him out.'

'Me?' I ask, though Thurloe's meaning is plain.

'You,' says Thurloe, who believes that things can never be quite plain enough. 'The Knot clearly trusts you. You have bought us time while we try to track down this man of theirs. But perhaps you can buy us more than time—names, dates, places. You have already unmasked Ripley. Who knows what else they will tell you?'

'I had hoped,' I say, 'that you would simply arrest Ripley and Brodrick in a manner that placed no blame on me, so that I could return to the study of law at Lincoln's Inn.'

Thurloe nods encouragingly. 'Unfortunately that will not be possible,' he says. 'We cannot arrest Ripley and Brodrick until we know what their design is. Arguably we have no grounds for arresting Ripley at all.'

'Arrest Brodrick then,' I say. 'You know he is the Secretary of the Sealed Knot.'

'The question would be,' says Thurloe, *'how* we knew he was the Secretary of the Sealed Knot. The answer is, of course, that we have bought ourselves a member of the Sealed Knot—I obviously cannot tell you who that is. It is unlikely, however, that our source of information would wish to give evidence in open court. Nor would we want him to. He would be able to provide us with little further information once he had done so.'

'They would kill him?'

'Probably.'

'Just as they will kill me if they find I have informed on them?'

'Almost certainly.'

'And if I simply decline to help you?'

'You would be free to leave,' says Thurloe.

'And you could protect me from the Sealed Knot?'

'I have many informants. I cannot possibly guard them all. Men who come here with information know the risks. Since you have worked here, you above all know that.'

'But if I agree to go to the Lord Protector's court, as I have promised Ripley I shall do?'

'Ah at court... That's a much better idea. Yes, we could watch over you there.'

'You appear to leave me with little choice.'

'That was certainly my intention.'

'Very well,' I say. 'I will go and I will ask questions. I shall see if any further intelligence slips into my hands. But that is all.'

'Good,' says Thurloe. 'You must not communicate with us under your own name. We will call you...'

'Mr Plautus?' says Probert.

'Mr Plautus,' says Thurloe.

I wonder whether I can at least ask to be Mr Cicero or Mr Virgil but it seems it is decided. This is to be a low comedy, not lyric poetry.

'We shall find you an obscure post at court—perhaps as a cook or serving man. You will tell the Knot that your cousin secured it for you.'

'I do not have a cousin,' I repeat. 'The Knot knows my family. It will be aware that I do not have a cousin.'

Thurloe ignores this reasonable objection. 'You will report back to them, as Mr Cardinal, from time to time, with harmless accounts of His Highness's past movements. In the meantime you will continue with your real task—to uncover this assassin, or assassins. You shall report to me whenever you can.'

I wonder whether to raise the delicate question of how the real courier might be stopped before he makes contact with Ripley. But much though my mother might enjoy the prospect of my father's detention by the authorities at Dover or elsewhere, I must stay silent and hope that his mission is blameless and that he will avoid the Sealed Knot, as he was apparently instructed to do. No mention has been made of Samuel Morland, who might also betray me. Perhaps he is on business elsewhere. If so, that is well. I shall not ask, at any event. I do not wish to stir *that* hornet's nest.

'*Iacta alia est,*' says Probert. 'The die is indeed cast. You are a brave man, Grey. The life of a double agent can be exciting but very short.'

'But I am not a double agent,' I say. 'I have never been a member of the Sealed Knot.'

'That is not how the Knot will see it,' says Probert. 'You have promised them that you will kill Cromwell. Now you have betrayed them to us in a most regrettable fashion. I salute your courage, Grey. I would not have taken such a risk myself.'

'*Morituri te salutant,*' I say. I hope Probert at least will appreciate my irony.

He nods approvingly. 'Of course, it is not death that is to be feared so much as the torture that will precede it. A pistol ball in the head may come as a blessed relief.'

So, I have the deep and abiding respect of both the Sealed Knot and of Cromwell's secret service. I must hope that I have not bought it at a cost that is greater than I can afford.

'I think Mr Grey is keen to get started,' says Thurloe. 'We must get him to Hampton Court, the moment his cousin has secured that post for him.'

'I have no cousin,' I repeat.

'Then find one, Mr Grey,' says Probert.

❀ ❀ ❀

I arrive back at my lodgings looking, I fear, as white as when I left Westminster, though not as white as the snow that is now falling. My landlady is waiting for me. She is strangely obsequious.

'You should have told me your cousin was coming,' she simpers. 'She is waiting for you in your chamber. I think you should go up at once.'

Aminta

'Are you not pleased to see me, Cousin John?' asks Aminta.

She is sitting in my best chair at her ease, her ample, lilac velvet skirts spread before her, her fair hair cascading down over her starched linen collar. I see that she has commanded my landlady's daughter to bring her wine, and Will to go out and buy her oranges. I do not know what they have cost, but I have no doubt that my landlady is already calculating what she can charge me. The snow on this occasion seems to have been no impediment.

'You are not my cousin,' I say.

'But almost,' she says. 'My mother was your father's whore for some years, before he found somebody younger and more agreeable. That must make us related in some way.'

'I do not think so.'

'That is very awkward then, because I doubt that your landlady would be at all happy that I was sharing these two rooms with you, possibly for some weeks, if we were not *very* closely related. Claiming to be your cousin was the least I could do to spare your blushes and your reputation. I am shocked you are not more grateful.'

'For some weeks?' I ask. I notice a large travelling box in the corner of the room. It is not mine.

'Or as long as I need to be in London.'

'When did you return to England?'

'I arrived in Dover yesterday. I am exhausted from my long journey. And frankly, cousin, I have nowhere else to go, even if the roads were not impassable, as I fear they soon will be. You could scarcely turn me out, however distantly related I was. I wondered whether to say you were my brother. I rather wish I had. Since Marius died I have missed having a brother. And you and Marius are alike in many ways. My being your cousin is probably acceptable, but nobody at all could object to your younger and much better-looking sister living with you.'

Aminta is becoming progressively near to me in blood. This must be checked.

'Much though I liked and still mourn Marius, I do not think I resemble him in person. I am pleased that you decided to be no more than my cousin. Other than to appease my landlady, we are no kin of any sort. At least you didn't claim I was your husband.'

'That would have been difficult,' she says. 'Because I am already married.'

'You are married?' I ask. My heart sinks but I am sure my face reveals nothing. Absolutely nothing.

'Yes. Don't look so amazed, John. You knew that I was contemplating it. And you knew that Roger was in Bruges, just as I and my father were obliged to be.'

Yes, I knew she was contemplating it. But that was no reason to do it.

'Married to Roger Pole?' I say. 'To that...' I am about to say 'to that buffoon', then I realise I am describing Aminta's husband, to whom she may be a little attached. In any case 'buffoon' does not do him justice in so many ways. He is Ripley with none of Ripley's charm. He is an arrogant, overdressed cut-throat with a taste for treachery and subterfuge. And now, as a fugitive Cavalier, he must even lack funds to indulge himself in velvet and silk doublets. 'To that...incorrigible Royalist,' I say.

'Yes,' says Aminta. 'To that…incorrigible Royalist.'

Aminta Clifford is not my cousin and it is no business of mine whom she marries—even if she chooses someone as unsuitable as Roger Pole. I could describe Aminta as a childhood friend. I could describe her as a life-long tormentor and corrector. I could describe her as the sort of person who would arrive after a long absence and assume that they could share your accommodation with no offer of payment. She is all of those things. But if she is suggesting that I regret not proposing to her myself during the many long years that we have been acquainted…well, she is mistaken. I do not deny that many find her pretty, that her nose is small and her hair blonde. I do not deny that she has appropriated my best chair with a certain grace and elegance. But I have never wished to be appropriated in the same way. And nothing has changed. Nothing. Except, of course, that she is no longer Aminta Clifford.

'In any case, my father and I were also forced to flee as Royalists,' Aminta continues, 'so you would do well not to criticise Roger on that count alone.'

'Then I must address you in future as Mistress Pole,' I say as cheerfully as I can.

'Viscountess Pole,' she says. 'At least, I will be once Roger's title and lands are restored.'

'The King is not coming back,' I say.

'As you have so wisely told me, so many times. No, Roger and I are very much of your opinion. The good Viscount is no longer the incorrigible Royalist that you describe. Indeed, we now look to Cromwell to restore both his property and his ancient title. Many former Royalists are returning. Roger has petitioned Cromwell before. I have come to renew his request that Parliament should reverse the attainder on Roger's father, allow me to pay whatever fines may be demanded of us and regain what is ours.'

'And it is safe for you to return to England?' I say.

'A lying report reached the authorities of our Royalist sympathies, hence our flight to the Spanish Netherlands, but I do not believe that my own arrest is still sought. Indeed, I am told that it is not. It is safer that I return than my father or Roger. Unless you know differently?'

She looks at me as if she knows more about me than I would wish. But she is unaware of any connection I have with Mr Thurloe.

'No,' I say. 'I do not know differently.'

'And if I do not take this risk now, then the chance may pass. But these things are not to be done without friends at court. Do you know anyone who might help me, my dear cousin?'

I pause longer than I should have done.

'*Who* do you know?' she demands.

'Nobody,' I say.

'I can tell when you are lying, John.'

'What do you mean?' I swallow hard.

'You know somebody with a position at court.'

I laugh, though it doesn't sound quite as a laugh should—not quite as my laugh normally sounds. 'Why should I choose to lie about that?' I ask.

'I have no idea,' she says. 'Like so many things you do, it makes no more sense to me than it does to you. But you are lying.'

I change the subject. 'Did you introduce yourself to my landlady as a viscountess?'

'Yes.'

I can see why I have gone up a little in her estimation and why Will must buy oranges in the snow: I have a cousin married to a viscount, albeit to the most conceited one alive, now happily exiled and, apparently, with no immediate prospect of a return.

'You are still in Bruges?' I ask, before she can return to the subject of my friends in Westminster. 'Or do you live in Brussels, now Charles Stuart has moved his court there?'

'Paris,' she says. 'We have left the Spanish Netherlands. It seemed wise to distance ourselves from the Stuart court if I am to portray us as loyal citizens of the State. France is now the ally of the Protectorate, just as Spain is our mortal enemy.'

'When you say "*our* mortal enemy" you mean...'

'Mine and Cromwell's. I am as loyal to the Republic as you are, cousin.'

'And do you enjoy living in Paris?'

'It is livelier than Essex.'

'I hear that the food there is good?'

'If you have money to pay for it.'

'Have you seen the new King—the young Louis?'

'From a distance.'

'What is the palace like?'

'Big.'

I had hoped for more, because I have never been to France, but Aminta is undoubtedly tired after her journey. I'm sure she will tell me more in due course. I enquire after the health of Aminta's father, Sir Felix Clifford, who has, she says, transferred with them to Paris, though he has no hopes of petitioning. His estates are sold and lost for ever.

'Gout,' Aminta replies, as if her father and swollen joints in some way deserved each other. 'But even without it, he could not have risked coming here.'

I ask after her mother, ex-mistress of my father and now a lady-in-waiting, it seems, of the Queen of Bohemia, another English exile in Brussels lacking the lands or the ready cash to go with her title. I do not ask further after Roger Pole, being simply relieved he is in Paris and not here in London. Since my father is now living with a Flemish slut, there is little point in asking whether Aminta or her mother have news of him. And he is, of course, dead. I must remember that. I wonder briefly whether he succeeded in landing at Dover and, if so, whether he is, even now, trying to make contact with his fellow Royalists in London.

I complete my account of family news by telling Aminta that my own mother has married Colonel Payne and is now living in a state of some smugness in the manor house; Aminta's family once lived there too, both hers and mine having been lords of the manor at different times. Which still does not make us cousins. The manor was also Roger Pole's home for a while, when he was secretary to my stepfather.

'If your father and husband have had to remain in Paris, who will offer you protection here?' I ask.

'Why, you, of course. To whom else would I turn but my cousin? My cousin and my late brother's dearest friend.' She places a hand on my shoulder. She knows that there is very little that I would not do for her. Still, one point must be cleared up.

'You are not my cousin,' I say for the third time.

'I would *not* say that too loudly. Otherwise your landlady might think you were living with a married woman who was in no way related to you—something the men in your family have an unfortunate habit of doing. She might gossip and that might attract the attention of the authorities. The Spanish are some-what lax in their suppression of vice in the Low Countries, but I think that the magistrates in London are made of sterner stuff. Wouldn't you agree, Cousin John?'

I sigh. 'How much protection exactly will you require?'

'Quite a lot. I'll let you know.'

'But...'

Tomorrow I am to start work at the Lord Protector's court, a place that I have claimed I do not have access to. How can I do that with both the Sealed Knot and Aminta watching my every move? I am the most watched man in London. And I am indebted to Aminta in a way that she cannot realise—cannot realise because if she did, she would have already mentioned it and in no uncertain terms.

'I think you owe me that much,' she says.

Our respective eyes meet. Aminta's do not blink. I have no choice. I have never had any choice.

'I shall of course give you every assistance,' I say.

I have departed from my lodgings in the most cowardly manner, slipping away at dawn before Aminta had risen and asking my landlady to look after any needs that she might have during the day, with due concern for the necessity for economy. No wine. No more oranges. I wear the only suit I have and hope that it will prove appropriate to the work that will be allocated to me.

To avoid any possibility of being followed, I set out east-wards and then hide in a cul de sac in case any viscountesses are in pursuit of me. None passes the end of the alley and I am able to double-back westwards and continue on my way. The snow is melting again and the streets are muddy, though not as completely impassable as Aminta predicted. It may be that she can be sent on her way sooner than she thinks.

I report to Whitehall Palace and am informed that I am to be a clerk in the Lord Protector's service. I am to answer to Mr John Milton, Latin Secretary and author of the *Defensio pro Populo Anglicano*—his *Defence of the People of England*. I shall perhaps meet him in due course. My pay is to be £30 a year plus whatever bribes I am able to solicit. I am sent to various other clerks in various other departments who write up my commission and arrange for it to be signed; they charge me for the privilege. Even though I am allowed to draw my first month's salary, I am quickly out of pocket.

But these to-ings and fro-ings have a purpose. If the Sealed Knot ever make enquiries, they will discover that I am properly employed by the State, assisting the blind and commendably Republican Mr Milton with his labours, whatever they are, as Latin Secretary.

I walk home having made little progress as to the identity of Cromwell's assassin, but well pleased with my day's work.

❋ ❋ ❋

I find myself running up the stairs two at a time, my heart beating quickly. It is not that I am anxious to see Aminta again, I tell myself, but merely that I am eager to get home and sit in front of a warm fire. I find her in my only comfortable chair again, but this time she is not drinking wine.

'What is in that cup?' I ask.

'Tea,' she says.

I take it and sniff it cautiously. Tea is, reputedly, more expensive than wine.

'You must have heard of tea,' she says.

'There is a merchant in Exchange Alley who sells it,' I say. 'I have never seen it before. It is newly arrived here in London. I am told that it costs ten Pounds a pound.'

'My father likes it,' she says.

'Is it much drunk in Paris?'

'Why in Paris?'

'I assume that is where you discovered it.'

'Oh, yes. In Paris. To be sure. The French drink it all the time. It is cheaper there, of course. I brought this with me as dried, shredded leaves.'

'Is that how it is sold?'

'Yes, like a dried herb. You infuse it in boiling water.'

I sniff the concoction again and take a very small sip. The liquid is very hot and slightly bitter. It is not unpleasant, but I would praise it no more highly than that. I pass the cup back to her.

'The French may enjoy it, but I question that many in England will wish to drink it,' I say.

'I doubt you could afford to, my dear cousin,' she says. 'You are, after all, still training to be a lawyer. How did your studies progress today?'

The last sentence appears innocent enough on the surface, but I can tell that dark currents lurk beneath.

'A lecture on tort, then study in the library,' I say cautiously.

It is hard to see how such a dull, brief and evasive answer could hold any peril. And yet it does.

'A lecture on tort?'

'A civil wrong that unfairly causes somebody to suffer harm or loss, resulting in a legal liability...'

'That wasn't what I meant.'

'Wasn't it?'

'My emphasis, my dear cousin, was on the word *lecture,* rather than on the word *tort.*'

'I don't see why. Lectures are common enough at Lincoln's Inn.'

'But they are not very common at Cromwell's court in Westminster.'

'You followed me!' I exclaim.

'Your face, John, is not well suited to indignation. I do understand the effect you are trying to achieve, but I must warn you that you simply look alarmed and constipated, as if surprised on the privy by a person bearing your tailor's account. Of course I did not follow you. I told you that I needed to gain access to Cromwell. And you may readily guess that I do not have funds to allow me to remain long in London. Where else would you suppose I would go today other than to court? And who should I see amongst the crowd of faces in Westminster Hall than your own?'

'Or somebody who looked like me,' I say. But I am merely playing for time. Even if I were to continue with my denials, Aminta would return to court tomorrow and every day thereafter until she discovered why I was there and what I had been doing. I would rather she did something else.

'So are you saying it wasn't you?' she asks. 'How strange because, when I enquired who that good-looking but rather bookish young man was, I was informed that he was called John Grey and that he had just been appointed to a clerkship in the office of the Latin Secretary. Or are you saying that he not only looked like you but also had the same name? So, what were you doing in Westminster, cousin?'

Now, I could point out to her that I am neither more nor less bookish than many others I saw at court. I could also point out that it is none of Aminta's business where I go and whether I choose to take up employment under Mr Milton or any other poet. I could point out that I am not her cousin.

'I was going about my lawful business,' I say.

'About which it was necessary to lie to me? I do still have some friends in London. I can ask questions in all sorts of places. It is only a matter of time until I find out. The question is, how many other people I have to tell in the process and how much you would wish them to know.'

I take a deep breath. 'I was there to kill Cromwell,' I say.

It is a brief victory—one of those very rare moments when Aminta is actually speechless. Of course, she is not speechless for long. That would be a great deal to expect.

'Kill *Cromwell*?' she says, not unreasonably. 'I don't understand.'

I scarcely understand it myself, but as an alternative to having Aminta pursue me through the corridors of Westminster like one of her father's bloodhounds, I tell her everything, from Sir Michael's invitation to my meeting with Thurloe.

'So you are not *in fact* going to kill Cromwell?' she says.

'You sound disappointed.'

'John, the idea of your killing anyone, other than through boredom during an unusually lengthy summing-up, is improbable.'

'Ripley and Thurloe both commented on my bravery,' I say. 'They clearly felt I had a certain devil-may-care recklessness.'

'Yes,' says Aminta, 'but I know you better than they. As for Cromwell's death by anyone's hand, that would be unfortunate at a time when he may finally be receptive to our petition. It would be very inconvenient if he were to be replaced by some Anabaptist or Fifth Monarchy Man like General Harrison, who might be less sympathetic to the idea of returning Cavalier property. But you say that Thurloe wants you to uncover the true assassin?'

'Yes,' I say. 'But I hope it can be done without causing my father to be arrested.' Then, remembering my mother's embarrassment on this point, I add: 'Of course, my father may be dead...'

'Dead? He was alive and well in Bruges not long ago, when we were there, as I am sure you and your mother are aware. I have no doubt that he is now in Brussels, with the King.'

'You know that much, then?'

'Whatever we Royalist exiles lack, it is certainly not gossip.'

'It might be better if you did not mention it to my stepfather.'

'I'm sure your mother will have told him,' says Aminta. 'So, an informant of Ripley's has told him that he overheard a conversation between your father and Hyde in which Hyde gave him some instructions, including that he should not make contact with the Sealed Knot when he was in London?'

'Yes. That's about it.'

'Then the Sealed Knot sent your father a letter here, requesting that he should see them after all?'

'Yes.'

'So, how would they have known to write to him here?'

'They didn't. They simply mistook me for my father. They sought news of somebody called Grey, newly arrived in London. They discovered I lived here.'

Aminta considers this for some time.

'And they overheard nothing of the purpose of your father's mission? Nothing that would be of help to you?'

'No. That is why I still fear he may have been persuaded to attempt to murder Cromwell.'

'But surely your father would not act as an assassin?'

'It is a while since I saw my father. I hope not.'

'I am certain of it. There is nothing of the assassin in your father. My mother might be a whore but she's no murderer's whore. And I don't say that simply out of love and affection for her. I think there is only one assassin that Thurloe needs to worry about.'

'And he will do nothing until the Knot is certain that I have failed,' I say. 'We have time on our side.'

'I'm not sure about that. Didn't Thurloe say that one attempt had already been made on Cromwell's life? The problem with people like Ripley's hireling is that they take instructions less willingly than you might imagine.'

I smile. 'And that is the sort of thing you know about?'

Aminta ignores this. 'What do you know about Ripley and Brodrick?' she asks.

'Very little—just what Thurloe told me.'

'And Sir Richard Willys? The Sealed Knot freely come and go from his premises. Did Thurloe not find that odd?'

'It would apparently be easy enough to gain access to his chambers in his absence,' I say. 'A porter could be bribed.'

'Perhaps,' says Aminta thoughtfully. 'What really puzzles me is this: Thurloe must have dozens of men at court to ask questions for him. Why does he need you?'

'Because the Knot trusts me?'

'Thurloe has half of the Sealed Knot spying on the other half. He has no shortage of informants—most of them would be well trusted. He could ask any of them to do what you are doing.'

I suppose this has worried me too. I am being sent to a place that I do not know and where I have few friends to help me. The Knot will be watching my every move. My father might arrive at any moment and inadvertently reveal me as an imposter. Why me?

'Thurloe has confidence in me?' I suggest.

'Why should he have that?'

'Perhaps he thinks that my abilities...'

Aminta shakes her head.

'Well, why do *you* think he has employed me?'

'If you are caught and executed by the Knot, what will Thurloe have lost?'

'Why...nothing,' I say. 'Nothing at all.'

We both ponder this.

'Do you know,' says Aminta, 'I'm beginning to think you may be rather brave after all.'

'Really?' I ask. 'My main aim is to get out of this alive.'

'And with good fortune you will,' says Aminta, taking my arm affectionately. 'But if you do meet with the Lord Protector, I should be grateful if you raised the question of Roger's title and lands with him sooner rather than later.'

'Of course,' I say. '*If* I meet him.'

I am up betimes and hurrying through the dark but already crowded streets towards Westminster. I have not slept well, and only partly because Aminta has taken my bed and left me on a mattress in my sitting room. I find Aminta drifting fragrantly through my dreams. I awake happy, only for the lead to enter my soul again as I roll over and open my eyes to a grey dawn. We shall forever be on opposite sides of that bedroom door. And that is entirely my fault. While I dithered, as my mother would point out, Roger Pole snatched her from under my nose.

I try to keep her out of my mind as I make my way through early-morning London. A coach driver curses me for almost being run over by him. I hear a shout of 'Gardy loo!' just in time to avoid a cascade of filthy dishwater from an upper storey. I try to find a short-cut down an alleyway only to discover that it twists and turns back on itself, ending up in a malodorous dead end. I am almost run over by another coach, which fails to comment on the fact in any way. I step in horse shit. It is, in short, a typical journey across London that deserves no comment or further description.

A bell is striking eight as I arrive in Whitehall. But at the entrance to the Lord Protector's offices I am detained by a lackey.

'Mr Grey? I am instructed to inform you that you are required at Hampton Court this morning.'

'Hampton Court?' I say. Even if I set off now, it will take most of the day on foot, and I do not know the way. The lackey sees my puzzlement and indicates, with a wave of his hand, a coach that is waiting hard by. That then is my transport. I had scarcely noticed it as I ran up the road. It is far from new and painted a dull grey—people will not look admiringly in my direction as I pass by. Still, I observe as I examine it more closely, the leather straps that support the body of the coach are new and shining. The axles also seem to have had recent attention from the grease pot. The iron bindings round the wooden wheels are solid enough too. The horses that are to pull the coach are not well matched for colour, and their reins are of ordinary plain leather, but all four are glossy and powerfully muscled. The driver wears a capacious leather coat that covers his legs completely. He says nothing, but frowns at me as if to hurry me on.

The lackey too is watching me, waiting for me to board. They could have lent me a horse if I was needed there soon. A coach is kind but a little too generous. Why am I chosen for so much good fortune?

I cautiously open the door and climb in. The gloom of the day extends to the interior of the carriage and it takes me a few moments to notice that a man is already sitting on one of the seats on the far side. He is wrapped in a cloak and his hat is pulled down over his face. Immediately I sense a trap, but it is too late. The door slams behind me and the driver whips the horses. We are away. I wonder if it is too late to open the door and jump, but we are picking up speed. Anyway, I do not wish to turn my back on the stranger in the cloak. There is something about him that is wholly untrustworthy. I wonder whether to tell him I am armed. It is a lie, but it may make him think twice about attacking me.

Then he looks up and tilts back his hat.

I open my mouth to speak but no words come out.

'Good morning, Mr Grey,' says Cromwell. 'Now, tell me, how am I to be killed?'

Cromwell

'Your Highness!' I say. 'Forgive me, I did not see you.'

Cromwell shakes his head. 'I'm a plain man,' he says. 'Addressing me as my Lord will suffice.'

'My Lord...' I say.

Cromwell laughs and punches me on the arm. (I wish people would stop doing that.)

'You are clearly a man who loves a title,' he says. 'Some Quakers came to petition me last week. They insisted on calling me Friend Oliver—but they meant it well. What should we all call each other under a Republic, Mr Grey? Shall we put aside everything except our baptismal names that we were given before God?'

'That we are a Republic does not eliminate distinctions of rank,' I say. 'Nobody could wish all men equal.'

Cromwell nods. He thinks so too. Cromwell was once overheard to say that he hoped to live to see not a single nobleman in England. But he has not said that for a long time.

'You are right. It is a fine thing, is it not, to be a citizen of a republic, answerable to no petty tyrant king? One hundred, two hundred, three hundred years hence, men of the English Republic as yet unborn will look back on us, just as the Romans of the Golden Age looked back on Brutus and Lucretius. And they will wish that they had had the good fortune to live in our time.'

'The advantages, sir, lie entirely with Republican government,' I say.

He frowns. Should I have called him 'my Lord' after all? But that is not it.

'Not entirely,' he says. 'If I were to be assassinated, what then? What happens to our Republic? A king may sleep easy knowing that, if he dies, his son will succeed without demur. A blow to the monarch, however hard, is no blow to the State. So who will feel it worthwhile to make the attempt on his life? And if he has *two* sons...'

I am not sure what he means. Cromwell does indeed have two sons—the amiable Richard and the efficient Henry. But our last King had three. And he is as dead as you could wish. His Highness seems to be rehearsing some argument in front of me—testing ideas that are still half-formed and might yet be re-shaped.

'Could you not argue,' I say, 'that a republic is more secure because it has tens of thousands of sons who might succeed? Anyone could rule a republic.'

'*Anyone?*'

'I am sorry, my Lord, I did not mean—'

Cromwell laughs. 'There are many who *think* they could do it.'

'Then I concede a monarchy is more secure,' I say cautiously.

'And a secure State is a blessing for the people,' says Cromwell.

'Indeed,' I agree quickly. 'A great blessing.'

'But were I to make myself King... The Roman republic endured four hundred years between the fall of Tarquin and the rise of Augustus. Is our own republic to last a lousy ten? Am I to be Caesar as well as Brutus...'

Again he stops in mid-sentence. He looks at me keenly, as if I might know how he intends to end it.

'There is also much to admire in the age of Augustus, Your Highness.'

'True,' he says thoughtfully. 'There is much to admire.' This time, he does not correct the way I have addressed him. He has grown more used to this appellation than he believes. I suspect that, most of the time, he scarcely notices what people call him. 'But Augustus had only to answer to the Roman Senate and people,' he continues. '*Senatus Populus Que Romanus.* I, on the other hand, have to answer to the Lord God of Israel. I have to divine His purpose. What is that, do you suppose?'

'His purpose must be the good of the English people,' I say.

'Of course,' he says. 'He wishes us well above all things. We are His Chosen People. He is on our side. How else would we have defeated the Scots at Dunbar?'

I had assumed the Scots had simply been out-gunned, but Cromwell was there and I was not. He'd know.

He gazes out of the window for a while. We are now passing through the suburbs of London. Some snow still lies by the sides of the road and on the roofs of houses. We see the same road and the same roofs, but we see them differently. I am not charged with the safety of their occupants. Perhaps in a moment he will speak again but in the meantime, there is something almost sacred about the silence that now reigns. Cromwell is deciding the fate of the nation. The coach continues to roll along on its well-oiled wheels, while Cromwell decides whether he wants to be King. Soon, I think, we shall be at Chelsea. This is not the fastest way, but that is the point; the fastest way is the way others will expect him to travel.

He turns back to me. 'We make good time,' he says.

'Do you always travel like this—with no guard?' I ask. For it strikes me that we are alone on the muddy road. At any point we may have to slow as the horses wade through the mire and melting snow. Time enough then for a man to fire a ball through the open window.

'A coach with a guard of twenty dragoons left Westminster ten minutes before us. The blinds were drawn and the troopers had instructions not to disturb me because I was suffering from an ague and would sleep. If the coach is attacked, I fear they may feel obliged to defend it with their lives, but it would be a prescient assassin who let that ostentatious crowd thunder past and waited to attack this modest and wholly innocent carriage.'

'But if they did...'

Cromwell reaches into a pocket in the door and pulls out a pistol.

'Do you know how to use one of these?' he asks.

'In principle,' I say.

'Then, should we be attacked, leave me to do the fighting. If by some ill chance I am shot and close to death—and I shall inform you very clearly if that is the case—there is a second pistol in the pocket of the other door. Aim it at somebody close by and pull the trigger. Use both hands, for these guns kick like a mule. Or surrender and take your chance.'

'Thank you,' I say.

I notice that he told me of the second pistol only once I had admitted that I had no idea how to use it. I also notice that he still holds the first pistol in his hands, stroking the grey, polished barrel. He takes no risks with strangers, even ones that are vouched for by the head of his secret service.

'Now,' says Cromwell, 'let us return to my first question: if I get safely to Hampton Court, how am I to die?'

'I do not know,' I say. 'Only that there is a plot by somebody close to you.'

He smiles. I wonder if he is close to anyone now: Ireton is dead. Lambert and Fairfax are estranged. His circle of friends grows smaller and smaller.

'But you don't know who?'

'The Sealed Knot are behind it.'

'They like to think they are behind everything. You have no more information than that?'

'Do *you* know who it might be?' I ask.

'I have upset General Lambert,' he says. 'He feels slighted. But I have also upset a great number of other generals. General Fairfax feels that I have treated his new son-in-law unfairly.'

'How?'

'I have ordered his detention.'

'And they would kill you for that?'

'No. Not for that. But if they view me as Caesar...'

'...encompassing your death would be a noble act?'

'A noble act? That is how you see it? These words are treason, Mr Grey. They will send you to the gallows!'

'No, my Lord!' I exclaim. 'I intended to give no offence.'

'I jest, Mr Grey,' says Cromwell, as if I have disappointed him greatly. 'I merely jest. And I wouldn't hang you just as a joke. Or probably not.'

I swallow hard. It is easy, it would seem, to become a traitor. I am not sure whether I prefer Cromwell's humour or Thurloe's lack of it.

'But of course,' I say. 'A jest. But surely neither my Lord Fairfax nor my Lord Lambert would contemplate your murder? I mean, however much you had offended them, they would not strike the blow themselves?'

'I think not. But if they were plotting with the Sealed Knot to remove me—if they were aiding some assassin hired by Sir Edward Hyde or recruited by the leaders of the Knot here in London... They know me well. They have, after a fashion, access that other men do not. As this man Ripley said to you, it has to be somebody with access to me, somebody whom I would not suspect.'

'But there must be many who have such access?'

'Those who wish me dead are too many to name. Those who could get close enough are fewer. It won't be Thurloe anyway. He knows which side his bread is buttered on. And Thurloe says I may trust *you*. He says you are honest.'

'Thank you.'

'It wasn't a compliment. Not from him. And you need not suspect my doctor. If he was going to kill me deliberately, he could have done so years ago. I expect him to kill me eventually in the normal course of his ministrations, but not yet. And you may trust my son Henry because he knows he still lacks the experience to rule. And you may trust Richard because he loves hunting and good company and doing nothing—and he knows he will have little of that if he succeeds me.'

'Is there anyone else whom we may trust?'

Cromwell shakes his head again. 'I *tell* others that I trust them,' he says. 'I tell them and they believe me.' He smiles at me as if he had made some great joke. I think he trusts nobody at all. Perhaps not even Thurloe. Certainly not me.

'It is true. I could stab you now,' I say.

'If you wish.' He carefully places the pistol back in its holster and opens his arm wide, as if inviting me to strike.

'But of course,' I say. 'You wear armour under that cloak.'

'Ah, that old lie,' he says. 'Punch me in the chest and prove if that is true!'

'So you do not?'

'Of course not. Punch me and see for yourself. Do not fear the consequences: I order you to do it.'

I draw back my fist and land what I hope is not too hard a blow at his chest. Then I double up in pain. I think I have bruised every finger.

'Ha!' he says. 'Thurloe was right. That was bravely done but, as an honest man yourself, you are far too trusting. It is fortunate that was a feeble lawyer's punch. If you were a soldier you would have broken your hand.'

'So you do wear armour,' I say.

'But not on my back,' he says. 'Too uncomfortable for travelling. Perhaps you would like to punch me there? This time I may be telling the truth.'

'Thank you, but no,' I say, rubbing my hand. 'I am happy to trust the word of Brutus.'

For a while we travel in silence, broken only by the occasional chuckle from Cromwell as he recalls either my discomfort or some particularly amusing incident from the Battle of Dunbar. Then he leans forward in his seat.

'The Royalists have faith in you, Mr Grey,' he says. 'Thurloe thinks their man, whoever it is, will approach you soon. Perhaps he will. You were told how disappointed he was not to share in the glory. I have faith in you too. You are, as Thurloe says, honest and frank. I think men will tell you things because they trust you. So talk to the other clerks. See what gossip there is. Talk to my doctor too. He's called Bate—George Bate. He was the late King's physician, but he's mine now. A bit like Hampton Court in that respect. A bit like the whole country in fact.'

Again he looks out of the window. We have passed through Chelsea and must be close to Hammersmith, though I do not know these roads well.

'Here we are,' he announces suddenly.

I notice we are approaching a jetty and that a boat is moored to it. 'We continue by river?' I ask. That we should switch to a boat is entirely consistent with Cromwell's way of travelling. It will be faster by water and the empty coach will doubtless continue, a second decoy.

'No,' says Cromwell. 'I get out here. You will remain in the coach. Remember where the pistols are if you are waylaid. Point them and tell your attackers to desist. Your voice carries authority, Mr Grey, though perhaps you do not yet realise it. You may be a Judge one day, if you live long enough.'

'But...' I say.

Cromwell laughs again. 'You think I send you into a trap? But you are supposed to be a junior clerk in the service of Mr Milton. It would look odd if you arrived in the same boat as the Lord Protector, would it not? Or at least, your new Royalist friends might start to wonder how you have made such progress and, more to the point, why you have not already taken the opportunity to kill me. From here you are safer alone. Your driver will slip quietly into Hampton Court shortly after the arrival of the first coach. You will disembark equally quietly and find the chamber that has been allocated to you. You will tell people, if they ask, that Mr Milton has instructed you to attend him here, but you do not know when he will arrive. I will send for you again if I need you. In the meantime, you will be warmer in the coach than I shall be on the river.'

And he is gone, striding down to the narrow wooden jetty. I look at the set of his cloak on his back. I see clearly that he wears no armour there. My driver waits long enough to watch him board the small boat and then, without consulting me in any way, whips the horses into a smart canter.

I would enjoy telling Aminta of my journey with Cromwell, but it may be as well not to say anything to her for the moment because, it now occurs to me, I have spent some time in his company without once raising the question of Roger Pole's title and lands, and I feel that she will think I should have cleared that up before proceeding to discuss the advantages of Republican government.

I sink back into the leather seat and, my hand still throbbing gently, allow the coach to carry me onwards towards Hampton Court. It is more than two hours before the great red-brick building emerges from the river mist that hangs around it, first as a vague shadow, then a dull brown stain, then a mass of fantastical turrets and walls. Finally we reach the two long rows of heraldic beasts between which we must pass before gaining admission through the rose-brick gateway. Somewhere on the other side is Dr Bate, once the royal physician, now Cromwell's, and the first man I must talk to if Cromwell and I are to stay alive for very long.

Dr Bate

Dr Bate is a man of medium height, plump and not entirely unhappy with the way that things have gone. He has outlasted his old master and gained a new one. He has good financial and professional reasons for keeping this one alive as long as he can.

We are walking together along a path by the Thames in the fast-fading light. Away to our left stretches a knot garden, its carefully pruned lines of box running north to south and east to west in a strict rectilinear pattern. Here and there, bedraggled lavender peeps over the top of the low hedging. Beyond is the long, crenellated red-brick wall of the Palace, softened by the mist and glowing with blurred candlelight from its many windows. On our right, where yellow vapour clings to the river, the countryside begins. The Thames here flows smoothly and darkly. The opposite shore, perhaps a hundred yards away, can be made out, but only just. Beyond this dark brown streak of riverbank and the skeletal willows balanced on it, there is nothing visible. We are several centuries away from London. The constant stink of sea coal is absent, as is the incessant calling of tradesmen and the rumble of their carts. The smells and sounds here are the ones that I grew up with in rural Essex. The bells I hear are from a single church, far across the water, not a multitude on every hand with parish crammed onto parish.

Dr Bate and I have walked some way. I check again that we are completely alone.

'His Highness recommended that I should seek your counsel,' I say. 'As his doctor, you know him as well as any man…'

Bate looks over his shoulder before replying. 'I know him better than he knows himself, for I see beneath his skin and into the very guts of the man. He is growing older than he believes. His health has not been good. That is no secret.'

I nod.

'I also know him well enough, Mr Grey, to be sure that he has asked you to sound me out on my loyalty.'

'I must protest he did no such thing.'

Bate laughs. He knows Cromwell. 'He trusts nobody, Mr Grey. We all spy on each other. It is more than likely he will ask me tomorrow if *you* are to be relied upon. But I shall do my best to reassure you—and him. I was informed you were coming. I think we need to work together. I gather there is yet another plot?'

'Is that what His Highness told you?'

'No. But there is always another plot. You look surprised. Let me tell you of a few of them. Last year, one Thomas Gardiner was arrested in Whitehall with two loaded pistols, for which he could not account to the satisfaction of the magistrates. He claimed he always carried pistols and that his question to a passer-by about whether the Lord Protector wore armour was entirely innocent. But a fellow lodger said he'd always been suspicious of him, which was regarded as proof enough of treason in these times. Before Gardiner there was Venner and before Venner there was Miles Sindercombe—that didn't go so well for Thurloe.'

'Why for Thurloe especially?'

'Because the authorities were slow to act and Thurloe was blamed for it. Sindercombe shouldn't have got close to succeeding. First he hired a shop in King Street from which he was going to fire on the Lord Protector as he passed. But then he discovered he'd hired a shop without a back door—no escape route. So he dropped that idea. Then he recruited one of the Lord Protector's own Life Guards—Toupe, he was called—who was to help him attack Cromwell when he changed from his horse to his coach, but that came to nothing either. Then he hired another house at Hammersmith—you'll have driven past it today. He had acquired a great gun from Flanders that could fire twelve bullets at a time. Twelve! I mean, one of them would have found its target. But in the end he went for setting fire to the chapel at the Palace of Westminster in the hope that the whole thing would burn down. A guard smelled the burning fuse and put it out. Another three hours and there might have been quite a nasty fire, according to Thurloe...'

'A three-hour fuse?'

'Assuming it hadn't already been burning for two, in which case it was a five-hour fuse.'

'It had to be discovered,' I say. 'It would be madness or incompetence to set a fuse that long.'

'Mr Thurloe was doubtful about Sindercombe from the very beginning because—and there is no polite way to say this—Sindercombe appears to have been a complete idiot. When Thurloe was first told—this was in Sindercombe's King Street days—he simply advised his informant to write to Brussels for further information.'

'Thurloe didn't believe in it, then?' I ask.

'No.'

'And from what you say, nor do you?'

'You are a wise and learned man, Mr Grey. Let me ask you a couple of questions. Why would anyone hire a shop without checking whether it had a back door, if that was its most important feature? And why set fire to the chapel on the off-chance that it would spread to the rest of the Palace and that the one person who wouldn't escape would be the Lord Protector, who would certainly have had a guard at his door who would have hustled him out on smelling the first whiff of smoke?'

'And the Lord Protector thought so too?'

'You would have thought that, as another wise and learned man, he would have done so, but that was not the case. Cromwell was furious with Thurloe. I've never seen him so cross. That's why I say, whatever Thurloe's plan was, it didn't go quite as he intended.'

'What happened to Sindercombe?'

'Thurloe interviewed him personally. Nobody else was allowed to go near him. He refused to talk, they say, but Toupe didn't. Toupe was quite helpful. Sindercombe was found dead in his cell on the morning he was to be executed. What a shame he never got to make a final speech on the gallows.'

'And Toupe? Was he executed?'

'He was working for Thurloe when I last heard. Funny old world, isn't it?'

'Are you saying that Thurloe had Sindercombe killed?'

'I'm told you are a lawyer. What do you think?'

'I think I'd like to hear all of the evidence before I made up my mind.'

'I doubt if anyone will ever get to hear that. Of course, Thurloe can't arrest people until they have done something—which means he often has to leave them until they have lit the fuse—or he has to get somebody to light it for them. I'm pleased my own job is so much simpler. You know where you are with a leech.'

'But you don't know who might be plotting the Lord Protector's death now?'

'You need not question my leeches,' says Bate. 'I'm happy to answer for them. Otherwise the whole court is open to your scrutiny, Mr Grey.'

'Did you know that somebody had tried to cut His Highness's saddle girth?'

'I'd heard. He could have had an unpleasant fall. What you have to understand, Mr Grey, is that most of the plots we have uncovered are so ill-conceived and futile that they are scarcely worth Mr Thurloe's notice. It is sometimes difficult to distinguish between the malign and the merely unfortunate. Undetectable murder requires real skill and application. Somebody who's not afraid to use a knife.'

'Do you know a Sir Michael de Ripley? Or a Mr Allen Brodrick?'

Bate's attention seems to be wandering. He is looking over my shoulder.

'Ripley? No, I don't think so.'

'Do you know who Sir Richard Willys might be?'

Bate shakes his head. I have perhaps tried his patience too far. Then he says: 'Willys? A common enough name. But Sir Richard Willys...no, I don't think I have ever met him.'

'He practises law in London.'

'Does he? Then you'd know him better than I.' Bate suddenly seems anxious to leave. He is finding this tedious. Or perhaps it is simply the coldness of the evening. 'I am acquainted with few baronets, I am afraid. As a mere doctor of medicine I do not move in such elevated company.'

'Not in elevated company? You are close to the Lord Protector himself.'

'That is another matter entirely. Good evening to you, Mr Grey. I think that must conclude our discussion for the moment, but I am at your service if you need me again.'

I am left with the feeling that Bate has not told me everything. I believe he does know Willys. He certainly knows he is a baronet, and I did not give him that information. But what I am to make of that is for the moment uncertain.

I realise it would be better to continue such thoughts in a different place. One where nobody can creep up on me in the mist. In the knot garden I can no longer make out the individual rows. Above me, the moon is no more than a pale yellow glow behind the gloomy clouds. It provides little comfort. I know I should have already returned to the safety of the Palace, whose lights still flicker in the distance. Then I hear a footstep behind me, then another, then a gentle cough. I turn suddenly.

It is Ripley.

CHAPTER 9

Sir Michael de Ripley

'Well met, Mr Cardinal,' he says.

'Good evening, Sir Michael,' I reply.

Where has he been during my recent conversation? Which words did he hear and which were blown away on the evening breeze? Did Dr Bate see him before I did? Bate certainly left quickly enough.

'You have obtained a post?' he asks.

'Clerk to Mr Milton,' I say.

Ripley whistles through his teeth. 'To gain such a post is a masterstroke—obscure yet close enough to Cromwell. You have exceeded my hopes. Well done, Mr Cardinal.'

I try to look modest, which is not difficult since the appointment was none of my work. Still, nobody is likely to tell Ripley if I don't.

'And you travelled here so quickly,' he purrs. 'Achilles himself would not have overtaken you this morning. Our man says that you were there one moment, in the middle of Whitehall, and gone the next.'

I am not deceived by these velvet tones. There is something that Ripley does not like.

'There was a carriage travelling empty to Hampton Court,' I say. 'I was able to obtain a seat in it.'

'Completely empty? How convenient.'

'I was fortunate. It was a decoy, to divert attention from Cromwell's own coach.'

It is inconceivable that the Sealed Knot is unaware that such things are done, and a good lie is often built on a little truth.

'That would have involved some danger to you—if the coach had been attacked, I mean.'

I smile. Soon laughing in the face of danger may be second nature to me. But smiling is a start.

Ripley ignores this. I am not commended on my bravery. 'It was just you in the coach then?'

Would Ripley's informant have seen Cromwell? I have no idea. I certainly didn't see him until I boarded. I am pleased that, in the dark of this Hampton Court evening, Ripley cannot see my expression.

'Nobody else needed to travel then,' I say.

'Again, how *very* convenient. A whole carriage to yourself. Your cousin has influence indeed. And you came straight here?'

'Yes.'

'You stopped nowhere?'

'The driver stopped somewhere near Hammersmith,' I say. 'A problem with the reins, I think. But we did not tarry long.'

'Didn't you?'

'Not for long.'

Close by where we are standing, the Thames still flows silently by. The dark surface looks smooth and untroubled but many currents doubtless contend in its muddy depths.

'You are fortunate indeed,' says Ripley. 'We must hope your luck continues.'

'Is there any reason why it should not?'

Ripley smiles as if I have made some choice jest. 'Was Dr Bate advising you on which poison to use?'

'No,' I say truthfully. 'Dr Bate has no knowledge of my real purpose here. We spoke in general terms of threats to His Highness's life.'

'There's no need to call that upstart farmer any sort of Highness in my hearing,' says Ripley. 'He's not the Duke of York or the Duke of Gloucester. He's not even one of His Majesty's royal bastards. He's no prince of any description unless he has changed his mind about accepting the crown?'

'If he has, he's said nothing to me about it.'

I smile but this time Ripley does not. 'You've spoken to Cromwell?' he says.

'Don't you think I'd tell you if I had?' I say.

Ripley's expression is difficult to gauge in this light. But he is not happy.

'So it was only you in the carriage?' he says again.

'And the driver,' I say.

'And the horses, presumably.'

'Yes. Four, though not well matched.'

Ripley can press me as many times as he wishes and employ as much sarcasm as he likes. All I have to do is to repeat that I was alone in the coach. He cannot prove otherwise—unless the coachman is in the pay of the Sealed Knot. That cannot be ruled out. In which case I'm as good as dead anyway.

Ripley looks towards the river. It's close enough that you could throw something from here and it would land in the water. Not something as big as a man, of course. You'd need to stab him first and then drag his body ten yards or so and finally give it a good push as it teetered on the edge, then flopped into the murky stream, drifting slowly away towards Putney, leaving a thin trail of watery blood. But it wouldn't take long. And you wouldn't hear the splash. It's really much more easily done than Dr Bate implied.

'Can I be honest with you?' he asks.

It's not a question that you can really answer 'no' to.

'If you would do me that honour,' I say.

'Brodrick thinks you're a scurvy piece of shit,' says Ripley.

A chill wind blows across the back of my neck.

'I'm sorry to hear that,' I say.

'Thank you. I'll let him know. He feels that we missed a chance to kill you at Gray's Inn. But I told him that you were dependable. I told him you were what you appeared to be and no double agent. I told him I knew your father.'

'Thank you,' I say.

'Absolutely dependable—that's what I told him. All that family—completely dependable.'

I think briefly of my mother. Does Ripley include her? It would be difficult to fault her long and unthinking adherence to the Stuart cause. I hope he does not know that my 'cousin' is now actively courting Cromwell.

'Thank you,' I say again.

'I told Brodrick how much your family has suffered in the King's service. You could scarcely be an adherent of the Republic.'

Suffered? I wonder what stories my father can have told Ripley. It is true that he followed the King's army as a surgeon and must have experienced the usual hardships of a long and ultimately unsuccessful campaign. But the decision to go into exile was his and his alone. I have no evidence that he regrets it or wishes himself home in Essex with my mother rather than in Brussels with his mistress.

'You know my father well?' I ask, if only to draw the conversation away from Brodrick and missed opportunities.

'Our paths have crossed occasionally. We have both spent some time in Bruges, and indeed more recently in Brussels.'

'We are not alike in temperament,' I add, not wishing him to think I am the whoring drunkard of whom my mother has spoken with so much pious regret.

Ripley looks me up and down.

'True. You are no soldier. Your courage is of another sort. You would undertake things that your father might not. And I trust your word. Of course, if you were deceiving us, I would look foolish. My judgement would have been sadly at fault. It would be a stain on my reputation that I would need to efface, *coûte que coûte.* Brodrick is rash and impulsive but ultimately forgiving. I, conversely...'

'You are different?'

'Exactly. I never forgive, Mr Cardinal. Forgiveness is a weakness that I cannot afford. If somebody betrays me, I hunt them down. If they run, I follow. If they go to earth, I dig them out. There is nowhere I cannot find them.'

I do not ask if that includes under the tables in the library of Lincoln's Inn.

'My own sentiments entirely, Sir Michael,' I say, with what I hope is a Cavalier swagger. 'I too never forgive a slight. But effecting Cromwell's death may not be as easy as I thought. This other person that you said would attempt the assassination if I failed...'

'Yes?'

'It might be better if we worked together, he and I.'

'Ah, I see. You'd like me to tell you his name?'

'If you would be so kind.'

'Hyde didn't tell you who it was?'

Another question whose answer I shall have to guess.

'No,' I say.

Ripley smiles. 'That's because we didn't tell him. And I can't tell you either.'

'Because?'

'Because if you fail, you will be captured and tortured. You know that. The less you can tell them, the better. You will die happier in the knowledge that you have not betrayed us in any way.'

'Is it Sir Richard Willys?' I ask.

Well, that has surprised Ripley. 'Willys? Why on earth would it be Willys?'

'We met in his chambers at Gray's Inn.'

'If you say so. I don't recall. Perhaps it would be better if you did not recall it either.'

'Who is he?'

'Sir Richard Willys? You surely know that at least?' Ripley looks at me oddly. Though it is dark I fancy I can see his hand tightening on the hilt of his sword.

For a moment I say nothing. Things look bad, but I can always make them worse.

'He's a lawyer,' I say tentatively. 'A lawyer...and a loyal supporter of the King.'

Ripley looks at me in puzzlement and not for the first time. 'Did Hyde recruit you specifically for this mission?'

'Yes,' I say.

'Because of your father?'

'Yes,' I say.

'You had no other contact with our party in Brussels?'

'No,' I say.

'Not ever?'

'No.'

Ripley stares at me again, then he finally releases the hilt of his sword. I hear it slither back an inch or two into the scabbard.

'Then Hyde might have briefed you better,' he says. 'He, or indeed your father, might have told you more, since your life might have depended on it.'

He shows, however, no sign of wishing to make up for Hyde's omission.

'But I have survived,' I say.

'I think,' says Ripley, 'that you have no idea how lucky you have been. Let us hope, Mr Cardinal, that your luck holds.'

✿ ✿ ✿

I have been allocated a small part of a small chamber in one of the more obscure recesses of Hampton Court. A tiny leaded window looks down, a long way down, on a dim and narrow courtyard, the function of which is unclear, but from which the smell of drains rises. I am to share this room, for as long as my presence is required at Hampton Court, with another junior member of the Protector's household.

'Esmond Underhill at your service,' he sniffs. I do not think he has caught a chill. I think this is the way he always speaks. 'Of Colchester in the fair county of Essex. Formerly

Corporal of Horse in the service of my Lord Lambert. I now serve His Highness the Lord Protector as a clerk in the Post Office.'

He seems unreasonably proud of each of these achievements. He does not have the air of a soldier, but Lambert's troops were noted for the soundness of their political principles as much as the strength of their arms. I wonder if he would be impressed if I told him I am here in a double capacity as a spy for the Sealed Knot and Mr Thurloe. I doubt it. I don't think he is impressed by things other people do.

'My name is Grey,' I say. 'John Grey. Clerk to Mr Milton.'

'Grey?'

'That's right,' I say.

Underhill wrinkles his nose and sniffs again, drawing up copious quantities of snot into some inner recess. 'What's Milton like to work for? He writes poetry, doesn't he?'

'So I'm told.'

'Takes all sorts.'

That could be an observation on Underhill himself. The constant activity of his nose, the sharp cheekbones, the thin, insipid face—they all recall to mind some nocturnal carrion-feeder. His claws are black with a nameless filth. His clothes are little better. But he is my companion for tonight at least.

'Which bed would you prefer?' I ask.

'Either is fine with me,' he says. 'But would you care for a drop of brandy first, Mr Grey?'

'You have brandy?'

He produces a glass bottle, stopped with a cork and three quarters full of a pale amber liquid. 'The very best,' he says. 'French.'

'Thank you but no,' I say. 'I occasionally tried brandy when I was at Cambridge, but my head will not stand it. Even a little makes me act like a brainless fool.'

Underhill smiles sympathetically. 'But just a sip?' he enquires. 'Surely that would do you no hurt?' He tips the bottle slightly so that he may better admire the golden liquid as it splashes to and fro behind the green glass. 'Smooth as a lady's cheek. From the

Lord Protector's own cellar. Don't ask me how I got it and I might even let you try a second sip. Come! You may never taste its like again.'

I shake my head, older and wiser than he. 'I'll take the bed on the right, then,' I say.

My Lady Pole

I am aware that the sun is shining brightly through the small window. I have been dreaming that somebody was winding a rope round my head, then pulling it tighter and tighter. The blood pounds in my ears. My mouth is dry. I could swallow the contents of a well at a single draught. I can't have had a drink of any sort for a week.

Except possibly, now I think of it, about half a bottle of brandy, allegedly from the Lord Protector's cellar.

Underhill has departed about his business and the left-hand bed is vacant. The right-hand bed is still full of me, although the day is well advanced and I should be somewhere else. I sit up suddenly and the room spins round. I stand and it is at least no worse. I am, I notice, fully clothed, so that is one potential problem solved with no expenditure of energy on my part.

Excellent.

In one corner of the room there is a basin of filthy cold water, the remains no doubt of Underhill's morning ablutions. I plunge my head into it, thus meeting the need for hygiene and penance at a stroke. Then I forget that I must not breathe when my head is under water and emerge coughing and spluttering. I go to the window and try to calculate the time of day. Ten of the clock, perhaps? The sun never rises high at this time of year but it has, it informs me, been up and doing for some time while I slumbered.

I dry my face on what I believe must be Underhill's spare shirt, for he deserves no less. I think back to twelve hours or so before. Surely (he said) I would at least take a sip of his brandy—politeness dictated that. Did I mean to insult him? Was it not (he said) some of the finest brandy I had tasted? And a second sip would only help me sleep, he said, taking the bottle back from me. I observed in passing that I knew a fine song about drinking brandy, suitable for any company except that of ladies and Puritans and priests and magistrates, such as my stepfather. Underhill said he was no Puritan and (he promised) no stepfather of mine. I said amen to that, thou good and trusty companion. And then...and then...

I think I may have asked him in a confidential fashion who might wish the Lord Protector dead. I remember that he reacted with shock—then, when I assured him (at my third attempt) that I spoke merely in a conjectural manner, he considered this carefully.

'My Lord Fairfax,' he said, 'has a great grudge against His Highness.'

'How so?' I asked, though perhaps (thinking about it) with less cunning than I then imagined.

His face approached mine in a conspiratorial manner.

'Fairfax was a better general than Cromwell. It was Fairfax that won Naseby. Cromwell was no more than his deputy. After that victory, Fairfax was ruler of England. Ask anybody who remembers those times. But Cromwell snatched the prize away. Fairfax knows *he* should be the Lord Protector. And he wouldn't be calling himself Highness or toying with a crown.'

'Would he not?'

'No. He's proper nobility, see. Lord Fairfax of Cameron, he's rightly called. Cromwell's just a jumped-up nobody, near blinded by his first sight of gold and ermine.'

This seemed to me no way for an officer of the State, however minor, to talk. A little brandy obviously loosened his tongue. I offered him the bottle back and he returned it to me.

'But Fairfax has married his daughter to the Duke of Buckingham,' I said. 'Is he too not dazzled by gold and ermine?'

'Black Tom Fairfax is a wily old fox,' said Underhill. 'He knows an alliance with Buckingham is the way back to power.'

'Cromwell is seeking to arrest Buckingham,' I said. I returned the bottle to Underhill. He tipped it back.

'Precisely,' he said, wiping his lips. 'A declaration of war if ever there was one. It's an insult to Fairfax, ain't it? It's showing him he don't have the power even to protect his own daughter's interests. A proud man like Fairfax won't be able to stand that. They was strangers before, but now he and Cromwell are mortal enemies.'

'Is that so?'

'That is so, my friend. Now, have some more brandy.'

If I stopped drinking, then Underhill would too, I reminded myself. I was drinking for England.

'What about General Lambert?' I passed the bottle back.

'An honourable man. Won't hear a word said against my Lord Lambert.'

'But an enemy of His Highness's?'

'He'd have cause enough, wouldn't he? Lambert was supposed to be Cromwell's chosen heir—perhaps the greatest general of them all and loyal to the Good Old Cause. Then all the talk started of Cromwell becoming King and his eldest son, Richard, succeeding him. Lambert spoke honestly to Cromwell and advised against it. Cromwell, to be fair, turned down the Crown but he never quite dropped the idea that he might be succeeded by a member of his own family. He rather liked that, in fact. So, he gave Lambert a pension and told him to piss off home. Lambert is in honourable exile, so-called, in Wimbledon. Not too far away to be out of touch with the court, though. He's too clever to fall for that.'

'So, he might be plotting to kill His Highness? He might see him as a threat to the Republic?'

'My Lord Lambert is too good, too high-minded to stoop to assassination.'

'Anyone else?' I asked.

'Have you considered Dr Bate?' he asked slyly.

I shook my head and Underhill chuckled as he passed the bottle back to me. I wiped his spittle from the neck and drank. Smooth as a viscountess's cheek.

'Did you hear that there was an attempt on His Highness's life?' I asked. 'Somebody tried to cut his saddle girth.'

'No, I've heard nothing about that. His saddle girth, you say? That's clever. Do they know who it was?'

'No.'

'They have no clue at all?'

'No,' I said.

And Underhill smiled.

Or at least, we spoke in something like that manner. I would not care to vouch for the precise words used, but that was the sense. I remember I later asked him about Sir Richard Willys and he laughed and said it was a difficult problem or an intractable problem or an awkward problem...but it was the exact phrase that seemed to so amuse him. It amused him even more that I failed to see the joke. And then... And then...

Doubtless it will all come back to me in due course. In the meantime I see that I have thrown Underhill's shirt into his basin of dirty water, which is a shame for him.

I descend the stairs quite slowly and set off for the kitchens and a large draught of small beer.

The dial, high on the gatehouse of Clock Court, shows that it lacks but one hour to a winter's midday. *Octava hora.* High above me, the sun shines on the red-brick battlements and their white stone capping. Down here, in the depths of this echoing quadrangle, shadows lie over the worn flagstone. The ground is still covered with a rime of frost, except for a line of footprints that slants across it. While I slept, others have been active in the Lord Protector's service. The air is bitingly cold and I think it may snow again very soon, but my thoughts are as clear and bright as the one small patch of blue sky above me. I even see Aminta before she sees me. As she leaves a side door, I stride over and greet her.

'Where have you been?' she demands. She wears a green riding costume, which fits snugly round her small waist. A large hat shades her eyes. In her hand there is a whip, which she taps against her soft leather glove.

'Here,' I say, indicating Middlesex in general.

'In bed, no doubt.'

'Underhill gave me too much brandy,' I say.

'Who or what is Underhill?'

'A clerk who gives me brandy.'

'To what end?' she asks.

'In a spirit of generosity,' I say. But I doubt I am right. It is a Christian act to give somebody drink when they are thirsty, but Underhill's actions were, judged by this very proper standard, almost saintly. 'I needed to keep him drinking. I needed to get information out of him,' I add.

'And what information did he get out of you?'

This is a question that I have asked myself several times this morning. What exactly did I tell Underhill? I certainly gave him my name—but then I am here as John Grey. The Sealed Knot know who I am. Thurloe knows who I am. There is no need to dissemble on that score. I'm fairly sure I did not tell Underhill that I had travelled here with Cromwell. Or did I? At one stage we were very good friends. There is something that troubles me slightly.

'I swore him to secrecy,' I say.

'About what?'

'I'm not sure.'

'Idiot. Who does Underhill work for?'

'The Post Office,' I say.

'Which reports to?'

'Mr Secretary Thurloe,' I say. 'But Underhill is merely...'

'Employed by Thurloe.'

'So word of this may get back to...'

'Thurloe. If you're lucky,' says Aminta.

'And if I'm not?' I ask.

'Then, dear cousin, to whoever he really works for.'

I wonder who the bill for the brandy will be sent to. Still, what he said about Fairfax was interesting for all that.

'Now, have you been able to talk to Cromwell about Roger's lands and titles?' says Aminta. 'Which of course are also *my* lands and titles, so I very much hope you have.'

'No,' I say. The longer answer is that I shared a coach with the Lord Protector for a couple of hours and forgot, but I find I prefer the shorter one.

'It is fortunate that I am now here in person then,' says Aminta.

'You travelled here this morning?'

'You failed to return home last night, suggesting that Cromwell had moved here for a few days. I hired a horse and followed, riding side-saddle in the freezing cold along muddy roads, while you travelled by coach.'

'You heard that?'

'It is the one thing that everybody seems to know about you.'

'So,' I say, 'you plan to gain access to Cromwell and speak to him about the reversal of the attainder?'

'No, I had planned that *you* should do that. You have, after all, impeccable Republican credentials and your stepfather fought on the winning side, albeit that your real father, like mine, instinctively supported the losing one. But there are also others whom I can approach, who may not have a position at court but who are not entirely lacking in influence. Roger's family is connected to that of the Duke of Buckingham, who in turn is married to the daughter of General Fairfax, who may well still have Cromwell's ear. Of course, the fact that there is a warrant out for the Duke's arrest does not help things, but the connection is there for all that.'

'Roger Pole is a cousin of the Duke of Buckingham?' I say.

'There's no need to sound quite so reverential. He is only a third or fourth cousin, cousin. I had thought that, as a Republican with impeccable credentials and so on, you would be unimpressed by mere titles. Otherwise I would have reminded you more often of my own. Lady Pole. I'm a viscountess.'

'But only in Brussels.'

'I thought I would remind you anyway.'

'You could remind my landlady, if you wish.'

'Oh, I do. All the time. She never tires of it. I think you will find that she now regards you almost as a gentleman.'

'Really?'

'No, not really. You are unquestionably a lawyer for all that. And a lawyer is regrettably... Well, I need scarcely tell you how low you have fallen, Cousin John. To study law is acceptable, but to work at it for money... Even the great Sir Edward Hyde flinches when anyone reminds him that he once actually practised law. The point of being a gentleman is to be capable of doing something useful but to choose not to. Make yourself serviceable and everyone will look down on you.'

'Then Charles Stuart must be the most respected man alive,' I say.

'There's more to him than he allows men to think,' says Aminta. 'If Cromwell believes His Majesty is a fool then he's more likely to leave him alone.'

'If you wish anyone to credit that your conversion to Republicanism is sincere and affected in no way by pecuniary considerations, then you must learn to call the Lord Protector "His Highness" and to call the man in Brussels "Charles Stuart" or, if you choose, "the titular King of the Scots". Either is acceptable if you sneer as you say it.'

'Charles Stuart,' says Aminta. She's good. That's the best sneer I've seen for some time. Then she adds: 'John Grey.'

'Yes,' I say. 'That's certainly the tone I had in mind.'

'Drunkard.'

'Excellent. Very sneering.'

'Loose-tongued drinker of cheap spirits.'

'Yes.'

'Lawyer.'

'Well, I think that's enough sneering practice for today,' I say.

'I'd be happy to continue sneering.'

'You are continuing.'

'So I am.'

'I must go and find Underhill,' I say.

'Good idea. You can let slip a few more secrets.'

'You can stop practising now,' I say.

'There are some things you can never be quite good enough at,' says Aminta.

I am fortunate that Probert is also at Hampton Court. As the Lord Protector moves from place to place he draws in his wake a crowd of greater and lesser officials. Probert it seems is one of them. I find him enjoying a long clay pipe in a sunny corner, his large frame propped up against a buttress of mellow red brick. He is dressed in brownish fustian, with some evidence of wear, especially to the knees and the elbows. His stockings are a pale buff colour that may once have been white. The broad brim of his hat flops in a way which its maker surely cannot have intended. It occurs to me that I have never seen him in a suit of clothes that appeared in any way new. Everything about him, other than his size, seems designed to draw attention to others rather than to himself. And yet even Probert's clothes must have been new once.

He listens to what I have to say about my meeting with Ripley, then breathes out a cloud of smoke.

'I have not seen him myself. Perhaps he has already left.'

'Is Mr Thurloe here?'

He shakes his head. 'Mr Secretary Thurloe is still in Westminster.'

'And his clerks?'

'I believe they are all hard at work in the same place, as they should be.'

'Could he have sent one ahead of him? A man named Underhill—Esmond Underhill?'

'Esmond Underhill? I know all of the clerks in the department and there is none of that name.'

'A sneaking ferret-like fellow,' I offer. 'Sallow of countenance as if long out of the sun, perhaps in some damp underground burrow. Slightly stooped. Sly, deceitful and grubby.'

Probert considers this with some care. He draws in smoke slowly, then releases it from the corner of his mouth. It hangs in the cold air for a moment, then dissolves.

'Not called Underhill,' he says eventually. 'Dickinson and Musgrave certainly fit the description you give. Slightly stooped? Grubby? Perhaps you would be describing Musgrave a little generously. Did he smell of cloves?'

'No,' I say.

'Not Dickinson then, who takes some tincture against the cold at times such as this. But why do you ask?'

'I met a man claiming to be such a person.'

'And you think he was not?'

'I am beginning to think that—yes.'

'Why? To be Esmond Underhill—it is a modest enough claim, surely?'

'He behaved...oddly.'

'That in itself is nothing. It is almost reassuring. Those who behave oddly are rarely concealing anything. It is those who behave normally that you should mistrust. Meet me at dinner. It is served for those such as you and me in the hall near the kitchen. Sit on the bench next to me as if we are not acquainted. I shall perhaps be able to tell you more.'

I spend the next hour wandering round Hampton Court. Other than Whitehall, I have never seen a palace before. There is a constant coming and going—messengers arrive, clerks dressed in black fustian run this way and that with bundles of papers. A group of men dressed in magnificent furs and long beards process to the Great Hall, preceded by a man holding a bow and arrows. Some say they are from Russia, some say they are from Turkey. Nobody quite knows why they are here. Serving men cross the court in the other direction carrying dark red sides of bacon, all following each other to a destination that the leading man at least appears to know. Two maids run after them, lifting their skirts to prevent them trailing across the ground, chattering as they go. One glances at me and grins but the other pulls at her arm and they are gone. A man in a blue silk suit emerges from a side door that I had not previously noticed, looks up at the sky, then vanishes again inside the building. It is like watching a vast ants' nest. There is constant activity but it is difficult to make much sense of what I see. For a while, like Probert, I find a sunny spot and just sit and watch the vast pageant that is the court.

My stomach rather than the giant one-handed clock tells me that dinnertime is approaching. By dint of asking every other person I see, I manage to work my way gradually to the dining hall, across courtyards and along low-ceilinged passageways, where my footsteps echo. I smell my destination long before I see it. A warm fug hits me as I finally pass through the door; indeed, there is so much steam, I can scarcely see the far end of the room. Oak tables and benches are set out and serving men rush backwards and forwards, some with full plates, some removing empty ones. Two or three clerks elbow past me without apology—I think they do not have much time to eat their dinner. There is activity everywhere. It is a microcosm of the court itself. Probert is already there and has been served with some roast mutton. I join him at the table. A wooden trencher is thrust unceremoniously in front of me.

'There has been another attempt on the Lord Protector's life,' says Probert as soon as the serving man departs. He does not look at me, but tears a hunk of greyish bread for himself and dips it into his gravy. 'It happened last night. Crude but ingenious. A dagger was rigged up on a long rope, hidden inside the canopy of His Highness's bed. The other end of the rope was nailed to the floor, with a candle close by. Once the candle had burned through the rope, the knife would fall, point first.'

'But His Highness is safe?'

'Of course. The rope burned through long before he retired for the night. He found a dagger embedded in the mattress and a length of smouldering rope. He smelled the rope burning even before he entered the room, by the way.'

'Not the best-laid of traps?'

'Not the best.'

'Who had access to the room?' I ask.

Probert looks round, but in the general hum of eating and talking, nobody pays us any attention. Still, he lowers his voice to no more than a normal volume. 'We are trying to find out. There were two entrances to the room, but apparently only one was guarded. *Latet anguis in herba*—and I believe the snake concerned may be named Underhill. He is definitely not one of our men. Do you know where he was last night?'

'Only for a part of it,' I say.

'Where is he now?'

I too survey the room, but see no Underhill.

'I don't know whether he is still at Hampton Court. He is certainly no longer in the chamber, though his shirt was there. Ripley, of course, was here,' I add.

'So you said. I do not think, from what you tell me, that Ripley is a man for games of the sort you describe. A dagger, by all means, or a rope, but not both together. We are making enquiries about him in Brussels and with our contacts in the Royalist camp. I think we may add Underhill's name to the list of those about whom we would like to know more—if Underhill is his real name. I shall leave you now, Grey, in case any observe us talking for longer than might seem plausible. The Sealed Knot will expect you to sound out Dr Bate but it will seem odd if you are friends with one such as I.'

'We could have met somewhere by chance.'

'I never meet anyone by chance, Grey.'

'Do you have further instructions for me?'

Probert stands and stretches.

'Watch and wait,' he says. '*Festina lente,* Mr Grey. There is no need for haste. I think the man you are seeking will come to you—if he hasn't already.'

Indeed—if he hasn't already. For I do not trust Underhill. But what could I have told him? Little more than my name, when you think about it.

Hampton Court was built for another less sophisticated age. Though it has one or two very grand chambers, much of it is Gothick and inconvenient. Few, I think, admire it now or will ever admire it again. For the spy, however, its small panelled rooms and narrow stone-floored passages afford many opportunities.

I am returning to my chamber after dinner when ahead of me I see Aminta and Dr Bate in earnest conversation, almost concealed in a window embrasure. Bate is half-sitting on the window seat and Aminta is standing over him. I think at first that she must be lost and has chanced to meet him and is now asking her way. But there is something about the way she is jabbing her finger into his chest that suggests she is telling rather than asking. She glances over her shoulder, without noticing me in this shadowy corridor, then continues her discussion. My greeting to her freezes on my lips. Bate looks worried and I am interested to see what Aminta plans to do with him.

I press myself into an alcove and try to make out what they are saying. I hear her ask something about Cromwell. Then I think I hear her mention Willys, though that seems unlikely. Bate shakes his head once or twice.

'I do not think it can be done,' he says.

'But you will think on it?'

'I have already said.' The good doctor is not happy.

In the ensuing silence, Bate makes a bow to Aminta, and not I think because of her claim to be a viscountess. For all his defiance, he has a beaten look about him. Then he creeps away. If he had a tail it would be between his legs.

Aminta gives a disgusted snort then turns to discover me just behind her.

'Was that Dr Bate?' I ask.

'Why are you trying to look innocent?' asks Aminta.

'I didn't know I was,' I say.

'Well, if you were, it wasn't very good,' she says. 'Yes, that was Dr Bate, as you are aware.'

'How are you acquainted?' I ask.

'My father knew him well many years ago. He is another possible friend to make our case to Cromwell.'

'But he won't?'

'He is the third or fourth most cowardly man I know. He will risk nothing. Nothing at all. He will merely think on it. Even that seems to carry too much danger. I must report back to my husband that we can expect little from Dr Bate. You know that he was formerly the King's chief physician?'

'I had heard that.'

'When the war started to go against the King, Bate was one of the first rats to jump ship. He crawled back to London from Oxford to resume his medical practice and soon had Oliver Cromwell as one of his patients. He's now chief physician to "His Highness" and his family. If the good doctor thinks you're a Royalist he will express all kinds of regret for the passing of the monarchy, but in between times he sucks up to Cromwell.'

'So, why won't Bate help you?' I ask.

'Help me?'

'You said he wouldn't help you make representations to Cromwell.'

'Oh, yes. He seems to think that being associated with delinquent Royalists may cost him his place here at court. He's treating Cromwell's daughter Elizabeth at the moment. I'm sure he's well paid for it.'

'I believe she is very ill.'

'She's dying of cancer. Bate's suggested cure is to take the waters at Tunbridge Wells. It will at least do nothing to hasten her death, unlike most of the other things he might advise.'

'It's as easy for a doctor to kill as cure,' I say.

'I suppose you would know,' says Aminta, 'since your father is a surgeon.'

When I return to my room I find a small sheet of paper there, neatly folded and placed in the centre of my bed.

> *Mr S. K. sends his greetings to Mr Cardinal and asks him to present himself on his return to London. Thursday night. Same time and place as before. The obliging porter has gone but you won't need him.*

Underhill's bed is carefully made up but his damp shirt is nowhere to be seen, any more than Underhill himself.

CHAPTER 11

Mr Cardinal

'Sir Richard is again called away?'

'You don't need to know that,' says Ripley.

The chill in the air is not due only to the lack of fire in Sir Richard's grate. We will not be here long enough to make it worthwhile fetching and lighting the coals. But I think that Ripley is, in any case, going to tell me no more than he has to. Something has changed.

Cold though it is in the chamber, it is by many degrees warmer than it is outside. Snow is piled against the windows, a brilliant white at the top where the sun shines through it, a deeper grey where it rests on the sill.

'So, have you yet formed a plan?' he asks.

'No,' I say.

'Even though you now have the post that you need? Even though you have access to Cromwell? You are not, I hope, planning to deceive us?'

I had little enough opportunity at Hampton Court, as he must realise. Something has happened. And whatever Ripley has learned is not to my credit.

'If it were easy, he would already be dead,' I say. 'Others have tried. He never tells anyone in advance when he is planning to travel, he never stays in a room unless there is more than one exit, he is cautious what he accepts to eat or drink, he wears plate armour, at least on his front, and he is guarded wherever he goes.'

'All things you presumably knew when you accepted the assignment?'

We look at each other. I think I can bluster my way out of this. In a moment I shall know for certain.

'Hyde doesn't want it to be an obvious assassination,' I say. 'He doesn't want the taint of Cromwell's death on himself or on His Majesty. It must be done subtly.'

I am impressed by my own powers of invention, but Ripley nods and, at that moment, we both know that what I have said is true. Cromwell lives forever under the shadow of having executed his predecessor. Charles Stuart will wish not to have the same stain on his character. He would prefer that assassinations of heads of states should continue to be regarded as rare and exceptional events. However Cromwell dies, it should not touch the court in Brussels or appear as a precedent that might inconvenience a future monarch. It must be done subtly indeed, and at the right time, when Hyde has gathered his forces to strike.

'But how long will it take?' demands Ripley. 'What you say is undoubtedly true, but I can't hold good men in a constant state of readiness for an uprising that may not happen for months. Hyde must realise that. I have five thousand foot and five thousand horse at my disposal—but it would take only one of them to betray us for all to be undone. And each day that passes is another four and twenty hours for one of them to fall victim to fear or avarice or stupidity and to walk up to the front door of his local magistrate with a wagging tongue and a purse open to receive Cromwell's silver.'

'My job,' I say, 'is to kill Cromwell. Yours is to ensure that the troops are ready when needed. Is that understood, Sir Michael?'

Ripley is still not happy, but he nods reluctantly.

'We have been preparing for some time,' he says. 'As Hyde is aware.'

'Where are they?' I ask. 'Your ten thousand men?'

'That's not something that Hyde needs to know. But I assure you they will be ready to fight.'

'Where do you store their equipment—helmets, breastplates, swords, pikes, muskets, powder, shot? Is there not a danger it will be discovered?'

'At the moment Parliament keeps it safe for us. We shall take it from them when we need it and not before.'

'So, you are relying on seizing arms in the possession of the State?'

'They are the best that money can buy.'

'I shall let Sir Edward know,' I say.

'Good,' says Ripley. 'And perhaps in return he will let *us* know what *he* is doing.'

'I don't know what you mean,' I say.

'Yes, you do. I told you: the only way that we knew you were coming was that our own man in Brussels told me. And we were able to contact you only because our man also overheard you telling Hyde where you could be contacted.'

'Contacted at Mistress Reynolds's house?'

'At that very address. The place you are staying.'

I wonder how my father can have been so far-sighted. My mother knows where I am, of course, but not he. Unless my mother has written to him. That is not impossible.

'That was careless of me,' I say.

'But useful to us,' says Ripley.

There is another silence, then I say: 'You are aware that an attempt was made on Cromwell's life while I was at Hampton Court? A knife was to drop on him while he slept.'

'A knife to drop on him? How?' Ripley seems genuinely puzzled. So, the knife was not ordered by him then.

'I know only what I was told,' I say. 'A very poor trap had been set for Cromwell in his own bed. So, this was not carried out by the man you say you had commissioned?'

'He has been told to desist. As Hyde instructed.'

We look at each other. 'Perhaps you should check whether he has,' I say.

Ripley nods. A point to me, I think. But then Ripley says: 'You went under the name of Grey at Hampton Court?' he asks.

I too have been wondering whether I was wise to use my real name. But others there might have recognised me. Aminta in fact *did* recognise me. The risk of using a false name was greater than inventing an alias, even if it does mean that people like Underhill can find me again.

'It seemed best,' I say.

'It would have been helpful if you had told us what you were going to do,' he says.

This is true, perhaps, but I do not need Ripley's permission to use my own name if I wish. There is something, however, in Ripley's tone that I do not understand. I am beginning to suspect that Underhill is in contact with him. I wonder what he has said.

'You need me, John,' says Ripley. 'You need me more than you seem to think. There's a lot that Hyde clearly hasn't told you, for all your loyalty to him. You have to keep me better informed. If you don't tell us everything...if you give Brodrick the slightest cause to doubt you, he'll cut your throat without a moment's hesitation.'

'And does he have any cause?' I ask.

'Nothing to speak of,' says Ripley. 'Not yet. Of course, if I thought you were lying to us, I'd have cut your throat before Brodrick had even drawn his knife.'

CHAPTER 12

Sir Richard Willys

Thurloe's expression gives nothing away. 'The information about their preparedness is helpful, of course.'

'But you do not believe in their ten thousand men?' I say.

'You clearly don't, Mr Grey. I doubt Hyde will believe in them either. He's no fool, for all that he has backed the wrong horse.'

'Or perhaps he will,' I say. 'Men tend to believe what they wish to believe, even when the evidence is against it.'

Thurloe nods thoughtfully. This is what men do. 'Yes, perhaps he will,' he says. 'You may be right. In which case...'

I wait for him to complete the sentence, but he does not.

'Who is Sir Richard Willys?' I ask. 'We always meet in his absence at his chambers. Ripley was amazed I did not know him.'

'As I told you,' says Thurloe patiently, 'he is a former Royalist. His family is from Fen Ditton in Cambridgeshire. He served in the King's army with some distinction in the Bishops' Wars and later at Shrewsbury. He was Governor of Newark for a while—in 1645, I think—and was made a baronet by King Charles. When the royal cause was lost, he left for Italy, but returned to England in 1652 to resume his legal practice.'

'I think we should investigate Willys further. I could make enquiries.'

'To what end, Mr Grey?'

'He could be the assassin.'

'Impossible,' says Thurloe. 'You must accept my word for that. No more on the subject, please. You have done well, Mr Grey, but you must take guidance from me.'

That may be good advice, but I wish to move things ahead faster than that. I am curious to discover what I will find if I visit Gray's Inn when Ripley is not there and the owner of the chambers is.

❀ ❀ ❀

'Why?' asks Aminta.

'Because I am convinced Willys lies somewhere at the heart of this plot,' I say. 'Thurloe knows him better than he claimed. He was able, without consulting any papers, to tell me who Willys was, in which battles he had fought and in what year he had become Governor of Newark. Why would all of that be at his fingertips?'

'Because that is his job?'

'That would be some feat of memory if he knows such detail for every inoffensive former Royalist.'

'So, who do *you* think Willys is?'

'He is clearly involved,' I say, 'in clandestine Royalist activity.'

'But he can't be the intended assassin.'

'Why?'

'Because you said that the assassin had access to the court. Willys does not. Anyway, I think my father knew him—years ago.'

I look at her curiously. 'Did I hear you mention Willys's name to Dr Bate?'

Aminta shakes her head. Her blonde curls swing to and fro.

'Bate knew him,' I say. 'He said that he didn't usually mix with baronets, and I hadn't told him whether Willys was a knight or a baronet.'

'A good guess?'

'Knights are more common, surely?'

'A knotty problem,' says Aminta. 'But not one that need detain us.'

I look at her, astounded.

'But of course!' I say. 'That was it precisely!'

'What have I said?'

'The words that Underhill used and I had forgot.'

'What words?'

'When we were talking about Willys he laughed and said it was a something-or-other problem. "Knotty"—that's what he said. "A knotty problem". And then he laughed because I was befuddled with drink and didn't understand.'

'Are you sure? You were, as you say, befuddled. You were still somewhat befuddled when I met you the following morning. Anyway, what would it signify?'

'A lot,' I say. 'It is clear that I did not, after all, consume Underhill's brandy in vain. Whatever I may have told him, he has let slip a secret of his own. "A knotty problem", he joked. I think Mr Underhill is familiar enough with the Sealed Knot. What if Willys is actually the head of the Sealed Knot in England? What if *that* is the point of his jest? Doesn't that fit all of the facts as I have related them? That is why Ripley was astounded that, coming as a courier from Hyde, I had no idea who Willys was.'

'That is a very large conclusion from very little evidence. And Thurloe has told you not to take this further.'

'Which is why I must do it quickly and quietly. I don't know when Willys will return to his chambers, but I shall try tonight and then every night until I find him.'

'It may be better not to interfere.' Aminta is tapping her foot, a sure sign that I have somehow incurred her displeasure.

'I won't interfere,' I say. 'I'll just ask some innocent questions and come away.'

'It still seems an unnecessary risk.'

'The risk is slight,' I say. 'If he is alone and unarmed anyway. And I shall check carefully that he is both of these things.'

Truly, winter has now arrived. The air chills to the bone. Snow falls slowly but insistently. Now it lies thick on the ground and shows no sign of melting. Carriages roll over it, leaving long, slightly glistening indentations and the marks of many horse-shoes, but these are rapidly smoothed out again and lost to view. Inch by inch, a layer of white is building up too on every rooftop, hanging there precariously until it looks ready to collapse under its own weight. My feet make a pleasant crunching sound as I walk, but that is all that is pleasant. This is cold that kills.

At Gray's Inn the one-eyed porter is still absent, but the other, huddled by a brazier, informs me that Sir Richard Willys is at home, if I care to ascend to his chambers.

I knock. The voice that answers is one used to command. I enter as instructed.

'Have I the honour of addressing Sir Richard Willys?' I ask.

The occupier of the chambers looks back at me with disdain. He is a little above average height and of a soldierly bearing. He is, I would say, between forty and fifty years of age. His long, slightly curly hair is starting to turn grey. His mous-tache is jet black, as is the little tuft of hair below his mouth. His mouth is slightly open as if ready to issue some reproof. But he is alone. And I see no evidence of weapons in the room.

'You read the sign by the door,' he says. 'Who precisely are you?'

'I am called Mr Cardinal,' I say.

'Are you?' Willys appears quite willing to believe that.

'I was here last night.'

'If you say so,' he says.

He does not query why I might have been in his chambers or think it odd.

'I met a gentleman named Ripley,' I say.

'Never heard of him.'

'Yes, you have. And his friend, Allen Brodrick. And I think you've heard of me—or, if not, you're remarkably incurious. I've burst into your chambers and you've asked me nothing about what my business is or where I come from.'

Willys considers this briefly. 'So, where *do* you come from and what precisely is your business here tonight, Mr Cardinal?'

I take a deep breath. 'Why should I deal with junior members of the Sealed Knot when I can speak to its head in England?'

'Why should you think that's who I am?'

'Because Hyde told me. Even if he hadn't, it would be self-evident. You have a natural authority that Ripley and Brodrick lack.'

Willys frowns but is not altogether displeased. There is a vanity in him that may be useful.

'Brodrick isn't convinced *you* are who you say you are,' he tells me. 'I hope for your sake, Mr Cardinal, that you told Brodrick the truth.'

Well, he knows who I am then.

'I've no instructions from Hyde to tell Brodrick anything,' I say. 'The truth or otherwise.'

'I assume that means that you do have something to tell me?'

I take another deep breath. 'As you know,' I say, 'my instructions were to act alone. Since I have made contact with your organisation, however, Sir Edward would wish me to reassure you personally of his confidence in your management of affairs here.'

Willys laughs. 'Would he?'

'That is his message. He—and the King—value you highly.'

'Ah,' says Willys.

We look at each other. We are playing some sort of game, the rules for which are not very clear to me. He has not admitted to being head of the Sealed Knot but nothing in what he has said denies it. I press on.

'It's Brodrick in particular that Hyde doesn't trust,' I say.

'Why?'

'A drunk and a womaniser, with a loose tongue. Not entirely a gentleman.'

I am relying on the character provided for Brodrick by Ripley. It would seem likely that it is a generally held view.

'Hyde has clearly taken you into his confidence quite remarkably, as a newly recruited courier, if he has told you that the Secretary of the Sealed Knot isn't a gentleman. Perhaps you shouldn't have repeated it if he did.'

I remember that Probert once advised me that, if I was going to lie, I should lie boldly. I therefore ignore Willys's rebuke entirely and round on him.

'I do not have time for idle chatter,' I say sharply. 'Though you personally have Hyde's confidence, he does not have any trust in the Sealed Knot, as you are aware. He has therefore asked me to report back on affairs here.'

'Without contacting us?'

'Just so.'

Willys is strangely unfazed. 'What does he wish to know?'

I consider this. What information would Thurloe wish for? What will Willys trust me with?

'How many men you actually have at your command,' I say. 'Ripley says five thousand horse and five thousand foot, all armed. Is that true?'

'You doubt it?'

'Yes.'

'What would you find believable, Mr Cardinal? Three thousand horse?'

'Maybe,' I say.

'Two thousand?'

'Probably.'

'And a few hundred foot?'

I have no idea.

'Yes,' I say. 'That is what I would have expected.'

'You are right, Mr Cardinal. We don't have the powder and shot that we need for more than that.'

'Was Ripley misleading me deliberately?'

Willys smiles. 'I would advise you not to turn your back on him unless you have to. Where can I find you if I need you?'

'I am staying at Mistress Reynolds's house. Ripley knows where it is.'

'I may have a message for you to take back to Brussels,' says Willys. 'If the opportunity arises. There is something I need to report. It will be for the King and the King alone.'

'Of course,' I say.

'Good,' says Willys. 'I know a great deal about you, Mr Cardinal. More than you think. And you do have my full trust and confidence. But now you must leave quietly and unobtrusively. You may prefer not to mention this visit to Ripley or Brodrick. I shall certainly say nothing to either. If questioned by the porter or anyone else, tell him you came to consult me on a legal matter—a breach of promise case. You behaved inadvisedly towards a young lady, who now seeks redress. It is always as well to have your story ready, just in case. You never know when somebody may decide to ask you awkward questions.'

As I leave Gray's Inn the heavy snow deadens the sound of my feet. I manage to startle the watchman, who does not hear my approach.

'You found Sir Richard?' he asks. 'I hope you obtained good advice.'

'Breach of promise case,' I say.

'Nasty business,' he says.

'It will get worse before it gets better,' I say.

Mr Plautus

Thurloe can make you believe, quite genuinely, that you are not there. He is staring out of the window of his office. He does not look at me or at Probert who is also present. He cannot have failed to hear what I have said, but I do not know if he plans to answer me or not. He is watching something or somebody in the road below. Eventually he sighs and turns to me.

'I said that Sir Richard was no concern of yours.'

'You said that he was an inactive former Royalist. He is in fact the leader of the Sealed Knot in England.'

'Why are you so sure?'

'He knew without my telling him that Brodrick was the Secretary.'

'Then that was an unfortunate slip on his part.'

'And he knows Brodrick's character.'

'That is well enough known.'

'I accused him to his face and he did not deny it,' I say.

'A good point in law, I grant you,' says Thurloe.

'Even if I am wrong that Willys is the leader—and I don't think I am—he is at the very least an active Royalist with a knowledge of the Knot's senior officers, and is in direct contact with Hyde. He confirmed the number of troops that the Royalists could raise. Two thousand horse. Maybe a few hundred foot. And he asked that I should be ready to take a message to Hyde. Though I do not understand why, he said I have his complete trust.'

Thurloe nods slowly.

'I apologise for doubting you. Once again you have done well,' he says. 'So, we now know that Willys is the leader of the Sealed Knot. We have a better idea of the forces at their disposal. Yes, you are to be congratulated.'

'The information was obtained easily enough,' I say.

'I am sure that it was due in no small part to your skill in questioning a witness.'

And yet, even as he says this, I am beginning to worry that it was too easy—that a little bluffing and flattery was enough to obtain even this much. How can Willys know enough about me to trust me, especially when Brodrick says he should not?

'What if we have been deceived?' I say. 'What if Willys was lying? What if that is merely what they wish me to report to you? What if Ripley, say, really is the head of the Sealed Knot? What if the rising is in fact imminent, with tens of thousands of troops?'

Thurloe shakes his head. 'What Willys told you is supported by other things that we know. We are certain, for example, that they lack arms and that Hyde is planning to land weapons of all sorts in Dorset or Cornwall.'

'So, the information I have provided is useful?'

'It is of the greatest value.'

'Then I hope you will agree that I have now done enough for you—that I should be allowed to retire to the country under your protection while you arrest Willys, who will undoubtedly give you enough information to hang Brodrick and Ripley too. Of course, you may require me to give evidence in court, I understand that.'

'If we arrest him,' says Thurloe.

'If?'

'It may not be opportune.'

'But we can bring down the Sealed Knot! Willys. Brodrick. Ripley. And maybe others besides.'

'The Knot is many things. It is rash, foolish and incompetent. But it does not lack men who believe they can lead it. Willys may be the leader now, but they will soon appoint another. And it may be that under another leader it will flourish as it has not under Willys.'

'Nevertheless,' I say, 'an organisation of that sort can only be taken apart bit by bit. Willys may only be the first step, but if we do not take it, where do we start?'

'You have already obtained much without the need for an arrest. From what you say, he has no idea what we suspect. That is to our advantage. Our own stores of arms are well guarded. And when they bring in weapons from the Spanish Netherlands, we will be watching the ports. You have done well, but I think you can do a great deal more for us.'

'You will take no action at all against Willys?' I say, astounded.

'We must act prudently. And we must ensure that we do nothing that will reveal to the Knot that you passed this information to me. We don't want another Manning.'

'Manning?'

'Henry Manning. A double agent and my best source of information at the Stuart court. He tipped us off that a prominent English Royalist had paid a visit to Charles Stuart. Cromwell couldn't resist letting the same Royalist know we were on to him. But the only possible source of that intelligence was Manning. It was Manning's death warrant. The Royalists seized him. Cromwell wanted us to bargain with Hyde but we could offer to exchange Manning for another prisoner only by admitting he was our man. We didn't, of course. They shot him through the head in some woods just outside Cologne. A great pity.'

I agree that it would be unfortunate if I met the same fate. Thurloe rubs his eyes. I wonder if he will weep for me if I am pistolled to death. It seems unlikely and it will be of no practical benefit to me anyway. Then I see that he is not crying for

Manning. He is simply rubbing his eyes. He reads many documents, including some actually intended for him.

'What do you require me to do next?' I ask.

'There is the question of whether Lambert or Fairfax could be implicated,' says Thurloe.

'Two of our most distinguished generals,' says Probert. 'We can scarcely send Mr Grey to interrogate them as he has interrogated Willys.'

'Can we not?' asks Thurloe. 'I could not. Henry Cromwell could not. But perhaps... Mr Grey is, after all, obscure and insignificant. He has done well with Sir Richard. Lambert and Fairfax would have no reason to suspect him. What if we were to send him with a message for Lambert from Cromwell? What if he were to ask General Lambert not if he had murderous designs but on what terms he would consider a reconciliation? Let us see what he says. We shall at least know his price. The information will not be without value. And I am sure that Lord Fairfax would wish to say something on behalf of his son-in-law.'

'Would the Lord Protector sanction such a thing?' asks Probert.

'He will not sanction it because I shall not ask him. The advantage of sending Mr Grey is that we could always claim later that a junior official had misunderstood or overstepped the mark. Lambert is in Wimbledon. Fairfax is currently here in London. The thing is not impossible. What do you say, Mr Grey?'

It seems safer than many of the things that Thurloe might suggest that I should do. I cannot imagine either general will shoot me dead on the spot.

'And this is the last thing you need me to do?' I say.

'Of course. The very last. Tomorrow then for Lambert. We'll find you a horse that is strong enough to get you there and back in a day even in this weather. When are you to meet Ripley again?'

'Not for some days. I can report back to you on the twenty-fifth of December.'

'Or before, if Lambert or Fairfax say anything of interest. Do you plan to attend church on Christmas Day?'

'You think that, as a purported Royalist, I should?'

'No. You are a purported Royalist but you are a cautious one who does not wish to draw the attention of the authorities to his presence. I would suggest you keep away from Christmas services this year at least,' says Thurloe.

'Is that general advice or just for me?'

'I would not repeat it to anyone, lest you are asked to reveal the source of your information.'

'I see. Thank you,' I say.

'On the contrary, my thanks are due to you, Mr Plautus. I think that you may, after all, have the makings of a good agent.'

'So, you are not to pursue Sir Richard Willys further?' asks Aminta. She is drinking tea from a cup made of porcelain. I think that she has indeed sent Will to Exchange Alley to obtain tea at ten Pounds a pound. Each sip would drain money from my purse if it actually had any money in it.

'No,' I say.

'But Thurloe thinks as you do? That Sir Richard is the leader of the Sealed Knot?'

'Yes. But he must have known all along. With his network of spies, it simply isn't possible that Thurloe was unaware who his main opponent was. At the very least he must have suspected, even if he lacked proof. So why didn't he tell me?'

'That is an interesting question. And he makes no effort to arrest him and question him?'

'No.'

'Sir Richard Willys knew who you were?'

'From the moment I came through the door. Ripley would have told him, of course. But he claimed to have information on me that made him trust me. That wouldn't have come from Ripley or Brodrick. So what is it?'

Aminta considers this. 'I think you should be worried about anything that doesn't quite add up,' she says. 'And there's a lot there that isn't quite as it should be. I certainly think Underhill has been talking to Ripley. And somebody has been talking to Willys. You will not see Sir Richard again?'

'No, Mr Thurloe does not wish it. But Sir Richard may send a message here for me to take to Brussels. Sadly, I shall be unable to deliver it, since I have no plans to travel to Brussels, but the contents may be helpful to Mr Thurloe.'

'I am sure they would be,' says Aminta. 'It also shows that Sir Richard believes you will come through this alive and return to Brussels. That is in itself interesting, because Ripley doubted it very strongly. When you learn anything further, perhaps you could let me know?'

'Why?' I ask.

'So that I may be of service to you in return for your hospitality. I am concerned for your safety. Two minds may be quicker to spot dangers than one alone—particularly if the one alone is yours.'

I look at Aminta. I have never seen a face so innocent and untroubled.

'Are you planning to attend church on the twenty-fifth of December?' I ask.

'Is there any reason why I should not?'

'It may not be advisable.'

'What's going to happen?'

'I don't know. Parliament may be planning one of its periodic round-ups of Royalist sympathisers. Christmas services would present a convenient opportunity.'

'Thank you for warning me, but I am, as you know, no longer a Royalist sympathiser. Unlike many of my friends, I speak of the titular King of the Scots with the utmost scorn.'

'If you mention this to anyone else, Thurloe will know I've told you.'

'Then I shall allow my friends to be arrested and fined or whatever His Highness has in mind for them. I should not dream of interfering.'

Again, a look of innocence of which an angel would be proud.

'Just so that you know,' I say, 'keep away from churches on Christmas Day. And tell nobody.'

A Letter

The Manor,
Clavershall West,
Essex

19 December 1657

My Dear John,

It was pleasant, as ever, to receive your rather brief note and to hear as much of your news as you are willing to tell me. I am glad that you have been able to provide Aminta with protection while she is in London. I had of course recommended to her that she should contact you when she returned to England, and I am pleased that she at least takes my advice. I had, as you well know, hoped that you and she would marry, but Lord Pole will, I am sure, make a very good husband, with a little training and direction from her. The loss, I think, is entirely yours, and if I recommend other young women to you in future, then I hope that you will be more effective in your pursuit of them. *Verb sap,* as Mr Probert would doubtless say.

As to your father's whereabouts—which seems to be your main reason for writing—I am not sure why you think I should have heard from him, still less written to him. He was living in Bruges with a female of tender years. I assume he left Bruges with the King and is now in Brussels. I have heard nothing of his travelling to England again, but I of course correspond with nobody at the King's court since you have forbidden it. If I had heard news of your father, it would not be a matter of great consequence for me or anyone else. But I haven't.

Your curiosity on the matter is, however, interesting. Am I right in suspecting that there are things that you have not told me? Obviously, you may prefer that Aminta lets me know in due course and in somewhat greater detail. The choice is yours.

We shall be celebrating Christmas here in the poor fashion that the law and your stepfather permit. I hope that you will fare better at Mistress Reynolds's and that we shall see you here in Essex in the New Year. In the meantime, I seal this with a mother's love and a mother's reasonable expectation to learn more, once you wish to tell her.

CHAPTER 15

My Lord Lambert

I have been given slightly more horse than I am comfortable with—a black stallion who has, I think, opinions on many things. Fortunately we are agreed that a journey south to Wimbledon, on a bright morning with the snow thick and soft on the ground, is in order. He makes light of the drifts that I fail to see until we are in them, and scarcely notices my weight as we toil up the long hill near Wandsworth. More usually he carries a dragoon with full equipment. He is perhaps wise enough to regard this as a holiday that may be repeated if he does not misbehave too badly. Certainly it is not my horsemanship that keeps him on the road. If he decides that he would like to dine in Putney, then I fear that I must needs dine in Putney too.

It is mid-morning when we arrive at General Lambert's house. The land is white and the air sparkling. I think that the merest breath of a wind would dislodge the covering of snow from the tree branches. But there is no wind. Everything is still. Even though the world is bound in ice, the sun warms my cheek.

This then is where you live when you have quarrelled with the Lord Protector. It is a very pleasant mansion made of soft red brick. Roses grow above the door, though I must return in May if I wish to discover what colour roses they are. Beds of bedraggled and snow-bound lavender stretch out before it. Neat box hedging makes pretty, angular patterns between. It is rumoured that two thousand Pounds a year comes with the house. I wonder if Lambert will wish to end a quarrel that has left him so comfortable.

I am not certain how I expected a retired general to pass his time, but not in this manner to be sure. He looks up from his needlework.

'It will be a rose,' he says, indicating the half-completed bloom. He selects a long strand of white silk from a tray before him and expertly threads a needle. He studies the design, head on one side.

'I noticed that you had roses above your door,' I say.

'*Rosa canina,*' he says without looking up. 'The dog rose. This that I am stitching now is *rosa alba*—the old rose of York. That is also in my garden, but elsewhere. I would show you round the gardens, Mr Grey, but they are not at their best at present. Indeed, I could not tell you precisely where the lawns end and the flower beds commence. The box hedges look very well, however, beneath their crust of snow.'

'That is true,' I say, 'but I had not come to see the gardens.'

'No, my man told me. You come with a message from Cromwell.' His hand smooths out the fabric in front of him. Something about the rose displeases him.

'I am, of course, grateful to you for seeing me,' I add.

'Why should I not see you? Did you think I would not cease my sewing for long enough to listen to what the Lord Protector has to say to me?'

'You haven't ceased your sewing,' I say.

'No, I haven't, have I? So, what does His Royal Highness require of me?'

'His Highness,' I say without thinking. 'Not His Royal Highness.'

Lambert smiles. 'A slip of the tongue,' he says. 'Which I hope is not treason at all, even now. The farmer's boy from Huntingdon is, of course, merely His Highness. Scarcely royal at all. He was proud once to be called General. Which would you rather be, Mr Grey? A General or a Highness?'

It is the sort of question Cromwell might have thrown at me—innocent enough but a test of some sort.

'If I were a Highness,' I say, 'I could make myself a General easily enough.'

Lambert frowns and for a moment I think that I may have insulted him, but he eventually nods grudgingly. 'Well said, Mr Grey. So you might. General is a discounted title these days. Its value drops in times of peace. We can be bought cheaply at market.'

I think that two thousand a year is not cheap, but I do not say this. Perhaps Cromwell is prepared to pay more than the going rate.

'The Lord Protector still values the services that you rendered the State.'

'*Values*? So he should. Men like me created the State. No army, no victories at Marston Moor or Dunbar. No victories at Marston Moor and Dunbar and we'd still have a throne and a Stuart arse on it. A Stuart arse on the throne, and Cromwell's head would just be one of many on a spike on London Bridge. That may still come to pass if he's not careful.'

'Nobody doubts your contribution, my Lord,' I say.

I wonder if he will spit the word 'contribution' back at me as he spat 'values'. But he simply sniffs at it.

'Do they not? I sometimes wonder if your master believes that he and his Cambridgeshire militia defeated the King on their own. He certainly seems to have convinced Parliament that that is the case. Harrison, Fairfax, Fleetwood, myself—we all count for nothing. The Good Old Cause counts for nothing. The will of the people counts for nothing. Cromwell thinks I can be bought for a house and a pension. We shall see.'

'The Republic is safe in His Highness's hands,' I say.

'Who told you that? Cromwell?'

'Yes.'

'Ha!' he says.

He starts to unpick the rose he was sewing. Something about it is not right. For a moment his needlework has his complete concentration. I wonder briefly who he reminds me of—then I realise that it is Cromwell whom he resembles. This is Cromwell as he would be if he had lost. But Cromwell would not have lost. That is the difference between them. Parliament was willing to let General Cromwell become their master. They would never have suffered my Lord Lambert to do the same.

'So, what is Cromwell's offer?' he asks, not looking up. 'More money? A bigger house? In return for which I agree to become Lord Lieutenant of Ireland or Governor of Jamaica or somewhere else obscure and far away, and I promise my allegiance in whatever terms they are demanded? Is that what His Highness requires?'

'There is no offer,' I say. 'Cromwell simply wishes to know under what circumstances you are willing to take an oath of allegiance to the State.'

'And by the State, he means His Majesty King Oliver the First?'

'The oath would be to the new constitution.'

'The difference is too small to matter. So, what were his precise words?'

'As I say, just what the circumstances would be that might lead you to reconsider your decision not to swear allegiance.'

'Those are the precise words?'

'Yes.'

'No, they're not. Those aren't Cromwell's words. Cautious circumlocutions of that sort come from Thurloe. It's Thurloe who's sent you, isn't it?'

'I have spoken to Mr Thurloe,' I say.

'I don't doubt it. Thurloe's behind this as he's been behind most things lately. It will have been Thurloe who calculated that a pension of two thousand—rather than one thousand or four thousand—was just enough to keep me quiet. And he was right, wasn't he? I have kept quiet. And it will have been Thurloe who suggested that Wimbledon was close enough to London not to look like exile, but far enough away to ensure that it was. And now he sends you to sound me out. Why?'

'Because His Highness asked him to do so.'

'I doubt Cromwell is even aware you've come here. Thurloe knows Cromwell is sick. We all know Cromwell is sick. Thurloe needs to decide who to back next—me or Richard Cromwell or Henry Cromwell or Fairfax or Charles Stuart. That's your real mission, in case you were wondering.'

'You mean he is preparing to back you? Not Richard?'

'Me. Richard. Richard and me. You can bet on more than one horse,' says Lambert.

'So, what would you have me say to Mr Secretary Thurloe?'

'Nothing,' says Lambert. 'I won't need him. If you speak to Cromwell, tell him I'm here in Wimbledon and that I can wait a long time. I've got longer than he has.'

'It would certainly be convenient to you if the Lord Protector should die.'

'You think so? It would be more convenient to everyone if the Lord Protector recognised who his true friends were. I am plotting no rebellion, if that is what Thurloe has sent you here to discover.'

'Do you,' I ask, 'know a man named Sir Michael de Ripley?'

There is no sign of recognition on his face—merely puzzlement. 'Who is he? Some aristocratic friend of Thurloe's? What role has Cromwell promoted him to?'

'Or Sir Richard Willys?'

'Willys? There was a Royalist general of that name. If he's still alive, he'll be a forgotten man. We all are. I doubt that Charles Stuart has any more loyalty to his generals than

Cromwell does. Except that Cromwell was one of us once, and should know better.'

'What about Esmond Underhill?' I ask.

Lambert pauses. I am not sure whether he will curse my impudence for questioning him so, or whether he will deny that he knows the man. Lambert is also unsure what he is about to do.

'A man of that name once served under me,' he says at length.

'You remember him then?'

He pauses again. 'He was a corporal.'

'You must have had many corporals.'

'A few.'

'Have you met with him lately?'

'I cannot see that is any concern of yours. Did Thurloe tell you to question me on him?'

'No,' I say.

'Then why do you ask after him?'

'I met him recently,' I say.

I watch Lambert's face. He is curious to know more, but I say nothing. Something tells me that Lambert remembers Underhill very well indeed.

'Where did you meet him?' he asks casually.

'At Hampton Court,' I reply.

'I trust that you found him in good spirits?'

'He seemed to be.'

Lambert appears relieved that I have not told him Underhill was in the Tower or worse.

'Ah,' he says.

Outside the window the sky is darkening. Unnoticed by me, the clouds have been gathering, gun-metal grey and ominous. By the time the sun sets on this short winter day, the roads may be impassable. I do not think I will learn more than I have.

'I must go,' I say.

'Back to your master.'

'We must all answer to somebody, my Lord.'

'Not all of us have to stoop to answering to a creature like Thurloe. Tell Mr Secretary Thurloe that I won't need him when Cromwell's gone. He can start packing his bags now.'

'I'll tell him, if those are your instructions to me.'

Lambert nods and turns again to his sewing. Then, as I am about to leave the room he calls: 'Wait!'

'Yes?' Perhaps after all he is going to tell me something about Underhill.

'Before you go, ask my cook to serve you some warm ale and a slice of smoked ham. You have a long journey back to London. One day, so will I.'

My Lord Fairfax

The snow lies deep on this day that was once known as Christmas Eve. There are few abroad in this white world. Black figures scuttle across the landscape, bundled up in long cloaks, hats pulled down against the wind that is sweeping the snow in heaps against the walls of houses. The black figure scurrying towards me, hat pulled down against who knows what, is a familiar one, however. When I was younger and more credulous, my mother would often warn me that if you speak of the devil, he will appear at your elbow. This is the first instance I can think of when he has done so.

'Underhill!' I say.

He pauses and seems to sniff me out rather than see me. 'Mr Grey,' he says.

'Indeed,' I say, regretting once again that I gave him my true name, rather than Plautus or Cardinal. 'You are well, I trust, Mr Underhill? You are some way from your office at Whitehall.'

'As indeed are you, Mr Grey,' he says. 'But we must both run errands for masters who are not ready to venture out on such a day. I am returning from Lambeth. And you, my friend, are bound for...'

'Somerset House,' I say, simply because I know that it lies in this direction but well beyond my actual destination. I see no reason to tell Underhill another truth, though I shall try to get him to tell me one or two.

He gives me a twisted smile. 'You have some way to go.'

'You left Hampton Court somewhat precipitously,' I say. 'Was there any reason for that?'

'I ran out of clean shirts,' he says.

'You tried to tell me that Sir Richard Willys was head of the Sealed Knot,' I say.

'I've no idea what you are talking about, Mr Grey.'

'You work for the Sealed Knot,' I say.

'You were drunk when I last saw you, Mr Grey. I am not sure that you have sobered up much in the meantime.'

'Except,' I say, 'perhaps you are no longer working for the Sealed Knot. Perhaps you are now working for somebody else entirely.'

'This is making my head spin, Mr Grey. First you say I'm working for a body that I've no knowledge of. Then you tell me I've left their service. Perhaps we should continue this conversation when you've made up your mind what it is I'm supposed to have done.'

'Just tell me who employs you. Is it General Lambert?'

He laughs. 'I work for Mr Thurloe.'

'You lie, Mr Underhill. Who do you really work for?' I grab his arm. 'I could make you tell me.'

'Oh, I doubt that, Mr Grey. I doubt you could make me do anything. And you need not hold my arm. I have no intention of running away or of starting a fight with you here in the middle of the road.'

I relax my grip slightly. Underhill makes no attempt to pull his arm away. Eventually I release him and take a step back.

'I can find out who you are,' I say.

'I'm Esmond Underhill,' he says. 'At your service, Mr Grey. Entirely at your service. But—and here's a funny thing—I did mention to somebody that I'd met you at Hampton Court. This person—a good friend of yours and mine—thought that you were really called John Clifford. So, I wondered, is "Grey" an assumed name? Or is "Clifford" an assumed name? Because you've obviously been lying to one of us.'

'Who was he, your friend?'

'You don't know? I wondered whether to tell the gentleman concerned that I thought your name really *was* Grey. That might have surprised him quite a lot. But I decided not to tell him. As a courtesy to you. So, let's leave it that we both know something about each other. I don't work for Mr Thurloe, and you're called John Grey. You see, I like you, Mr Grey—not enough to incommode myself on your behalf, but enough to be willing to keep your secrets for the time being. As long as I'm not questioned too closely by anyone, then my knowing who you are need not worry either of us. Any more than what *you* know about *me* need trouble anyone except ourselves. On the whole, I'd rather not hang and you'd probably rather not be stabbed from behind in an alleyway one fine morning. What do you say, Mr Grey? Shall we be friends? I should like that above all things. Oh, and I know where you live, by the way.'

'No, you don't.'

'Yes, I do. And I know who lives with you too. Clifford, eh? *Very* good.'

He gives me another grin and is on his way, with no formal farewell.

For a moment I stand there. What exactly did Underhill mean? He knows who lives with me. And Aminta has been very free in describing herself as my cousin—that may not have been helpful. So a misunderstanding concerning my name might have occurred. But what common friends do Underhill and I have except common friend Ripley, and Brodrick? And Ripley knows my father, so how can he think that I am called Clifford? I actually told Ripley that I was John Grey.

Or, then again…thinking about it, was I less explicit on that matter than I thought? I certainly told them I was the son of the man they were expecting. As for their many questions to me, a purported John Clifford, close kinsman of Aminta, would have answered much the same. The Cliffords for example once owned the manor as we did before their time. But surely Ripley and Brodrick have had time to make enquiries, in which case they would have been told that Sir Felix had no living son called John, merely a dead one called Marius? Yet it all begins to make sense. I think that in my conversations with Thurloe it is Aminta's father rather than my own that I have been protecting so carefully. It is he who was expected from Brussels. In which case, where is he now?

I look at the line of footprints in the snow, all that remains of Underhill. They are coming from where I am going. No doubt about that. They lead me on, backward step by backward step, towards the south. But there are many other tracks that cross his and soon I lose any sense of what is his and what belongs to the feet of others. Has Underhill been this way? I cannot tell. Where was he going? I do not know.

Too many questions. Too few answers.

I press on towards the river and another meeting.

Thurloe has given me directions to a house in the Strand, where he says Lord Fairfax may be found. I am glad that I am not riding out to Wimbledon today. The snow is deep and soft, and a few errant flakes continue to drift down from the sky. My mount is doubtless munching hay in a warm stable while I trudge the streets of London.

I think the years have been kinder to Fairfax than to Cromwell. The hair and beard that gave him the nickname 'Black Tom' are only slightly tinged with grey. The brow is unfurrowed. He rises easily as I enter the room and motions me towards a chair by the fire. There is a self-assurance about him that Lambert and even Cromwell lack. Here is a man who has grown up knowing his place in the social order and knowing that it was a good one. He may rank many places below the Duke of Buckingham in the Order of Precedence, but they would speak the same language, have the same interests, marry into the same families. Lambert chafes in the country, away from the court for a few months. Fairfax knows that power is a long game that may be played over many generations. He views me with amused suspicion. He has the measure of his opponent.

'Cromwell sent you?' he asks.

'In a manner of speaking.'

He raises an eyebrow, but he does not ask which manner I refer to. 'What does the Lord Protector want? Does he plan to arrest me as well as my son-in-law? The Duke's only crime was to visit London. I am clearly in London too. Or would it please His Highness to arrest my daughter? Or my wife? Or my cook? They are here. In London.'

'He has not arrested your son-in-law,' I say. 'The whereabouts of the Duke are unknown.'

'And Cromwell expects me to tell him where he is?'

'The Lord Protector understands the importance of loyalty. I doubt he expects that.'

'The Lord Protector understands the importance of loyalty to himself. I am not sure that he has considered any other aspects of it. And he really believes the Duke plots against him? Just because he has returned to England? Why in God's name would the Duke wish to do that?'

'I don't know,' I say. 'Buckingham has long been a Royalist—indeed, he was Charles Stuart's closest friend, just as his father was close to King James. He is almost an adopted member of the Stuart family. He fought at Worcester. He accompanied the Pretender for many years in exile. His conversion to the cause of Parliament is unexpected—a great blow to the Royalist cause.'

'Just so. And a great victory for Cromwell, if he would only accept the Duke as one of his most sincere and devoted supporters.'

'His conversion might look cynical,' I add, 'to those who are cynical themselves. The Duke has secured his position.'

'Provided Cromwell does not make him spend the rest of his life in the Tower.'

'He would be in more danger of that if the Stuarts returned,' I say.

'Or perhaps he would charm his way back into favour. His family has never lacked charm. Or good looks.'

'You are gambling that he would? He is your guarantee of safety if Charles Stuart returns?'

Fairfax shoots me a glance. Just for an instant he is no longer a wealthy country gentleman with no concerns other than the state of his crops and his cattle. He is a general surveying the battlefield, not unpleased with his state of readiness.

'Do not think for a moment that I would sacrifice my daughter's happiness for personal ambition,' he says. 'I no longer have any personal ambition. But, as you say, my grandchildren's future is assured whatever happens. Cromwell too has forged alliances with the old nobility. It is simply that I have scooped the biggest prize. That perhaps is what he resents. It is I, not he, who has extracted the Duke from the Spanish Netherlands. It is with my family, not Cromwell's, that he has made his pact.'

'Does Buckingham expect you to succeed Cromwell? Is that *his* gamble?'

'I have never led him to believe that.'

'Or,' I say, 'do *you* expect Buckingham to succeed? He is the closest thing this country has to royalty other than the Stuarts.'

'He is a man of ability. I would expect that to be recognised. Eventually.'

'So, if Cromwell dies...'

Fairfax gives me a crooked smile. 'Tell me, Mr Grey, why are you sent? Not, I think, to test my loyalty. His Highness knows he has that as long as he lives and I live. I lack for nothing. I am content with my estate in Yorkshire. Were he to grant me another, I would not know what to do with it. I doubt that he has sent you with any concession for my son-in-law. So what is this about?'

'He wishes for some reassurance that you remain friends.'

'Friends...' He smiles and looks into a distance that I cannot see, because I was never there. 'And what mark of friendship does he plan to bestow on me?'

'What would you like?'

'To be left alone. To have my family left alone. To see my fruit trees deliver a prodigious harvest next autumn. Can he do that? Caesar after all became a god as well as an Emperor. A good crop of peaches should not be beyond him. He might also suspend the warrant for the arrest of my son-in-law.'

'I shall tell him.'

'I still have some influence with Parliament, Mr Grey. One day Cromwell may need that.'

I pause, then say: 'There are rumours of a plot against His Highness's life. By somebody close to him.'

'Nobody is close to him now.'

'Then by somebody who might easily gain access to him.'

'He is guarded.'

'There have been two attempts this month.'

I watch Fairfax carefully. His expression does not change.

'Cromwell will die in his bed, just as Buckingham will one day govern the country. There are some things of which one can be certain, even if one cannot see quite how they will be done or when.'

❀ ❀ ❀

Thurloe nods thoughtfully. 'So, Fairfax is not to be feared but Lambert is dangerously discontented with Wimbledon? I think you are right about both. And Lambert communicates with Underhill?'

'Lambert should have damned my impertinence for questioning him about a corporal who served him many years ago but he was studiously polite, trying to discover what I, and therefore you, knew of the man.'

'I agree that is interesting.'

'Underhill must be arrested,' I say. 'I met him here in London. I fear that he may make another attempt on the Lord Protector's life.'

'We know exactly where Underhill is and we shall arrest him at a time of our choosing, just as Lambert dreads we will. We think he will provide us with a great deal of information and not just about Lambert.'

'Underhill said something else that I did not understand at first. He told me that there were those who thought that Grey was a name I had assumed—that I was really called Clifford.'

'Does he mean Ripley and Brodrick think that?'

'I think that they believe I am the son of Sir Felix Clifford. His daughter, Lady Pole, is temporarily staying with me at Mistress Reynolds's house—hence the confusion in their minds.'

Thurloe frowns. 'Aminta Clifford? She and her father, as you know, left England hurriedly as proscribed Royalists. They left moreover as a result of information that you provided when you were working for me.'

'Yes,' I say. I do not care to be reminded of this. 'But she is now completely loyal to the State, and comes to petition for the return of property forfeit by Lord Pole's father.'

'Is this lady aware of your role in her exile?'

'No,' I say. 'Nor is anyone else except you and Mr Probert and Mr Morland.'

I do not add that my mother knows too. Thurloe looks at me as if trying to decide where to file this piece of information. 'As a member of the Clifford family, I can see why they might trust you. It could be inconvenient if Underhill—or anyone else—told Ripley that you were John Grey.'

'Underhill wishes to be my friend. In return for my not informing on him, he will not inform on me.'

'A bargain you have not kept.'

'A bargain that I never made.'

'At some point I am sure he will decide to inform Ripley. I think your days as Mr Clifford are numbered.'

'Then, with your permission, I would now like to retire to the country, as you promised I should, until such time as you have arrested Lambert and Underhill and Ripley and Brodrick.'

Thurloe considers this. 'Did I say that? We should not be precipitous. I said that your days were numbered—not that they were over. They clearly do not suspect you yet.'

'I would not wish to delay my departure until after they suspect me. It might not then happen at all.'

'But to withdraw you to the country now might simply arouse the very suspicions you fear—especially when we are close to making some arrests. I think we need you to continue as Mr Clifford for a little longer—for your own safety, you understand. We need to ensure that we have cut this plot off at the very roots. Another week may be enough for that. Underhill will soon be safely under lock and key. Whatever danger he poses will then be of no account. And, in the meantime, Ripley clearly still trusts you, because you are happily still alive.'

'Yes,' I say. 'I am happily still alive.'

But for how much longer?

CHAPTER 17

A Former Physician of the King

'So, Mr Thurloe does not release you?' asks Aminta. 'Like some over-trusting knight in a fairy tale, you are given just one more task before you can marry the princess. Your labours continue.'

'I think their conclusion is in sight,' I say. 'Aminta, your father—he *is* still in Paris?'

I had hoped that my question was guileless, but Aminta's expression suggests that it wasn't.

'Yes, of course,' she says. 'I have told you. With his gout he would find it difficult to travel anywhere.'

'Has he travelled to Brussels lately? Or London?'

'London? Why should he? Even if it were not for his health, he would probably face arrest as a delinquent Royalist. I am the only member of my family who could visit England in reasonable safety. That is why I am here.'

We look at each other. If there is something she has not told me, then she is still not telling me.

'Of course,' I say nonchalantly. 'That is why you are here. I suppose, by the way, that you haven't said anything to anyone that would have convinced them I was your brother? That my own name might be Clifford?'

'You are asking me some very odd questions this afternoon. Has something happened?'

'No,' I say. 'All is well. And how have your own labours progressed?'

'My labours?'

'Your petition. Is that not also a Herculean task?'

'Ah, that. I have submitted my request to Cromwell. It is well written and its arguments are irrefutable. But I fear it will just sit there unloved unless somebody speaks for me. It would have been better if you had used your influence...'

'I truly have none,' I say.

'I think, however, that I may be able to get somebody else to speak for me. Sir Richard Willys has chambers at Gray's Inn?'

'Yes,' I say. 'But surely you are not seeking *his* assistance? Thurloe could arrest him any day.'

'As I told you, I think my father knew him. He is clearly out of favour with the Republic, but he will in turn have friends—former Royalists who have now gone over to Cromwell. I think that he may be able to help me if I explain things properly.'

'But why would he? Your father may have known him, but... You will, of course, not reveal to him any part of our conversation?'

'You mean would I threaten to expose him as the head of the Sealed Knot if he doesn't help me?'

'It would be pointless—I have already revealed all to Thurloe.'

'Sir Richard doesn't know that, though, does he?'

'You must not let him know that you know he is part of the Sealed Knot.'

'Then, of course, I shall do no such thing.'

But there is something about the way she says it that I do not entirely trust.

'I'll speak to Thurloe,' I say. 'After Christmas, I shall speak to Thurloe. I'll tell him it is important that you receive help. There is no need for you to go anywhere near Gray's Inn.'

I shall indeed speak to Thurloe at the first opportunity. But by the next time I see him, I hope that some arrests will have been made. The sooner Lambert is arrested the better—and I think I know who may provide the last piece of information that will speed Thurloe on his way. I must speak again to the good Dr Bate. I believe I can find him at the College of Physicians, of which body he is a Fellow. Both Cromwell and Thurloe have said I may confide in him, and so I shall.

'Lambert?' he says. 'I would not have believed it possible. He lives in exile in Wimbledon, does he not?'

Bate's room is full of many objects that I recognise—the saws and probes and forceps; the tall blue and white jars with labels in abbreviated Latin. There is a glass jar full of leeches, wriggling and squirming. I wonder if they are hungry, but they are fat and black and sleek. I think they have eaten well today.

'Lambert has an accomplice,' I say. 'A former soldier, who was under his command and still, it would seem, has his loyalty. This man travels freely. Did you meet Esmond Underhill when you were at Hampton Court? A sneaking little ferret-like fellow. He claimed to work for Mr Thurloe.'

Bate considers. 'Yes, I think I did. He engaged me in conversation more than once, enquiring about His Highness's health.'

'What did you tell him?'

'Perhaps more than I should, had I known who sent him. He asked me with which drugs I was treating His Highness. As you say, he had a very convincing story that he was employed by the State. Have you told Mr Thurloe of your suspicions about Underhill?'

'Of course.'

If Dr Bate could be thus cozened, perhaps I should feel less guilty about what I had told Underhill—whatever that was. Still, I shall not criticise Dr Bate for whatever trifles he may have let slip.

'Did Underhill mention General Lambert?' I ask next.

'At one point I mentioned something and the wretch muttered to himself that he must needs report it to my Lord Lambert.' Bate pauses and looks at me carefully.

'So, contrary to what Lambert said, they are in touch with each other.'

'There can be little doubt,' says Bate.

'Thank you. I shall let Mr Thurloe know,' I say.

'Did you meet with Sir Richard Willys?' Bate asks. 'When we last spoke, you seemed to think that he played some role in this.'

'Yes,' I say. 'I found him.'

Bate looks as if he would like to know more but, even though Cromwell says I may trust his physician, I doubt that I should tell him I now know Willys is the leader of the Sealed Knot.

'Then whatever you have found out, you doubtless also reported that back to Mr Thurloe?'

'Of course,' I say.

'And to the Lord Protector?'

'Not as yet,' I say.

'Thurloe does intend to inform His Highness? He has proved slow in the past to act, as I have described to you. It would be unfortunate if he kept this information to himself for too long.'

'I am sure Mr Thurloe knows what he is doing,' I say.

The College of Physicians is close to St Paul's and I do not have far to travel to reach my lodgings. The lanes are, however, not familiar to me and I pause for a moment, trying to decide whether to go right or left.

'Are you lost, Mr Cardinal?'

I turn to see Brodrick and two other men whom I do not recognise.

'No,' I say instinctively. These lanes are almost empty and somehow I would feel safer back on the main road.

'I think we should see you back to your lodgings,' says Brodrick.

'That's kind,' I say, 'but I'm sure I can find my way back.'

'Why don't we come with you anyway?'

'I wouldn't want to inconvenience you...'

'It won't be inconvenient. And we can have a little conversation as we go.'

A large hand pushes me from behind, directing me neither left nor right but into a narrow passageway straight ahead. Any thought that this might be the quickest way home is extinguished quickly when it proves to be a dead-end. And any thought that Brodrick wishes me well is extinguished when I am forced against a sooty wall.

'You've lied to us,' he says, getting straight to his point.

'Of course I haven't,' I say, wondering which of my lies he is referring to. Has Underhill already told them I am not John Clifford? So much for Thurloe's theory that it would be safer for me not to flee to Essex.

'Who sent you?' asks Brodrick.

Ah, that lie.

'Hyde,' I say.

'Why?'

'You know that.'

'Do I?'

'I explained before.'

'You gave us Hyde's answer to our question about Cromwell's assassination.'

'Yes.'

'How odd then that we have since received a letter from him. He asks us to desist from any such scheme. There is no mention of you at all. And—before you waste any more of my time—the letter is genuine. The question is: are *you* genuine, Mr Cardinal? Or have you lied to us since we first met? I don't like being lied to, Mr Cardinal. Nor do the gentlemen who accompany me. None of us likes being lied to. And if you *have* lied to me you will regret it very much indeed.'

As Thurloe said, Brodrick talks when he would be better advised to hold his tongue. When he commenced his sermon against lying, I still had no idea what to say. By the time he had finished I had had all the time I needed to think.

'Hyde's letter does not contradict what I told you,' I say. 'He wants *me* to arrange the thing—not you or Ripley. I wasn't even intended to see you. Of course there was a letter to you telling you to desist, or you might have marred my plan.'

'Why did Hyde tell you not to involve us? We are his representatives here. I don't believe he would cut us out.'

'He doesn't trust you,' I say. 'You know that.'

Brodrick nods. Tell people what they have already told you and they will believe it.

'So, why doesn't Hyde trust me?' he asks.

'Because you're a whoring papist,' I say.

Well, it might have been better if I'd had more time to think of that answer. Still, it suffices. Brodrick nods again. 'No shortage of those in Brussels,' he says.

'Does Ripley know you have me pinned against a wall in an alleyway?' I ask. 'Or is this your own little plan?'

'Ripley's not my master,' he says, but he gestures to his two companions, who back off a pace or two.

Still, it clearly isn't just that Hyde doesn't trust Brodrick. Brodrick doesn't quite trust Ripley, it would seem. And I think Ripley does not entirely trust Willys. And I'm sure Hyde doesn't trust any of them. Long years of Thurloe buying their agents one by one has rightly made the Sealed Knot suspect everybody. It's what cripples every Royalist plot. Brodrick has decided to try a little bluster on his own account, it would seem. And he hasn't addressed me as 'Grey'. Not yet.

'Thank you,' I say. 'I take it I am now allowed to find my own way home?'

Brodrick shakes his head. My interrogation isn't over.

'The lady who is staying with you,' he says, narrowing his eyes. 'Who is she?'

But surely the Sealed Knot know who Aminta is? Because that's why they think I'm a Clifford myself? I realise that there is still much I do not know. The sooner I can finish this conversation, the less chance there is that I will give myself away.

'She is my cousin,' I say cautiously.

'Has she also come over from Brussels?'

'No, Paris,' I say. 'She and her husband and her father live in exile in Paris.'

'What's she doing in London then?'

'She has business here.'

'Come to compound with Parliament?' Brodrick pushes his face close to mine. I really ought to be able to identify the vintage that he has been drinking. 'A pair of turncoats then, your cousin and her husband?'

'No more than the Duke of Buckingham.'

'He'll live to regret his desertion of the King. Why is your cousin staying at Mistress Reynolds's?'

'She had been told I would be there.'

'By whom?'

'My mother,' I say.

'Your mother has a very loose tongue.'

'That is undeniable.'

'So do you if you have written to your mother to say that you were travelling to London on the King's business.'

For a moment I had forgotten that I am not studying law in London, free to write to my mother as I choose. I recall it now. It also occurs to me that my mother may at some stage in the past have corresponded with Brodrick. But I cannot raise that mitigating factor now without revealing that I am John Grey. And I have no idea whether Brodrick trusted my mother any more than he trusts Hyde.

'I didn't tell her that,' I say. 'She simply knows this is where I stay in London. When I'm here.'

'So, she has no idea that you have just travelled over from Brussels?'

'It would surprise her very much indeed to learn that I had.'

I am losing track of what is true and what is not, but there is no doubting this last statement.

'Then perhaps you should have chosen other lodgings this time. Don't tell this cousin of yours more than you have to.'

I nod. Not telling Aminta more than you have to is always a good plan. Not telling Brodrick more than I have to is an even better one.

'So which way do I need to go now?' I ask.

'Speaking as a whoring papist,' says Brodrick, 'I don't give a fig which way you go. Good day, Mr Cardinal. We'll meet again soon.'

I wait until Brodrick and his companions have left. Then I set off by what seems to me to be the best route. I hadn't noticed before—perhaps there were more pressing matters—but it has certainly started snowing again. If Brodrick plans to follow me, he will have a clear trail of footprints to guide him.

Saint Nicholas

The snow continues to fall. Dirty London is again covered with a carpet of white, though grey smoke rises from chimneys and black smuts of soot fall with the snow. It drifts against the walls of houses. Even the great coaches are now impeded by the sheer mass of it, their painted wheels choked and blocked. I, on foot, plod onwards, my shoes and stockings caked with ice. The lane that Mistress Reynolds's residence occupies is a narrow strait of gently undulating snow between the dark cliffs of the houses. Glistening icicles have sprouted in clusters and now dangle murderously above my head.

I sense an illicit jollity even before I open the front door. A burst of heat from the fireplace in the hall hits me as I enter. Then I notice the candlelight glinting on the dark, glossy leaves of holly and mistletoe. The scent of spices and wine greets my nose. Coming from the cold air outside, I find this intoxicating. Intoxicating and dangerous.

'You are celebrating Christmas!' I say.

'Tush,' says Aminta. 'Half the households in London will eat goose tomorrow.'

'It is not the goose they eat,' I say. 'It is the blasphemy that is mixed into the sauce.'

'Then eat of the goose and leave the blasphemy on the side of your plate,' says Aminta. 'In any case, I think that it is our pudding that is truly Arminian. Goose with a plain sauce, as we shall serve, is almost puritanical in comparison.'

'And what harm could there be in a cup of mulled wine on a cold evening?' asks Mistress Reynolds. 'That cannot threaten the Republic in any way.'

'Not at all,' says Aminta. 'Let us make this Puritan take wine with us, Mistress Reynolds.'

I accept the cup from her and sip cautiously, not out of religious considerations but because I fear Aminta will have used too much nutmeg and billed it to my account.

'Well?'

'Very good,' I say.

'See?' says Aminta. 'It has not turned you into a Royalist. You are merely a slightly less sour Puritan.'

'I am no Puritan,' I say. 'Did you visit Gray's Inn this afternoon?'

'Yes,' she says.

This is not good news.

'Did you find Sir Richard?'

'Yes,' she says.

'Was he helpful?'

'How could he be otherwise?' she asks. 'This is, after all, the season of goodwill, is it not?'

'Indeed,' says Mistress Reynolds. 'And you should attend church with me tomorrow, Mr Grey.'

'Neither of you should attend church,' I say very firmly. 'It would be most inadvisable.'

'Tush,' Aminta says again.

Aminta knows I cannot say more in front of Mistress Reynolds. I hope she is merely teasing me.

'I certainly shall not attend,' I tell them. 'Nor should you.'

'More spiced wine for the Puritan lawyer,' says Aminta. 'I think he still needs a great deal of sweetening.'

At first I can hear nothing at all. No carts or carriages are abroad. I get up from the pallet on which I now sleep and go to the small, leaded window. I rub my finger on the icy surface until I have a circle that I can see through. The snow in the lane must be a foot deep at least. One set of footprints runs towards the main road, but this is not a day for people to stir. And yet, I fear that somebody may have done so. I knock gently on the door of what was my bedroom but there is no reply. I turn the handle and peep in. The bed is empty and unmade. I look out of the bedroom window and at the footsteps, leading away from this very house. Is it my imagination or do I see the mark of a long skirt that has, here and there, trailed through the snow?

I pull on my breeches and button my doublet and run down the stairs.

'You are eager to attend church this morning,' says my landlady, 'but I fear that I cannot accompany you. The snow is too deep for one of my age and sex to venture out.'

'Aminta...' I say.

'When I see her, I shall forbid her to go out in the snow too,' says Mistress Reynolds, thus destroying my hope that Aminta has actually gone on some innocent errand for her or indeed that she is safely in the kitchen, plucking a goose or preparing an Arminian pudding.

'Where is the nearest church?' I ask. I do not doubt that Aminta is there at this very moment, warning the congregation to disperse before the authorities arrive.

'St Mary's is our parish church. But...' My landlady looks at me, and not for the first time, with puzzlement.

'And the service begins...?'

'In half an hour.'

'I must go at once,' I say.

'But—'

'It is essential that I am there.'

'Had I known my wine would have such an effect, I would have given you some on your very first evening,' says Mistress Reynolds.

But I am already out of the door.

St Mary's is not hard to find. It is a tiny stone building without a spire, wedged between two mean and dirty houses. I burst in through the door. The narrow nave has half a dozen rows of pews, no more. Two candles are burning on the altar. I detect the merest whiff of incense. The handful of worshippers who are already there turn in mild surprise. Aminta is not amongst them. There is nowhere for her to hide. She is not there. Then I remember my landlady saying 'but'. What was she about to tell me? That she did not attend this small church herself? In which case…

'Is there some larger church near here?' I ask. I sound unappreciative and ungrateful.

'St Michael's,' says a man, frowning. 'But will you not stay, now you are here? Our welcome is as warm as theirs, and the service is about to begin.'

In a moment soldiers will burst in here and arrest them all. Yet, if I tell them and Thurloe finds out, I risk my own safety. Only an idiot would warn them.

'There are soldiers on their way,' I say. 'However warm your welcome, it would be better if they did not find you here. Now, where is St Michael's?'

St Michael's is very much bigger and the service has already started. I edge in at the rear of the congregation and scan people's backs to see where Aminta might be. I do not sing, but I do remember some of the Christmas hymns from when I was young. The harmonies are almost as intoxicating as Mistress Reynolds's wine.

And all the bells on earth shall ring,
On Christmas Day, on Christmas Day;
And all the bells on earth shall ring,
On Christmas Day in the morning.

How easy would it be to fall into sinful and superstitious
ways! Yet I resist and see this spectacle for what it is—a crude
puppet show unworthy of the church that houses it.

And all the Angels in Heaven shall sing,
On Christmas Day, on Christmas Day;
And all the Angels in Heaven shall sing,
On Christmas Day in the morning.

But here too I cannot see Aminta. Then at last it occurs to
me. If she had time to warn only one congregation, where would
that be? St Paul's! London's great cathedral! This is a Christmas
goose chase and no mistake. I start to edge towards the outside.
I must go at once. But this time I cannot stop another service
and announce to the congregation that it should flee. They were
foolish enough to come here and must take their own chances.
Only those of us wise enough to stay away will avoid their just
punishment.

Then let us all rejoice again,
On Christmas Day, on Christmas Day;
Then let us all rejoice again,
On Christmas Day in the morning.

The heavy wooden door creaks open as I push it. The cold
air rushes in. There is also a smell of horse shit in the air—no
surprise when I see the number of horses that block the road.
The army is out in force. There will, sadly, be no escape for the
minister or for the congregation. Well, that is after all what they
deserve. The sooner I am away from here the better.

But I find a large red hand forced against my chest.

'Not so fast, you Cavalier whelp,' says the trooper.

'I was just looking for a friend in there,' I say. 'I'm not a Royalist myself, obviously. If you'll excuse me I must go.'

'Hear that?' he says to somebody behind him. 'He's not a Royalist. He must go.'

There is a gruff chuckle.

'But you don't need to arrest me...'

'You think not?'

'I'm not here for the service. I believe Christmas is a superstitious pagan festival.'

The trooper smiles. 'Save it for the magistrate,' he says.

'I'm a lawyer,' I say.

'Then you should know better.'

'I work for Mr Secretary Thurloe. He warned me this was going to happen.'

'Of course. That's why you're here then. Because you knew you'd get arrested.'

'But I wasn't even singing.'

'That's what they all say. Take him and lock him up with the others, Ned.'

Back at Mistress Reynolds's they will soon be sitting down to goose. I doubt they will serve goose where I am going.

Then let us all rejoice again on Christmas Day in the morning.

❃ ❃ ❃

I am being held in the Tower of London. I am not optimistic that I can escape.

At first I was in a large comfortable room with many of the rest of the congregation. Then I explained to the officer in charge that I was, in a manner of speaking, a secret agent. That caused a small and gratifying amount of excitement. I was pleased to be taken from the room and marched away from the Royalist rabble, through the snowy streets. Only as the melancholy walls of the Tower began to loom above me, did I realise that perhaps things were not turning out as I had hoped. We passed beneath a great stone gateway and a heavy door closed behind me.

Now I am in a narrow, malodorous room that is more underground than not. The only window is high up in the stone wall—a small, barred square of light, which is already fading fast. Christmas Day is as short under Parliament as it was under the King. The floor is damp and icy. There is a stool to sit on and an old and filthy straw mattress, which I hope I shall not be here long enough to need. I believe most of the others will have already been fined and released.

My patch of sky, which was slate grey, slowly grows pink, then fades slowly to nothing. I can scarce make out the bars. Only the icy draught from above reminds me that there is a gap in the solid stone. I have not been fed goose or any other thing. Even if I were a Puritan, I could not have wished for a more miserable Christmas Day.

Then, in the depths of my darkness, I see a flicker of red beneath the door. The gaoler is approaching with a candle and perhaps some bread and beer. A face peers through the grill.

'Stand away from the door, you. Gentleman to see you.'

'*Salve!*' announces my visitor. 'You are not good at taking advice, Mr Grey.'

'I was looking for somebody,' I say.

'I hope you found her and that she was pretty,' says Probert.

'I did not find her,' I say.

'Then you have suffered imprisonment in vain.'

'At least you have come to release me now,' I say.

'Perhaps not quite yet,' says Probert.

'Why?'

'We have new intelligence. We think that the Sealed Knot is having doubts about you.'

'I know. Brodrick cornered me yesterday. But it was mere bluster. They have had a letter from Brussels that failed to mention me, that is all. I merely fear Underhill. He thinks he has the power to undo me and he may not be wrong. Have you arrested him yet?'

'No. He has proved more elusive than we thought. Did Brodrick say anything else to you?'

'He asked about my cousin—Aminta Clifford, now married to Roger Pole and living in Paris. She is staying with me. Indeed, she was the lady I went in search of.'

'Mr Thurloe said that she had reappeared in London,' says Probert with a frown. 'So, Pole wishes to change sides again?'

'Like Buckingham and many others, he has given up hope of a restoration of the Stuarts. He is in Paris with Aminta's father.'

'If the two families are now united… Mr Thurloe told me that you thought you had perhaps been mistaken for Sir Felix's son. But could Ripley in fact have been expecting Pole? His son-in-law, in other words?'

I think back to our conversation. Pole also lived in the same village, for a time at least. He was secretary to my stepfather, the Colonel. He lived at the manor house.

'Why would Ripley think I was then called Clifford?'

'It is an obvious alias for you to choose. His wife's maiden name.'

'I do not resemble him in any way,' I say.

'That might explain their puzzlement.'

We both consider this. I shake my head. 'I don't think so.'

'Why did you not inform us earlier about Lady Pole?' asks Probert.

'About Aminta? Because it has no relevance to the matter at hand.'

'I beg to differ. She could endanger your safety if she knew too much about your activities. She may bear you a grudge.'

'I do not think she would give me away,' I say.

'Better not to give her the chance. *Variam et mutabile semper femina.*'

'That saying may be true of some women but not Aminta. She rarely changes her mind about anything. And I am sure she is telling the truth about her allegiance. She and her family have no communication with the Stuart court. And she knows nothing of my part in her exile.'

'Let us hope so. She could not have met Ripley or Brodrick before?'

'No, but she said that her father formerly knew Sir Richard Willys,' I say reluctantly. 'I believe she has had contact with him.'

'Otherwise she shows no other residual Royalist leanings?'

'Only, as I say, that she may have gone to church on Christmas Day. Is it possible she was arrested as well as me?'

Probert shakes his head. Wherever Aminta went, it was not to church, or if it was, she was more cautious than I. She is not in some foul dungeon. Of course she isn't.

'When can I be released?' I ask.

'As I say, we have received fresh intelligence that the Knot is suspicious of you. It is possible that Underhill has been speaking to them. It is also possible that, contrary to what you suppose, your cousin Aminta Clifford has lied to you and told the Sealed Knot all she knows about you. We hope not, because there is one final task we need you to perform—one that will ensure not only your own safety but the whole country's safety. The problem is what to do with you in the meantime. It may be that here in prison is the only place that we can truly protect you. But there is a further reason for keeping you here. Your arrest will also give credence to your purported status as a Royalist. Whatever they believe now, Brodrick and Ripley will reason that we would not arrest one of our own, or if we did that we would treat him well.'

'So, I am to be detained and not treated well?' I say.

Probert nods. 'Precisely. Another few days, or say a week at the most, will assist you greatly. We shall try to ensure that you are not too uncomfortable—I think we may spare you the usual interrogation—but we must give your imprisonment some semblance of reality.'

'Thank you.'

'Not at all. It also seems to me that it would be wise in any case to remove you from Mistress Reynolds's and the prying eyes of Aminta Pole.'

'So, I am to stay here in the meantime eating dry bread and drinking filthy water?'

'Of course not. We shall instruct the gaoler to give you water that is reasonably clean. But not so clean of course as to arouse the suspicions of Brodrick and Ripley.'

'Will the Sealed Knot even know I am here?'

'Yes, we shall make sure they do. And I must remember to get the gaolers to address you as Mr Clifford in case the Knot make enquiries. We shall not stint in our efforts to impress upon them that you have suffered greatly. On your release you can tell him them you were threatened in all sorts of ways, but revealed nothing about the Knot. Or we can make you a little less heroic, if you are of a modest disposition.'

'No. Tell them that you threatened to torture me, but that I laughed in your face.'

'I have never witnessed such a thing myself, but if that is what you would wish me to say, I shall certainly do it.'

'Lay it on as thick as you like,' I say.

It is, I think, Thursday. Time moves slowly here in prison and the winter night and day are often as one. Few sounds reach me down here, and most of those that do echo strangely on the cold stone. I hear the clink of keys, the sound of locks turning smoothly, footsteps receding into the distance. Occasionally I can make out the cries of one who has been here a little too long—the despairing sobs of somebody who is truly forgotten by the world. But I shall be here a short time only. Probert has returned.

'A little longer, Mr Grey,' he says apologetically. 'I had expected Mr Thurloe to order your release, but he is reluctant for reasons I cannot fully understand. Underhill has, however, been arrested. He has as yet provided us with few facts. He refuses to implicate General Lambert in any way. But nothing he tells us makes us think that he has betrayed you to Ripley, whom he of course denies knowing.'

'Then perhaps it would be safe to let me go?'

'As I say, Mr Thurloe has ordered it otherwise. We still have a large number of dangerous Royalists in prison. Perhaps that is his reason. If we were to release you before the others, it would imply that you had friends working for you. Clearly, as a hardened Royalist, you have no friends at all.'

'So it would appear,' I say.

'Friend to see you,' says the gaoler.

I have been dozing, dreaming of flocks of roast geese, flying across the sky, dripping a rich, dark sauce. They vanish into a vapour, which is rising warmly from innumerable plum puddings. I rub my eyes.

'Thank you,' says Aminta to the gaoler, handing him a discreet coin or two. She looks at me, head on one side, and smiles. The gaoler touches his cap to her, a thing he had never done for me. I suspect that, even in this Republican gaol, an ancient title carries some weight. Any residual fear that she too may have been arrested is dissipated by the way the gaoler backs out of her presence, mumbling his thanks to Her Ladyship. She is certainly not here as a prisoner, however many Christmas services she may have attended. She waits patiently until he has gone before she addresses me. Perhaps she at least brings news.

'I think I like your other chambers better,' says Aminta, wrinkling her nose. 'They are warmer and lack the green slime that seems such an important feature of this one. Your present accommodation also smells of unwashed lawyer.'

I struggle to my feet in order to be slightly less at a disadvantage. My muscles are stiffer than I thought. I rub my chin, which I have not shaved for some days. And I doubt that she would wash that often if the water was as cold as that which I am offered.

'I am not here by choice,' I say, glancing towards the door. 'Mr Thurloe believes—'

'It has been explained to me,' she interrupts, 'by one in Mr Thurloe's office. I am of course touched that you should have come looking for me, but otherwise the less we talk of that the better. We need to maintain the pretence that you are a Royalist prisoner and that I am graciously visiting you as an act of charity.'

'Who in Mr Thurloe's office has explained my incarceration?' I ask. Probert would scarcely have explained anything to her.

'I forget the name,' she says unconvincingly. 'But he made clear the necessity of it. He also provided me with a pass to enter here.'

'And this is an act of charity?'

'I have unfortunately had to bribe the gaolers with the cakes that were to form the outward and visible part of my charitable act. The pass alone proved insufficient. But as a Puritan you probably enjoy fasting. The gaolers assured me that they belonged to the Church of England. However, since I have seen you, I can report to your mother that you are in good spirits and that your cell is no worse than it might be. Of course you can give her a fuller report when you are released.'

'I am to be released then?' I ask.

'I so wish I could bring you better news, but sadly not, my dear cousin. As you know, there are good reasons for holding you here for a little while longer. There are, however, things happening in the great world outside. Do you know a Mr Daniel O'Neill?'

'No,' I say.

'One of Hyde's couriers, according to my contact. He has been over here on some business for Hyde. Thurloe has been trying to arrest him, but every time he sends some soldiers round to pick him up, O'Neill has gone. Somebody seems to be tipping him off. Has Ripley mentioned him? Or Sir Richard Willys?'

'No,' I say. 'But if there is a leak, then it is Sam Morland's work.'

'That is your view?'

'Most certainly.'

Aminta considers this, a lilac-gloved finger against her red lips. It is weeks since I have seen anyone so beautiful.

'Is it Willys who has told you this?' I ask.

Aminta shakes her head. I am not sure I believe her.

'Has Willys been arrested?' I ask.

'Not as far as I know.' Aminta looks round the cell again, though there is little enough to see. 'Well, cousin, that is enough charity for one day. Mistress Reynolds is cooking roast lamb for dinner—tender baby lamb cooked with rosemary and a steaming hot apple pie with a golden crust to follow. I would not wish her to burn it all just because I had selfishly loitered here. But be of good cheer. You are not forgotten here. Far from it.'

'You are sure of that?'

'Absolutely.'

It is, I think, still January. Time moves slowly here in prison and one month is much like another—damp and unpleasant.

The gaoler delivers a note to me. It is from Probert. He regrets being unable to visit me in person, but he does not wish to arouse suspicion, and a further visit by him without my being tortured would seem odd. He makes no mention of Aminta's visit to me but does say that she has departed my lodgings, for France in all likelihood, leaving behind a large bill for me to pay at Mistress Reynolds's. It is only a matter of a few more days until I shall find out. I am instructed to eat the note. I do so. It at least tastes better than the bread.

It is, I think, February. My cell remains damp, but it is a little warmer. I receive a letter from my mother, much delayed by the authorities. It bears greetings for the New Year. My mother says that she has received a full (word underlined three times) report from Mr Probert and regrets that I am detained. She wonders why I did not adhere to my plan to study law, which would have been altogether more convenient. She compares me to my father in a way that compliments neither of us. Finally, she reports that she and my stepfather enjoyed a pleasant Christmas and hopes that I shall be home next year.

It is, I think, March. The breeze that blows through my barred and glassless window is fresher and sometimes almost warm. I receive a letter from Aminta, addressed simply from Paris, thanking me for my hospitality. She is well but her petition makes no further progress. She is sure that I will bear my imprisonment with the same fortitude that she bears having to live in France. If I meet anyone of importance in gaol, who might have the ear of the Lord Protector, she would be grateful if, etc etc. They have had to move house in Paris several times to avoid their creditors. I may reply to her via my mother if I need to.

It is, I think, April. I receive a bill from my landlady for wine, oranges, tea and four months' rent. She begs to remain, as ever, my obedient servant and hopes for early payment.

It is, I think, late spring or early summer—at least it is in the world outside. Here in prison it is always bleak mid-winter. I have eaten nothing since a note I received yesterday from Thurloe—a brief message but finally there is hope. My incarceration will shortly be at an end. Underhill has been released, having given the State no assistance of any sort. Almost all of the other Royalists have also now been freed. There is no reason to keep me here any longer. My stomach is rumbling but, unless I am released today, it will be at least another hour before the next hunk of dry bread is thrust at me.

Outside, I hear footsteps—not just the heavy plod of the gaoler but another lighter pair of feet accompanying him. I wonder if one of Mr Thurloe's agents has come to conduct me back to his office at Westminster or to my lodgings. Either would be good provided we can stop off at an inn on the way and procure a roast chicken and some slices of ham and a grilled trout and a flagon of ale and a basket of apples and…

But the lace-bedecked figure who strides through the door does not come from Thurloe.

'Sir Michael…' I begin. But Ripley quickly holds a finger to his lips. I wonder who he has told the gaoler he is. I somehow doubt if he has said that he is a renegade Cavalier.

'Mr Clifford,' he says pleasantly. 'I have been arguing to this good man that you present no threat to anyone. He assures me, however, that you are a dangerous agent of Charles Stuart.'

'I've had word from the Secretary's office to detain him until further notice,' says the gaoler. 'Bread and water diet. No visitors.'

Should I say that I am in fact about to be released? I am not supposed to know that and suspect that Ripley should not know either.

'That is true,' I say cautiously. 'My diet and other conditions are as you describe.'

'But perhaps I might be permitted to talk to this gentleman in private?' says Ripley. He plays a little with his purse as if acquiescence on the part of the gaoler might result in gold changing hands.

'You know I can't,' says the gaoler, though not without considerable regret. He watches the purse vanish back into Ripley's pocket. 'As a magistrate yourself you would know that, Mr Jones. I have to guard the prisoner.'

'Since I am a magistrate,' says Ripley, flashing a lace cuff, 'I could instruct you to allow me to examine the prisoner alone.'

His voice carries great authority but Ripley's mistake was to put the purse away. The gaoler shakes his head. 'You're not a City magistrate,' he says. 'I'd know you if you were. You'll need to get an order from a London Justice of the Peace.'

'You mean the one coming down the corridor?' asks Ripley.

The gaoler turns to look, squinting into the darkness. A big mistake. You'd have thought he would have exercised some caution in dealing with out-of-town magistrates.

The wooden stool crashes down on the back of his head. He collapses to the floor without a word. Though I had seen Ripley make his move, I am shocked by the weight of the blow.

'What have you done?' I ask, horrified.

'I've just obtained a *habeas corpus*,' says Ripley.

'I was in no danger. If this poor man is badly hurt, when he recovers he may now give evidence that I attacked him and tried to escape.'

Ripley bends over the bloody figure and places his hand carefully in front of the gaoler's face. I wait anxiously for a minute, then another.

'Don't worry. It's fine,' says Ripley, getting to his feet.

'Thank God for that.'

'Stone cold dead,' he continues. 'He won't be giving evidence against anyone. Still, it would be inadvisable for either of us to stay here longer than we need to. We have, after all, just murdered an officer of the State, albeit a minor one. If you'd be kind enough to pick up that candle, I'll lock the door behind us and we can leave quietly. If anyone asks, I'm Henry Jones, Justice of the Peace in the County of Surrey and you're my prisoner. Happy Christmas, by the way, Mr Cardinal. And a Happy Easter, too.'

Mr Allen Brodrick

'So, the gaoler is dead?' Brodrick is not happy. 'Did you not consider the consequences before you decided to hit him with a stool?'

'That's my concern,' Ripley snaps back at him. He was quite jaunty on our journey from the gaol, but he is less so now. 'It seemed for the best.'

We are ensconced in a tavern near Aldgate. It is a modest establishment, and the food is bad, but its bill of fare is not limited to the stale bread I have grown used to. And I think we cannot remain here long enough for the quality of the meals to matter greatly. For the moment, Ripley and Brodrick have consented to eat with me on condition that I strip off my verminous clothing and hose myself down for a full ten minutes under the pump in the courtyard. I am now dressed in the second best suit of one of the serving boys, which Ripley has improbably promised to return to him at some later date. I am not sure that it smells much better than my prison garb, and both gentlemen have elected to sit on the far side of the table from me. Brodrick's expression has, however, nothing to do with any residual odour of the kitchen that may be emanating from my shirt, breeches or stockings.

'It is my concern if it means that the authorities are seeking you,' says Brodrick. 'Or seeking *him*. Even if Clifford had been tortured, what he could have told them was old news. This whole action was unnecessary.'

For once I am with Brodrick, at least as concerns the general principle. 'There was no need to rescue me,' I say. 'I had already been told that I would be released soon.'

'Told by whom?' asks Brodrick.

'Other Royalists had been freed,' I say. 'They had no reason to keep me.'

'Some have indeed already been released,' Ripley concedes. 'But the more daring adherents of His Majesty have been detained longer. We had heard—from our own sources—that you had been closely confined and were likely to be tortured. They said you seemed to imagine that you could easily endure torture, which we doubted you could. Once we had discovered which prison you were in, we could not take the risk of leaving you where you were, even for another day.'

'Whoever you are,' says Brodrick.

A nasty silence follows this. It would seem that my imprisonment has counted for less than Thurloe imagined. Has rumour spread that I am John Grey?

'You know who I am,' I begin. 'I have been sent by Hyde...'

I look from one to the other wondering exactly what Hyde may have said about me in the interim. But Ripley comes to my rescue. 'Do not fear, Mr Clifford. Though Mr Brodrick retains some doubts, Sir Richard Willys made extensive enquiries about you in Brussels.'

'Did he?'

'He confirms that you are indeed John Clifford and a man of sound Royalist sentiment.'

I try not to show too much surprise. John Clifford after all does not exist—in Brussels or anywhere else. 'Then all is well,' I say.

'But why haven't we heard of you before?' asks Brodrick. 'That's what I mean. Even if you were told not to contact us this time, we know you're not one of Hyde's usual couriers.'

'It isn't a job for a courier.'

'How were you recruited?'

I have at least had time to think before I tell the next lie.

'My father was originally due to undertake the mission,' I say, 'but was unable to travel on account of his gout. I was asked to take his place. I travelled to Brussels, where I was briefed as you know.'

The mention of gout is, I think, a nice touch. With luck, if they know anything about him, they will have heard that Sir Felix is a sufferer. I have been careful not to say where Sir Felix is now, because I do not know and they may.

'Enough,' says Ripley. 'Willys says Mr Clifford's known in Brussels. That will have to be sufficient. You must concede that he has done all he can for us. He will be wanted for the murder of his gaoler, so we must get him out of the country. I can obtain papers for him and, since I am wanted too, I shall accompany him back to Brussels.'

'Brussels?' I say. 'But...'

'It will be safer than remaining here.'

'I'll take that risk.'

'We can't. If you are recaptured they will certainly torture you this time, and I do not share Mr Brodrick's view that you could tell them nothing of value. Brussels will surely not be that much of a hardship after prison?'

Brussels will be my death, but I cannot explain that truthfully. Very well then, I must lie again.

'You are right,' I say. 'I will accompany you to Brussels, Sir Michael. But I must return to Mistress Reynolds's first.'

'Impossible. '

'I have...I have documents there. I cannot risk leaving them behind. Thurloe will search my lodgings once he knows I have fled. They will incriminate us all.'

'Very well. We shall send a man with you.'

'No, I shall be safer alone. Thurloe will know most of your men and may be looking out for them. I'll go now and return tonight, when it is dark.'

'How do we know we can trust you to return?'

'Because, as you say, if I am recaptured I shall be tortured then hanged for murdering my gaoler. On reflection, Brussels is better. I shall need the forged papers of which you speak if I am to get away to the Spanish Netherlands. What else can I do but return here?'

'Then it shall be as you wish,' says Brodrick, 'but if you are taken, do not betray us. You would be better dead.'

That, of course, is only his opinion.

I am back in my own room at last. A light breeze wafts through the open window, carrying the happy noises of free people, going about their business in the street below. I have shaved and exchanged the serving boy's second best suit for some clothing of my own. Will Atkins has been sent out to run another errand and Probert is now sitting there with me, in my chamber, gnawing on a chicken leg that Mistress Reynolds had cooked for me. It will have been added to my bill. Outside, a warm day is drawing to an end. Soon Ripley will be expecting me back.

'The gaoler will live,' says Probert. 'The blow that Ripley struck was hard, but the skulls of our gaolers are harder, it would seem. We found him dazed and cursing the duplicity of Surrey magistrates. The State is, of course, put to the expense of purchasing a new stool, but otherwise no harm was done. Now we have explained the full circumstances to him, the man bears Ripley a grudge but reluctantly forgives you. There is no arrest warrant for murder.'

'Then all is well,' I say. 'There is a full moon to aid my journey. I shall leave tonight for Cambridge. I doubt Ripley will feel inclined to search for me—he will be too anxious for his own safety. I am of no further use to the Knot. I can be of no further use to you. Ripley wishes to send me to Brussels, for my protection as he sees it, but where I will most certainly be found out. They still think I am the son of Sir Felix Clifford because Willys has received confirmation from Brussels that that is who I am. I do not know how he was so misinformed, but let us simply be thankful that that is the case. Once I get to Brussels, however, I shall not be able to continue my pretence. My fear is that Sir Felix, far from accompanying Aminta and Roger to Paris as I was told, is in Brussels with Charles Stuart. I may be able to deceive Ripley into thinking I am his son, but I shall certainly not be able to convince Sir Felix.'

Probert is nodding thoughtfully. 'Then it has worked out well,' he says.

'Well?'

'I mean our trick has worked. We knew that the Knot would, in due course, make enquiries of you in Brussels. It would have been no more than prudent. But we do, of course, also have agents there. We were able to ensure that Sir Richard Willys was told that you were indeed John Clifford. It will therefore be safe for you to travel to Brussels.'

'But I've said—there are people there who simply know I am not—'

'We can take care of that too.'

'But Ripley will speak to them!'

'Only if he gets there,' says Probert.

'And he may not?'

'It will be arranged.'

'So, you wish me to travel to Brussels?' I say.

'Mr Thurloe feels that this is an opportunity,' says Probert. 'Sir Richard said that he would send a message by you, did he not?'

'Yes...'

'We need you to receive the message; then, having read the thing, take it to Brussels as proposed. Sir Richard will have no idea that we know his designs. The little incident with the gaoler this afternoon is an unexpected bonus. As I say, no arrest warrant has been issued, but it could be. It would in fact be prudent to do so. As a wanted man, your journey to Brussels would be very natural.'

'But even if Ripley is stopped, Sir Felix may still recognise me.'

'You will not be in Brussels for very long. All you have to do is deliver the message, as John Clifford, and return here as quickly as you can. If you meet Sir Felix, he won't need to know what name you have given Hyde. But you probably won't meet him, not if he is at home stricken with gout.'

'I think his gout may be as fictitious as his Paris address.'

'Then greet him in a friendly fashion and tell him as little as possible. We simply need you to travel to Brussels, deliver a letter and come back. It is very easy, Grey.'

'Why not let Ripley take the message? He wants to go to Brussels. Willys must trust him. Why am I needed at all?'

'That is the point, Mr Grey. Willys does not trust Ripley. He trusts you. Your arrest has allayed any suspicions he might have had. So your time in gaol was not wasted. And we think Hyde is expecting a young man of precisely your description.'

'So Ripley is not even to know that I have the letter?'

'That is correct.'

'There's one small problem you have overlooked. Even if I were willing to take the letter, how will Willys get it to me without Ripley seeing it?'

Probert produces a sealed sheet of paper from his doublet. 'I rather think I have it here. There is somebody within the Sealed Knot who is in our pay and to whom Willys gave this for delivery to you. He then gave it to me. We have, of course, already opened and copied it. The difficult part is done. Now all that remains is for you to deliver it.'

'So; you already know what is in it?'

'Yes, it is not in code. We have read it. Now we wish Hyde to read it too, because he will then act upon it and we will be waiting for him. There is a further consideration: if it is not deliv-ered by you, then the Knot will know that it has been intercepted by us and that there is a traitor in their midst. They will probably guess who it is. It is you, Mr Grey. I do not need to describe what happens then. So it is essential that it is delivered.'

'And you can really ensure that Ripley is stopped?'

'Ripley will, of course, begin the journey with you. He shall, I promise you, not get beyond Dover. We shall take care of that. You will arrive in Brussels alone as the trusted messenger of Sir Richard Willys—whom you have fortunately met, should they ask you any questions about him. You shall then travel back under the protection of the Sealed Knot as far as Ostend and under the protection of Mr Thurloe from the Kent coast. What could be safer?'

'And if I do not go?'

'We had hoped you would be happy to do this for us. But if you are not, Mr Thurloe asked me to remind you that there could be an arrest warrant out for you by tomorrow morning.'

'But you put me in gaol for my own safety and the gaoler is in fact alive and well. I am neither an escaper nor a murderer.'

'Of course not. And you will be able to argue that when you come to trial in a few months' or few years' time.'

'You would not arrest me again!'

'If we did not, then the Knot will be very suspicious,' says Probert. 'They will wonder how you can injure a gaoler with impunity. They will certainly wonder what can become of Sir Richard's letter. They will wonder if you have not gone over to our side. Of course, we would not betray your whereabouts to Mr Brodrick if you did not cooperate with us. I would not wish you even to think that we might. But we really do need you to do this, and there is nobody else who can help us.'

'Does Samuel Morland know that I am going?'

'I do not understand your fears. Sam Morland is to be trusted. But it has not been necessary for him to know.'

'The fewer people who know…' I say.

'You are right,' says Probert. 'The fewer who know, the better. Did Mr Thurloe ever tell you about Manning?'

'Yes. He was shot because Cromwell made a slip and inadvertently gave him away.'

'It wasn't a slip, it was a joke,' says Probert. 'As a lawyer it may appeal to you. A former Cavalier had been given leave to go abroad on condition that he did not see Charles Stuart. Note the precise wording. In order that he should not have to lie on his return, this gentleman's meeting with Charles Stuart took place in the dark. Manning heard and reported this to Whitehall. Once back in London, the Cavalier told Cromwell he had not seen Charles. Cromwell replied, "No wonder, since the candles were out". He was arrested but got a message back to the court that there was a spy amongst them. That was what did for Manning. Of course, Manning was careless with his ciphers. I suspect they were on to him anyway. Otherwise how would they have known which of them it was? And Manning made things up. You could never be sure what he reported was true. He wasn't a great loss. There was probably no need to have shot him.'

'Thurloe doesn't make jokes,' I say.

'It's safer that way,' says Probert.

Through the windows I can now see a glorious sunset. The red glow seems to reflect off Probert's weather-beaten face. He looks an honest man, which (as he would no doubt point out himself) is no reason for trusting him. Would Thurloe betray me to Brodrick if I don't cooperate? Only if he had to. Only if there was no better way of getting the job done.

'Very well,' I say at length. 'I shall go as you request. But this is the very last thing I do for you. And I would ask one favour in return.'

'Anything within reason.'

'It is, like my journey to Brussels, easy enough. I would request that the Lord Protector gives careful consideration to Lady Pole's petition requesting that the attainder should be reversed and her husband's estates restored. I think I owe her that.'

'Yes, you probably do owe her that. Very well. I shall do all I can to ensure that her request is well received. I cannot guarantee the outcome.'

'Nor, for my part, can I guarantee I will reach Brussels safely, but I intend to try. Surely, however, I do not need to go through this charade of skulking in the shadows with Ripley as far as Dover? Could he not be stopped here in London and I travel to Dover as myself? I would reach Brussels before they heard of Ripley's detention.'

Probert shakes his head. 'Who knows who may be watching you as you go? We would not wish the Sealed Knot to think that we do not take our trade seriously.'

I am therefore hurrying again through the dark streets, carrying a leather satchel with a change of clothes and Willys's letter. Brussels lies ahead of me. But first I must make my way to Dover with the threat of arrest helpfully hanging over me.

And there is one mystery that still troubles me. If the person Ripley and Brodrick were expecting really was Sir Felix, where has he been for the past few months? And where is he now? London? Paris? Essex? It would be so much better if it were not Brussels.

Mr Black of Thaxted

I am sitting in a dark corner of an inn. Through an open window I can see the ghostly moon-lit clouds riding across a starry sky and hear the slap of the sea against the harbour wall. From somewhere in the distance comes the insistent rush and hiss of water hitting a pebble beach. In my right-hand pocket is a passport bearing a good forgery of the Lord Protector's signature and seal, and begging that Jeremy Black, wool merchant of Thaxted, should be allowed free and unhindered passage to the Low Countries.

Ripley and I have taken four days to reach Dover, and all that time I have been lost in too many layers of duplicity for me to count. I have a false and lying passport provided by the Sealed Knot, when I might have had an honest one provided by Cromwell himself. I hide from Thurloe's agents even though they wish me well. I aid Ripley in his concealment, even though I anxiously await his arrest. I have pretended to start at every shadow, even though I suspected that we faced no danger until we reached Dover. After all, why should Thurloe waste his assets hunting us through Kent when he knows he can take Ripley at the port? But I have played my part well, I think.

We hid in the stables of an inn at Rochester when soldiers came to search for fleeing felons. Then we had to spend two nights in a barn just outside Canterbury because of troopers patrolling the road. But neither group was, I think, searching for us. Or, then again, perhaps they were. There may be layers of duplicity that I have not yet fathomed. It could be that the local magistrates are looking for all absconding Royalists, unaware of any plan of Thurloe's. If so, I may yet be arrested and perhaps hanged before Mr Thurloe can explain the stratagem.

The door of the inn opens and three men enter. Two, in red jackets and with their hands hovering pointedly about their swords, take up guard at the door. The third, an officer of some sort, scrutinises those assembled in front of him. He removes a rolled-up sheet of paper from his doublet and consults it. This far from London, the simple ability to read commands respect in its own right—though being accompanied by two armed men commands a reasonable amount of respect too.

'Is there a John Clifford here?' he demands, the open paper still in his hand. He holds up his other hand as if to shield his eyes from the glare of the candlelight and scans the room.

I assume this is part of Thurloe's plan to establish my credentials as a runaway, but surely only Ripley will be aware of my presence and he will soon be under arrest? I wonder again whether Thurloe has shared his plan with enough people. I am careful not to look at Ripley, who is sitting on the far side of the inn.

The company, both those who might be called John Clifford and those who might not, are suddenly silent. It is obvious to all that the question bodes no good for somebody. A sailor, seated at a table with a small group of friends, answers on my behalf. A pint or so of bad rum has emboldened him. 'Who wants to know?'

'I do,' says the officer. He speaks softly, in a voice that we have to strain to hear. He knows we will listen even if he whispers. It could be dangerous for us not to. 'Does anyone know the whereabouts of John Clifford?'

'What's he supposed to have done?' asks the sailor. He is too drunk to know how strangely loud his voice sounds after the silence.

'Thank you for asking,' says the officer. 'I am much obliged to you for raising that point. Mr Clifford is wanted for murder. Now, would anyone here like to admit to being John Clifford?' For some reason he looks in my direction and raises an eyebrow.

I look the man in the face. I hope he will not ask me to speak because my mouth is suddenly completely dry.

'You, young fellow,' he says to me, 'what is your name?'

Without taking my eye off him for a second, I pick up my tankard and take a swig. Is this man privy to Thurloe's thoughts or no? Whether I am lying to save my skin or merely to play a part, I intend to employ insolence at a level that will suggest innocence, but hopefully without inciting incarceration in its own right.

'What's it to you what my name is?' I say.

'I am paid to be curious about the affairs of other men,' he says. 'Are you travelling to France?'

'Ostend,' I say.

'I'll see your papers then,' he says. 'Maybe your name will be written there, if you don't have a mind to tell me straight, like an honest man.'

'I never claimed to be an honest man,' I say. I take a folded paper from my pocket and hand it to him, hopeful that a forgery of Cromwell's signature will be good enough.

'Jeremy Black?' he says.

'Yes,' I say.

'Of Thaxted?'

'Of the finest town in the county of Essex.'

'If you say so. What are you travelling to Ostend for?'

'I'm a wool merchant. I have business there.'

'What manner of business?'

'We make fine wool for tapestry work. They make tapestries in Brussels.'

'So I've heard,' he says. 'What's in the bag?'

I open the pack that is on the ground beside me and take out skeins of wool that I have been supplied with. They are dyed crimson and ochre and emerald green and cobalt blue and a dark blue that is almost black and a soft creamy white and (my favourite) a rich and shimmering gold. Though the Sealed Knot lacks powder and shot, it has provided me with these goods at short notice.

I expect the officer to stretch out his hand and rub the yarn with his fingers, marvelling at the quality, but he merely waves it away and yawns. He does not arrest me.

'Does anyone else know the whereabouts of John Clifford?' he enquires.

Nobody does. He bids us good night.

On his own side of the room, Sir Michael de Ripley, baronet, who is not for some reason being sought for the murder of anyone, briefly glances in my direction and winks. Then he buries his face in his tankard again.

If that was Thurloe's idea of stopping Ripley, I am not impressed. Slowly and carefully I put my samples back in my pack and pull the leather straps tight. I fold my passport and place it in my pocket.

The door of the inn opens suddenly and a large man is silhouetted in the frame, his back to the starry sky. But this too is not the leader of a troop of dragoons with a warrant for my companion. He has been sent to tell us that our boat is about to depart. The tide and the wind are with us. We sail at midnight.

I turn to see if Ripley has also heard this, but he is no longer there. He has vanished without trace.

CHAPTER

21

Mr Shufflebottom of Nowhere in Particular

Never having been to sea before, I had imagined our boat skimming across the surface of the water, a bird in flight. But, in what the captain is pleased to call a fair wind, we rise and fall and surge ahead and are checked, then surge forth again. The cold, dark waters of the Channel foam beneath us. Twice I have leaned over the side of the boat to vomit into them, the first time copiously and with some surprise, the second with weary resignation. All this without the pleasure of being drunk first. Now I stand here on the bleached wooden deck, watching it continue to rise and fall and rise and fall and rise and fall, while the stars slowly fade away.

Though my stomach tells me all is far from well, I feel a strange elation. Thurloe's plan, whatever it was, has succeeded. I should never have doubted him. I have left Ripley behind in Dover and can now travel on alone to Brussels and deliver Willys's letter to Hyde. In two or three days' time I shall travel back by the same route. Thurloe will be grateful, if not eternally then at least long enough to let me go back to Essex or Cambridge until it is safe to live in London again. I have never visited Brussels before, nor any other city on that side of the English Channel. There will be no Ripley there to betray me. This is to be a pleasant adventure.

The sails above me rustle, then crack like a gunshot, and the deck lurches again. The ship is going about. We are sailing into the dawn. The vast red day creeps westwards to engulf us.

The captain is a small king, or perhaps I should say tyrant, within his miniature state. Here on board nobody may say him nay. His word is law, and it may be death to disobey, though I think he will hang none from the yardarm who have the money and the inclination for a return journey. He nods in my direction as he strolls on his deck. I enquire, with all due respect, what is the name of the town that we can see off our starboard bow.

'Dunkirk,' he observes, with a patronising smile.

'Which is now in English hands,' I say.

'Indeed, Dunkirk is ours. God be praised. Not only did we defeat the Spanish, but our French allies handed the town over to us as agreed—both miraculous events. Cromwell's writ now runs there as well as at Dover. Which is inconvenient for some.'

'It matters not to me,' I say.

'Of course not, Mr Black,' he says. 'You are an honest dealer in wool. Why should you have anything to fear from the officers of the State? I can assure you, however, that we have no intention of docking there.'

He touches his hat and I touch mine. It would seem that there is some belief on board that I am a fleeing Royalist, so all is as it should be. The little comedy enacted at the inn may have been of some value after all, though I am still not entirely sure who the audience was.

I see relatively little of my fellow passengers, many of whom have chosen to remain below. One man, however, has joined me here beneath the masts and the vast bulging sails. I notice that he has a small pointed beard and a scar on his cheek. He wears a sword. He has been watching me for some time, as if he thinks I may be of some interest to him. He strolls across the deck—not a great distance.

'Aubrey Smithson,' he says, offering his hand.

His voice is familiar but I cannot place it.

'Jeremy Black,' I say.

He gives me a crooked grin in return as if he knows I am John Clifford or indeed John Grey or Mr Cardinal or Mr Plautus. I think he may know all of these gentlemen.

'I'm travelling to Brussels,' I say. 'I deal in wool. And you?'

'I'll be with you as far as Brussels,' he says.

'Have you travelled there before?'

'Brussels? As often as I have to.'

'And you deal in...?'

'Whatever seems best.'

I wait to see if he will tell me what seems best. He does not. Is he a member of the Sealed Knot—a back-up for Ripley? Or is he an officer of the State, searching for absconding felons? Or is he simply a merchant, as I purport to be?

'Do you know His Majesty's court?' I ask. I wish to see how he will respond to my reference to the Pretender—which may help me to place him and the side that he is on. But I am also more than a little curious to gain further information about the place—how I shall gain admittance and how I need to conduct myself. Probert was vague on the subject and Ripley suspicious of questions that he could see no reason for my asking. After all, he would be accompanying me to court.

'The English court in Brussels? Well enough,' he replies. He spits over the side of the boat. Perhaps this is in contempt for the titular King of the Scots or perhaps he just wants to spit. His allegiance remains unclear.

'If I needed to gain admission to that place—to speak to the King—what would I have to do?'

'You were given no instructions?'

'No.'

'I am surprised that nobody in Thaxted thought fit to brief you, if that's what you need to do. It is, of course, not difficult to gain entry. People come and go freely. But it is Hyde you will need to see first. He controls access to the King and much else.'

Smithson stares out to sea again. He is clearly not a great talker. But he shows no inclination to go elsewhere. We stand at the rail, shoulder to shoulder. For a while we both watch the waves. They are grey and larger than I would like them to be.

'You are travelling alone?' I ask.

'Yes. And you?'

'I seem to be,' I say.

'I thought I saw you arrive at the inn with another gentleman.'

'Did you?'

Smithson smiles. 'I do not see him on board anyway.'

'Perhaps he missed the boat,' I say.

Smithson smiles again. 'It is easily done. A moment's lack of attention… We shall speak again, Mr Black. We have a long journey together and it may be that I can be of service to you.'

I watch him stroll to the other end of the boat—still not a great distance. He now stands with his back to me, looking out at the same sea. He adjusts his sword belt slightly. I am no longer being watched by him, but then, there is nowhere that I can go.

We arrive off Ostend as their clocks are striking ten in the still-distant town. The bells ring the hour across the oily swell that separates us from the mole. The captain orders that the sails should be lowered and informs us that the wind is blowing offshore and that we cannot get into the harbour, not for all his skill and experience (which is great) but that he will signal for the shore-boat to take us to the beach. His manner is both ingratiating and contemptuous. He knows that I cannot tell whether a ship can be sailed into harbour, and I suspect that transferring us to a small boat will be of financial advantage both to him and to the owner of the small boat. I do not think that, in these seas, it will be of benefit to me or to the other passengers, unless it is our desire to get cold and wet and have our baggage spoiled. I think that this aspect of the situation pleases him too, because his pleasures are small and quite low.

We agree to this blatant imposition and climb with some difficulty down a rope ladder and into a bobbing boat below. The boat's owner greets us with a smile that is pure greed, hauling one of us after another into his craft with a tar-caked hand. The first boat will apparently not take all of us. Presumably splitting us into two groups will make it easier to charge the passengers of one boat more than the other, depending on the good captain's assessment of our purses and our stupidity. We set off, riding the swell with an ill grace. Though we had all assumed that we could not be seasick again, some of us are. But we are assured by the boatman that there is no other way and no better shore-boat in Ostend.

We are surprised, therefore, as we disembark and struggle up the slippery stone steps, to see our ship raising its anchor and proceeding towards the quay. It slowly rounds the mole, now towed by two of the ship's rowing boats, and is eventually tied up in the very place that the captain assured us it could not go. The few remaining passengers disembark via the gangplank. They are too far away for me to see if they are smiling, but I suspect they may be. I watch carefully in case one is dressed in red velvet and lace cuffs, but I am relieved to see that they all wear dress of sombre hue and have nothing of the Cavalier about their person. Ripley has not evaded Thurloe's men and slipped aboard.

There is a delay before the coaches set out for Brussels. I can see no reason why they should not depart at once, but we are told it is simply impossible. It is quite probably forbidden by some ordinance or other from the Spanish authorities. We therefore retire to the nearest inn, where the food is expensive, the wine sour and the landlord is, it seems, a good friend of the owner of the carriages. As soon as we have paid our bills, we find that the carriages are anxious to depart. They are crowded.

'I thought there were three,' I say.

The coachman shrugs. 'An English milord. He took the first coach.'

'I was told none were ready.'

He shrugs again. The milord will have paid well, no doubt, and the rest of us are paying no less for a sixth of a carriage than we would for a quarter. So nobody is worse off than they might have been. Or nobody who matters.

There is some pushing and shoving as we board the coaches. There should be just enough seats, but some are better than others, it would seem, and one coach appears a little more comfortable than the other. I find myself in one of the less favoured seats in the middle of the less popular carriage. Mr Smithson, I notice, has elbowed his way into my coach and into one of the corner seats. We are to travel together. He winks at me in some sort of complicity that I do not yet understand.

It's hotter here than in London. A summer sun beats down. Pale dust is whipped up by the giant wheels as we bowl along. Some of the dust drifts in through the windows. Those who elbowed their way to window seats are beginning to regret it. A gentleman, travelling with his wife, suggests that we close the blinds. We do so. We stifle in the heat. His wife proposes that we open the blinds. We do so. We are blinded by the dust.

Conversation is becoming difficult. I am thrown first against my right-hand neighbour, then against my left-hand neighbour, then almost into the lap of the lady opposite, who is holding a lace handkerchief to nose and mouth and does not notice me until my knee strikes hers with some force. I am reprimanded by her husband, but I think that the lady has scarce noticed. She will vomit again very soon, but hopefully over somebody else. Mr Smithson appears to be dozing in his seat, but I think I see him watching me through almost closed eyelids, in which case he will have seen me pitched on top of my right-hand neighbour. I extricate myself with some difficulty and many apologies. A change of direction throws me back into my seat. The husband of the lady is now banging on the roof of the coach to get it to stop; the lady needs to descend. But the coach does not stop.

Then the road gets bad.

Eventually we stop at a small town halfway between Ostend and Brussels. At first we are too numb even to notice. Only slowly does the absence of further dust or new injuries alert us to the fact that we are no longer in motion. We need fresh horses, and that will take time, so we are allowed to disembark and buy more bad wine, rye bread and rubbery cheese from another good friend of the coachman. The lady declines everything except a few sips of water.

I get out and experimentally stretch each of my limbs in turn, wondering how long this respite can be extended. Though I wish us in Brussels, I do not by any means wish us back in the coach. I decide that the coach will (surely?) not leave without me and that I can perhaps slip away and enjoy this relative peace for a little longer. With only a quick backward glance at the coachman, who appears to be receiving a small gift from the innkeeper, I walk quickly and purposefully down one of the side streets.

Under different circumstances, I might have said that this town offered little by way of entertainment. It is neither large nor well planned. There are few buildings of note. But I stroll through the narrow lanes, viewing with curiosity the strange and much decayed plasterwork on the houses. Women sit in their doorways, making lace on small frames. They do not glance in my direction as I pass. I do not look like a customer.

I am not sure at what point I become aware that I am being followed by Smithson. He seems disinclined to run after me but his pace is as rapid as mine and increases when mine does. When I slow, he does too. Eventually, reaching a small square, I turn and face him.

He gives me an encouraging smile. 'Mr Grey, I think?' he says.

'I'm called Black,' I reply.

'You are most certainly called Black and many other things, but I think that it is sufficiently private here for me to address you by your real name, though perhaps not private enough to hold the conversation that we need to have,' he says. 'We are not at present overheard, but others may choose to walk this way—and not by chance. Perhaps if you would care to accompany me we may find somewhere more convenient?'

The invitation sounds honest enough, but so did Ripley's letter inviting me to Gray's Inn. And I think back to Brodrick's invitation to walk with him and his friends for a while and converse. That did not work out well either. This proposed conversation with the gentleman who knows my real name may prove to be harmless, but recent experience suggests that it will not be. I have escaped Ripley, who perhaps had some suspicions of me, in exchange for this swordsman, who knows full well that I have been lying.

'There is an alleyway yonder,' I say. 'Go there now. I shall follow in a few minutes.'

He nods a little too trustingly. As soon as his back is turned, I take off as quickly as I can in the other direction. I will later plead, if necessary, a genuine misunderstanding. But that will be in the company of the other passengers, in front of whom he may be reluctant to run me through with his rapier. For the moment, I would rather not be alone with him, unarmed and in a dark alley in a strange country.

As I slip into a narrow lane, I hear a shout behind me. He has seen me, then. But I have a lead of a hundred yards at least, and the path is obligingly twisting and deceitful. The footsteps behind me falter at a crossroads and then fade away. Of the three choices he had, he has made a wrong one. I lean against a wall and regain my breath, then set off on what seems to be the right bearing. My plan is to circle round and back to the safety of the inn, but my sense of direction now fails me utterly. When I do finally reach an inn it is a different one. This one is smaller and more decrepit and has only a single carriage drawn up under its gently swinging sign. The carriage is familiar. It looks indeed like the missing carriage from Ostend—the one commandeered by the English milord.

A man is leaving the inn in a leisurely manner. He is dressed in dark stuff and a large hat, pulled low over his eyes. He approaches the carriage as if he owns it rather than merely leases it by the hour—indeed, as if he owns a number of carriages, of which this is not the grandest. The coachman runs round and opens the door in as obsequious a manner as you could wish. But his passenger stops and turns, as if suddenly aware of my presence. He raises the brim of his hat. And Ripley smiles and winks at me.

I have already cut and run once this afternoon. And in any case, he knows I am bound for Brussels. Running may help me in the short term, but in the longer term must confirm whatever suspicions have been growing in his mind. I remove my hat with a flourish and bow very low.

'Your servant, Sir Michael,' I say.

'Good afternoon, Mr Clifford,' he replies.

'I thought I had lost you at Dover,' I say.

'To your great distress, no doubt,' says Ripley.

'Your departure was very sudden.'

'I was concerned at the behaviour of the officer who came in search of us,' he says. 'Though he called out your name and yours alone, I noticed that he glanced several times in my direction and once indicated me to his sergeant when he thought I was looking the other way. For the avoidance of doubt, Mr Clifford, I am never looking the other way. I thought, by the bye, that you answered his questions well.'

'Thank you,' I say.

'A nice touch of insolence. I could not have done better myself. But, to continue my story, I felt it was odd that my name was not mentioned at all. It occurred to me—though I would never have previously suspected it of an officer of the State—that they might be playing some kind of low trick. I therefore slipped away and left the inn by the back door. I ascertained that the soldiers, on leaving the inn, had not gone as far as they might have done. Indeed, they were waiting on the path to the ship, poorly concealed behind some bales of wool. I therefore hung back from the main party as you went towards the boat. I might have delayed and caught the next boat across, but a gentleman of about my size and height decided to visit the privy before he boarded. Once I had him stripped of his doublet and breeches, gagged and trussed, I discovered from his passport that he was called Obadiah Shufflebottom. Ever since I was a small boy, it has been my ambition to be called Obadiah Shufflebottom, so I took the opportunity to impersonate him.' Ripley pauses, perhaps wondering if he has stretched my credulity a little too far. If he is willing to believe that I am pleased to see him, however, I am quite happy to accept his regret that he was not baptised Obadiah. I therefore say nothing and allow Ripley to continue the tale.

'Since the soldiers were searching for a Cavalier in a red silk suit, they paid Mr Shufflebottom scant attention as he hurried to the boat, his hat pulled down over his eyes. I apologised to the captain for my late arrival and spent the night sleeping out of the way of the other passengers, on a badly stowed heap of rope. The tar may have spoiled Mr Shufflebottom's breeches a little, but I have no plans to return them to him. I think that I overheard you vomiting, so I did not disturb you. I trust you passed an otherwise pleasant night on board?'

'Indifferently bad,' I say. 'I did not see you leave the ship. You were not on the small boat with us.'

'No, I had no wish to get cold and wet. While the first group was joining the rowing boat, I thought to engage the captain in conversation. I told him how the ship might be brought in.'

'You knew how? He said it was impossible.'

'I told him that I had served with Prince Rupert and that I had commanded my own ship at the age of sixteen and sailed her to the West Indies and safe home to France. I assured him that manoeuvring in these calm coastal waters was easy enough and that I could issue the necessary commands to his crew if he wished.'

'And he accepted?'

'No, surprisingly he declined. I rather think that he knew all along how it might be done, but was too modest to say so. Or perhaps he thought you would enjoy the ride in a small, leaking boat on a choppy sea.'

'He was wrong.'

'Then he clearly didn't realise his mistake until it was too late to offer you a more comfortable arrival in Ostend. You see how badly you do when we are separated. I think I will take greater care to ensure that it does not happen again. I shall watch you in future as a mother hawk watches her chicks.'

'Thank you,' I say. 'But as you can see, I have in fact got this far without your help.'

'But in less comfort.'

'True.'

'Well, we are both here now, by our various routes, and no harm has been done. I do think your carriage is slightly more crowded than mine. Why don't you join me for the rest of our journey to Brussels?'

So, Ripley is not as easy to shake off as Probert had thought. I hope that Thurloe has another plan up his sleeve, though I fear he may not. I am at least safe until we reach Brussels. I have heard it is a large city and I believe my father lives there with his Flemish whore. I think I can give Ripley the slip long enough to deliver my letter and find sanctuary at my father's residence. Then I shall hire a horse and ride as fast as I can for the coast. All is not yet lost.

'Did you really serve under Rupert?' I ask. 'Or was that Mr Shufflebottom?'

'Rupert would employ no officer called Obadiah Shufflebottom,' says Ripley. 'A baronet, on the other hand, would always be welcome in his service.'

'So that was not invented?'

'I have no objection in principle to telling the truth,' he replies.

His face gives nothing away. I think Ripley has indeed been on a boat before but whether that was with Rupert or somebody else is unclear. What I am sure of is that he would have taken the helm of our ship without the slightest doubt in his mind, sailing us into port or dashing us to pieces against the mole with equal confidence.

'You are looking over your shoulder,' says Ripley.

'There was a man in the carriage...' I begin.

'With a pointed beard?' asks Ripley.

'Exactly. Do you know him?'

'After a fashion. I saw him on board the ship. I took care that he should not see me. You would do well to avoid him.'

'Who does he work for? Thurloe?'

'I don't know, but I am certain that he is no friend of mine. Nor do I think he is any friend of yours. I imagine that his plan may be to ensure that an absconding felon, such as yourself, does not reach Brussels alive. Did he invite you to converse with him in a dark alleyway?'

'Yes,' I say.

'Then we should leave as soon as we can. You may choose to return and face your pursuer if you wish. I would merely ask you not to mention my name in your dying breath. It might be inconvenient if he knew I had also reached these shores. But I should, as I say, be honoured to offer you a seat in my coach, which would not involve your meeting the bearded gentleman again. Really, I think that would be best.'

If Smithson works for Thurloe then it might in fact be best if I travelled with him. On the other hand, if I opt to continue the journey with an officer of the State in preference to himself, Ripley may find that strange. Anyway, Smithson may work for somebody else entirely. At least with Ripley I know which lies I must tell in order to stay alive.

'It must be expensive to hire a carriage all to yourself,' I say.

'Mr Shufflebottom's purse proved to be full,' says Ripley.

'And the King will recompense him once he is restored. If we can find him.'

Ripley has arranged for my bag to be quietly collected from my own carriage and transferred to his own. The roads over which we now travel are no better than before and the dust is much the same colour—these things are beyond Ripley's control—but I have more space to be thrown around in and we bump over the ruts and crash through potholes at a surprising speed. We have just sent a harmless flock of geese flying and have been cursed by bystanders in Flemish and French.

'Did you promise the driver more money to get us there quickly?' I ask.

'Of course,' says Ripley. 'I fear that, in his greed, he may damage his conveyance beyond repair. But I think it will get us to Brussels before nightfall. Or very close to Brussels anyway.'

'I'm pleased to hear it,' I say.

'I am sure you are. But why have you come at all?' he asks.

'What do you mean?'

'You chose to come with me to Brussels.'

'I had no choice. You killed my gaoler. Do you not remember?'

'Of course I remember. But the world is full of places to hide; it did not have to be Brussels.'

'I need to report to Sir Edward.'

'I could have taken your message. Whatever it was. There must be little enough to report.'

Our eyes meet and he holds my gaze for longer than is comfortable. Is it my imagination, or can he see the slight bulge in my doublet where Willys's letter resides? Does he know I bear this package? Does he know Willys did not trust him with it?

'I've told you what Brodrick thinks of you?' he says.

'A scurvy piece of shit?'

'Yes, a scurvy piece of shit. But he also thinks you work for Thurloe.'

'Why?'

'Brodrick has a nose for double agents. In his opinion, you move a little too easily amongst the officers of the Republic and have told us very little that is of value. He believes that you were in the carriage with Cromwell on your way to Hampton Court and that you not only failed to kill him but did not even think to mention it to us. He opines that you are coming to Brussels because Thurloe has sent you.'

'And what do you think?'

'I think it odd that you were allowed to stroll onto the boat at Dover, while I was required to bind and gag Mr Shufflebottom.'

'You believe that is a cause for concern?'

'Wouldn't you?'

'Not at all. The officer searching for me would have had only the slightest idea what I looked like. You, I suspect, are better known. And of greater value. There is every reason why they should have overlooked me while continuing to watch you. But, if you are so suspicious, why didn't you kill me and dump my body in the harbour at Ostend?'

'Because my own personal preferences are not to be considered. Willys has ordered that I should see you safely to the King's court. I don't understand why, but Willys is your friend. Your very good friend. He says that you were imprisoned by Thurloe. He places a great weight on this, having been imprisoned by Thurloe himself and for much longer. It is his touchstone of credibility.'

Again, Ripley's gaze is better informed than I would like it to be.

'He is right. Thurloe would scarcely imprison one of his own agents,' I say.

'But you *were* one of Thurloe's agents once,' he says.

'Who told you that?'

'Willys,' he says. 'Brodrick asked him how you could gain access to Cromwell so easily if you weren't a double agent. Willys said you'd worked for Thurloe before but had deserted him. Is that true?'

'Yes,' I say. 'I worked for Sam Morland.'

'Thurloe's right-hand man?'

'Yes,' I say.

'And then you left?'

'Yes,' I say.

'Why?'

'I changed my mind.'

'And now you work for Sir Edward Hyde?'

'Yes.'

'Changes of allegiance are not uncommon, as you know. But more often we lose our agents to Thurloe rather than the other way round.'

'My father fought for the King.'

He looks at me. The statement is equally true of Surgeon Matthew Grey and Sir Felix Clifford. I do not think he will detect a lie there.

'That usually counts for little. Only a fool repeats all of his father's mistakes. I never served in Rupert's cavalry, for example. Some might say you have chosen a very bad time to change sides. The King has no ready money, no credit and a Spanish ally who is less bountiful than we had hoped. When the Duke of Buckingham quit His Majesty's camp, it should have been a sign to all of us that the game was up.'

'And you?' I say.

'My father fought for the last King too,' he says. 'As you know. I fought for this one at Worcester and saw him onto the boat at Shoreham. That was an interesting night—riding through the dark, dodging the Roundheads, making the King see sense, making him understand that he had to flee—all acts fraught with difficulty.'

'You fought at Worcester?' I ask. I think Thurloe told me that, but I had forgotten. In that case he fought with Marius Clifford. Does he know therefore that Marius had no brother—that there is no John Clifford and never was? Probably not. He would scarcely know every officer in the Royalist ranks.

'I was at the King's side throughout the battle,' Ripley replies. 'That was my choice.'

I nod. That would be Ripley's place, no doubt about that. But all the time I am thinking: Ripley's right. Why have I come? I know, as Ripley doesn't, that the gaoler is not dead and that I am in no danger of being hanged for murder. In those few minutes, when I had to make a decision in the fading light of my London chamber, Probert's assertion that there was a task that only I could perform made sense. But here under a warm Flemish sun, I am beginning to have doubts. Surely another messenger could have been found? Even if Hyde is expecting somebody of my age and height, Thurloe could have produced a suitable person to go to Brussels and say he was John Clifford—or merely that he had been sent in his place. Am I not simply travelling into danger for no clear purpose? Does Thurloe have a plan about which I as yet know nothing? If so, is it better than his plan to stop Ripley at Dover?

The answer to Aminta's question all those months ago, that will Thurloe have lost nothing if I am discovered, still rings in my ears. And yet, I find I do want to go to Brussels more than anywhere else in the world.

'And I chose to come to Brussels,' I say to Ripley. 'That is all you need to know.'

Ripley touches his hat. 'I'll be the judge of what I need to know, Mr Clifford,' he says.

At last we pass through one of the great gates in the walls of the city. We have arrived.

The carriage sets us down in the main square. There is a brief altercation between the driver and Ripley as to what the agreed price was. Ripley, it seems, is being more careful with Mr Shufflebottom's money than he implied. My French is just good enough for me to understand that Ripley is explaining very patiently that he had offered the driver ten times the legal fare, not ten times the fare that I and the other English passengers were being charged. The difference between the two sums is quite large. The driver argues forcefully, but Ripley merely smiles politely and keeps his purse in his pocket. Eventually a few coins change hands and the horses are whipped harder than necessary as the carriage quits the square.

Brussels is not, I think, as great or fine a place as London, though the main square is large and possesses some pretty buildings in what I take to be the Flemish style—red-brick, many storeys high, with stepped gables and proud statues of saints and gods and goddesses adorning their facades. But behind this grandeur there are narrow lanes and dark alleys; and the shouting and the grinding of carriage wheels on the cobbles seem to be the same everywhere.

Ripley has taken himself off, I know not where, and directed me to an inn in the back streets, where I have been served horse stew and black bread. I have arranged to meet him at nine tomorrow, when we shall both wait on Sir Edward Hyde. But I have no intention of allowing Hyde and Ripley to compare notes on my character and origins. I shall therefore seek out Sir Edward tonight. By nine tomorrow I shall be gone from this city—but I must pay one visit to somebody else before I leave.

For, while I do not fully understand Thurloe's reason for sending me here, I do begin to comprehend my own reason for coming. Somewhere in this city is my father, who may or may not be delighted to see me. Before I leave Flanders, I shall most certainly go and seek him out. My mother may have been happy with the idea that he was dead, but I never was.

CHAPTER

22

The Tyrant Charles Stuart, Titular King of the Scots

Hyde is a soft, fat little man, with arms that seem rather too short. He holds them now in front of his plump belly. He must be fifty years old at least, and aware that time is running out for him and for his master. Five more years here and the younger Cavaliers will be baying for him to be replaced by one of their number; ten more years here and he'll be dead. I think Ripley is right: Hyde is probably wondering whether he was really wise to go into exile when he might just as easily have taken a well-paid post under Cromwell. Of course, the Chancellor of an exiled King is still important—just not quite as important as he thinks he deserves. If you are less important than he is, he lets you know pretty quickly. He's already silently informed me of my status here. It isn't high.

He looks me up and down—mainly up, since he is a good two or three inches shorter than I.

'My name is Black,' I begin. 'I bear a message from one at Gray's Inn…'

Hyde smirks and nods. 'Thank you, Mr Clifford.' His voice, now that I finally hear it, is quite high. That final word almost disappeared into a squeak. And there was just a hint of impatience in it. 'We know who you are,' he continues. 'Sir Richard wrote to us some time ago to say that he would be entrusting you with a message that he would not send with anyone else. He said that you might introduce yourself to us as Clifford or Cardinal or some other name—but he gave us a good description of you.'

I wonder if the description was flattering. If it was, Hyde would certainly not tell me so.

'I am happy to go under whichever name you prefer,' I say.

'We'll use your real one, Mr Clifford, unless you've any objection?'

Clifford is perfectly acceptable. It is Grey that might prove awkward.

'Of course,' I say.

'You have not previously been noted as a friend of His Majesty's. It is not at all clear to us why Sir Richard trusts you in this way.'

'Many of His Majesty's friends have had to conceal their true loyalties,' I say.

Hyde considers the truth of this and then holds out a podgy hand for the message. I take the sealed letter from my pocket. Hyde opens it, wheezing slightly. It is a blank sheet of paper but inside there is a second sheet, also sealed and addressed to His Majesty King Charles, to be opened by him alone.

'What am I to do with this?' Hyde asks. 'Does that upstart Willys not trust me to read the King's correspondence?'

'I don't know,' I say. 'I was simply given the letter to bring over. Sir Richard must intend it for the King's eyes only.'

'I can see that, you fool. Who in God's name does Willys imagine he is?' Hyde is not happy. He may be about to stamp his little foot.

'I think I made him head of the Sealed Knot,' says a tall, dark man, who has silently entered the room without our noticing. 'On your advice, of course, Sir Edward. As for reading post addressed to me, I concur that that is your job. Since I am here, however, you may as well give me the letter, then this young gentleman will have fulfilled his duties as Sir Richard required.' He rubs his eyes and yawns.

Hyde has already turned and bowed to the newcomer. I now do the same. So, this is what a tyrant looks like.

The tall man winces slightly as if the late-afternoon sun in this room is much too strong. He does not seem to have slept well of late. His long, black hair is disordered, as though he has just risen from his bed. He is dressed in a grubby white shirt and shabby blue breeches. The breeches are decorated with bunches of ribbon, though not as many bunches as might be expected; there seem to be gaps where ribbons have become unstitched and mislaid. His red heels are worn down. He has not shaved today. With a beard as dark as his, that is a mistake. But perhaps whoever he has been with recently is of a forgiving nature. Three spaniels follow in his wake. They appear very much at home.

'This person, Your Majesty...' Hyde begins.

Charles Stuart waves his hand, dismissing whatever it was Hyde was about to say. They have been in exile together for a long time. He has already heard most of the things Hyde says. He takes the letter and breaks the seal. He reads and then frowns. For a moment or two he stares at the paper in silence as if he doesn't quite understand.

'If it is in cipher,' says Hyde, 'I can easily get it—'

'It isn't,' says Charles Stuart. 'So you don't.' He scans it a third time, then passes the document to Hyde.

Hyde reads it. 'But of course,' he says.

'Do you know the contents of the letter you have carried here, Mr Clifford?' asks the man with the dark stubble.

'No, Your Majesty,' I say.

'Truly?'

'Truly, Your Majesty,' I say, with growing nervousness.

Hyde and Charles Stuart look at each other again.

'You are too young to have fought in the war,' says Charles Stuart. 'Did your father fight for my father or for Parliament?'

'For Your Majesty's father, Your Majesty,' I say.

'As I should hope. And where is he now?'

'He is here in the Spanish Netherlands.'

'A poor exile, like me?'

'Indeed, Your Majesty.'

'But you have been living in England?'

'Yes.'

'Then let us walk in the shade of the limes, for there are some questions that I wish to ask you. Fairfax! Ireton! Cromwell!' He calls his three dogs to him. They wag their tails. We set off.

I have not met a monarch before, any more than I have sailed across the Channel. He is in many ways reassuringly like other men. He is polite. He is courteous. As we walk, he asks me questions. He listens attentively to my answers. He asks if England is a happy place and I tell him it is not. He asks whether the common people yearn for his return and I say that they do. He asks whether Cromwell is hated and I say that he is.

'Thank you,' says the King. 'That was kind of you. I am grateful to you for telling me what you think I wish to hear. Now, let us start again and this time you may tell me the truth.'

We start again. I tell him the truth. The people get by under Cromwell just as they got by under his father. Haymaking under a Republic is much like haymaking under a King appointed by God. People love Cromwell's taxes as much as they loved royal taxes—no more, no less. Different people are rich, but much the same people are poor. The rain still waters the corn. The apples still grow in the orchard. Fields still need to be weeded and birds scared off the young crops. People still get married, have children, get ill, get better, get worse, die. He asks me other questions. I answer as well as I can. I find it best to keep my answers short. In reply, he addresses his remarks sometimes to me and sometimes to his dogs. He is a fair and reasonable man.

As I complete an answer that is perhaps slightly longer than was required, he nods and yawns. 'Thank you,' he says. 'You show greater honesty than most men here. It is helpful to know that. And now, you say that you really do not know the contents of the letter you have brought here?'

Though, I realise, efforts have been made to put me at my ease, I am immediately aware of the dangers hidden in that question.

'No,' I say. 'Not at all.'

It would seem that I am about to rely on my wits again if I wish to live, but Charles Stuart smiles and slaps me on the shoulder. 'Then I shall tell you what it says, Mr Clifford. Sir Richard Willys claims that he has an army of two thousand horse and five hundred foot that he can put in the field at any time. He is inviting me to go over to England now and lead them. Is it true? Does he have them? The Sealed Knot is in the habit of counting every man they have as ten. I do not doubt their loyalty, merely their ability to add up.'

I think of Ripley's five thousand horse and five thousand foot. I think of Willys's question to me: what numbers would I consider believable. The forces he claims to have are not unlike those we agreed.

'They have a certain plausibility, Your Majesty,' I say cautiously.

'Only four hundred men gathered for Penruddock's rising three years ago. He too thought he would have thousands. Those who weren't killed by Cromwell's troops were hanged or transported. If I had gone over then, I'd have joined them on the scaffold... Is Willys sure he has even his two thousand horse?'

'Why do you ask me?'

'Because you have an honest face. I am sorry for you, but there it is. You will always go through life with that handicap. My father trusted men if their religion and principles were in accordance with his beliefs. I scarcely need to tell you where that got him. I trust men if I see honesty in their faces. You can see where that has got *me*—but I think I shall have another throw of the dice or two before the end. And I do trust you. So—and think very carefully before you answer—*does Willys have two thousand horse?*'

I had imagined myself being asked all manner of questions here in Brussels to prove I was who I said I was, but I had not expected this. I have no idea how many troops Sir Richard really has. Was I chosen as messenger by Sir Richard because he thought I would confirm these figures and that my honest face would convince the King that his claims were true? If so, to what end? How will it help the Royalist cause to deceive their own man? Thurloe knows the contents of this letter. Charles Stuart, if he acts on Willys's assurances, will be captured as soon as he lands in England. This letter is sending this amiable person in faded blue breeches to his death.

My duty to the Republic is clear. I must tell the King that Willys has the troops. They are armed to the teeth. They are ready and willing to serve. Because that surely is what Thurloe would want me to do.

'I don't know,' I say.

The King considers things for a moment. 'This letter definitely comes from Willys?'

'Yes...' I say.

And then suddenly I see it all. This is not Willys's letter. It is all a trap set by Thurloe.

Probert brought me the letter. Thurloe knew that Willys intended to give me a message to carry over. Willys had told Hyde to expect me. So, Thurloe has forged a letter, nominally from Willys, and entrusted it to my hands and indeed to my honest face. Charles Stuart is thus to be lured across the Channel with the promise of a phantom army and then...then the Royalist cause will be struck a blow from which it could never recover.

Each step has been carefully prepared—my arrest and imprisonment, my 'escape' from England. But nobody has thought fit to tell me any of this. And if the plan fails, then, just as Aminta foresaw, Thurloe will be no worse off. But he has miscalculated badly. Nobody is going to believe this improbable offer and I genuinely fear for the safety of its bearer. Though I now understand the plan, I am not sure, on mature reflection, that I am indebted enough to Mr Secretary Thurloe to die for him in such a hopeless cause.

The King is looking at me curiously. There is something about my honest face that interests him. 'You are absolutely certain that the letter is from Sir Richard Willys?' he says again.

'No, Your Majesty,' I say. 'I rather think it is a trick.'

'It is a forgery?'

'I cannot rule that out.'

'Thank you, Mr Grey,' he says. 'That was my view too. There was something not quite believable about it. A rising of this sort is something to be planned, coordinated over many months, not simply sprung on us in a single letter. And in any case, we had been expecting this—we had been warned we would receive an offer that was not to be trusted. Had you lied to me, you would not have left Brussels alive. But since you have told the truth—since I see that you have been deceived as much as we have—I do not hold this against you. In fact, you may be of use to us. Precisely how you might help us is something we shall let you know shortly, but in the meantime I must discuss this with Sir Edward. Fairfax! Cromwell! Good dogs... And Ireton, would you please not do that to Fairfax? He doesn't like it.'

I have been given permission to return to my inn and am required to attend upon Hyde in the morning, when I shall be told how I may be useful. I have promised faithfully to be there without fail.

But I shall not be there at all. Though I no longer trust Thurloe, I trust Hyde only a little more. I do not know how I may be of use to the King, but I would rather not find out. I have been of use to both Thurloe and the Sealed Knot and have gained nothing by it. I think it is time to look after my own interests. That is why I am walking rapidly through the streets of Brussels with my leather satchel, having paid a somewhat surprised innkeeper for a night that I have not spent with him. I had taken the precaution of finding out in which part of the city my father lives—or rather in which part he was last known to live, for he clearly has had little contact with his fellow Royalists of late. Perhaps, like others, he is distancing himself from a lost cause in order to return to England, with or without his mistress. He will be surprised to see his only son on a warm summer evening. He may be pleased or he may not. He can, however, scarcely refuse to shelter me until morning.

I have to ask for directions several times in very imperfect French. Eventually, as the last of the daylight is fading, I am directed to a narrow, tumbledown house in a narrow, tumbledown street. My heart is beating hard as I hammer at the door. There are footsteps on bare floorboards and the door is opened by a woman of, as far as I can judge, about thirty or thirty-five. If this is the filthy Flemish whore of whom my mother speaks so affectionately, then she is older than I was led to believe.

'I am seeking Matthew Grey,' I say.

She looks at me blankly.

Je cherche Matthew Grey,' I say. *'Il est mon père.'*

She shakes her head.

Je suis le fils de Matthew Grey,' I say. *'Il est...dedans?'*

I wonder if I shall have to try Flemish, which I am ill-equipped to do.

'Mijn naam is John Grey...' I begin.

'My man is dead,' she says. 'Mathieu is dead.'

For a long time neither of us says anything. Then I say: 'When?'

'Five weeks? Six weeks? He is sick for a long time. No money. I ask Milord Hyde for money. He says he has none. I ask his friends for money. They say they have none. I ask that evil old woman who follows the Queen of Bohemia...'

'Lady Clifford?' I ask.

'Her. Milady Clifford. She sends me away. She will not see me. She too has no money. The Queen of Bohemia has no money, but then she is English. None of you English have any money. Ever. Do you have no money in England? Are you all paupers? I cannot pay for the doctor. I cannot pay for Mathieu to be buried. The city has buried him. He has no grave of his own, but he is buried with others who also could not afford to pay. It is done. That is all there is to it.'

For a long time I say nothing, because, as soon as I do say something, then everything she has said will be true. It is done.

That is all there is to it. I look beyond her into the shadows. There is nobody there.

'I am his son,' I repeat. 'John Grey.'

She puts her head on one side, considering this proposition. 'His son? You are not, I think, much like him.'

'But that is nevertheless who I am.'

'Lisette,' she says eventually, pointing to her ample chest. 'You have money?'

'A little.'

She pulls a face. 'A little is better than nothing at all, but you come too late with your gold. Where were you?'

'In gaol,' I say. 'For attending church.'

She nods. This is what she would have expected of England. 'What did he die of?' I ask.

'Am I a doctor? How should I know what he died of? The rich die of things. The poor just die.'

I too may just die unless I can escape the men who will soon be pursuing me. I edge closer to her and away from the street.

'I need somewhere to stay tonight,' I say. 'And, much though I hate to inconvenience you, it has to be here. Then tomorrow I would like to visit where my father is buried.'

'And then?'

'Then I must leave Brussels very quickly. There are men here who wish me dead—or rather who will wish me dead once they have discovered the full extent of my deception. Do you know where I can hire a horse to get me to Ostend?'

'I know where you can hire one. Also where you can steal one. It is up to you. Stealing is cheaper and the horse will be better.'

'I have money to hire one.'

'Then you have a choice. Many people do not. How little money do you have?' Lisette asks.

'I have enough,' I say cautiously, for I think she shows undue interest in my purse. 'I'll need most of it for the journey back to England but I'll give you what I can.'

'You look over your shoulder as if people are chasing you. Why? Have you been going to church again?'

'It would be best if we could discuss this inside.'

Lisette smiles. 'Then you had better come in,' she says.

She moves to one side and I take one more backward glance before entering. The street, I am pleased to see, is completely empty.

'They are English, the people who chase you? Or Spanish?' asks Lisette, closing the door.

'English,' I say, dropping my bag to the sawdust-covered floor. 'I'll explain later.'

'You do not need to explain why. Your father tells me. You English all hate each other. As long as it is not the Spanish who chase you. I will not hide you from them but I do not fear the English. And in a way you are my son. In a way, I am your mother. That is right, yes? You can stay here. You will be safe until morning. Then your mother will teach you to steal a horse. Be a good boy and give your mother money and she will go and buy food, and maybe some gin.'

The inside of the house, now I have a chance to look at my surroundings, is no better than the exterior. On the ground floor the small room contains a table and two broken chairs in front of a brick fireplace, within which is suspended an empty cooking pot. The light is dim, both because the day is drawing to an end and because the small windows are caked with grime, which Lisette has not thought to have removed. In the same way, it may be some days or weeks since the floor was last swept and the sawdust renewed. I do not see a broom. A single candle stands on the table ready for the night. A steep wooden staircase leads to another floor.

'Did my father live here with you for long?' I ask.

'All the time,' she says.

'Was he happy?' I ask.

She shakes her head impatiently. 'Soon the shops will close. We talk about happiness later.'

I take out my purse and count over to her some good English silver. She watches me carefully, willing one bright coin to follow another.

'You wait here,' says Lisette, tucking my money into her pocket. 'I come back with a chicken. Bread. Some beer. A little gin.'

I nod. I am not hungry, but a meal for her, and a glass or two of gin, in exchange for a night's concealment strikes me as a good bargain at the moment. Where can you be safer than with your late father's whore? She closes the door carefully after her but does not lock it. I suspect it has no lock. Locks cost money. There is, however, a large wooden bolt, which I push into place. Who knows when they will start looking for me and whether they will think to come here tonight?

So this is where my father spent his final days. Though my mother wished many misfortunes upon him, I doubt she ever thought of this. This is where you live when only the gutter is a degradation. I climb the stairs carefully and glance into the only other room. The dormer window gives slightly more light than in the chamber below. There is an old bed, unmade and strewn with various items of women's clothing. Under the bed are some unsaleable medical textbooks in English and a leather case containing the tools of my father's trade—knives, a saw, pincers, a spatula, a drill, some probes and a hammer—all a little rusty. There is also a sword in a leather scabbard, which I am surprised has not been turned into cash. I take the last of these items and examine it. It too has clearly not been used for a while, but it may be better than nothing if I am obliged to fight my way out of this city. I carry it downstairs and prop it against the table. Then I sit and wait.

I must have dozed because, without hearing footsteps, I am suddenly aware of a rattling of the door. Of course, I have bolted it and Lisette is locked out. I pick up my father's sword and walk softly over to the door.

'Lisette?' I say. 'Is that you?'

'Of course it is me, stupid boy. Why have you locked me out? Open the door!'

I slide back the bolt. It is indeed Lisette, but it is also other people.

'Is this the man you want?' she asks Ripley.

'That's him,' Ripley replies.

'Then give me what you said.'

Ripley takes out his purse and hands over two small gold coins. Lisette has done well out of my visit.

'I think you should give me that sword, Mr Grey,' he says. 'I have half a dozen men at the end of the street. Even if you were to kill me, and I doubt that you could, you would not reach the main road alive. Still, you were wise to attempt to escape. Your treachery has been revealed in full. If you would care to accompany me, we will explain things to you and you will have a chance to make your defence. Then we will take you out and shoot you.'

I could try to run Ripley through the guts. It would give me a certain amount of pleasure to do so. Ripley has clearly had a chance to talk to Hyde and, in comparing notes, they have discovered discrepancies in my story, as I feared they would. Thurloe's plan has failed utterly. Any small remaining debt I might have felt towards him for protecting me from Ripley has been cancelled out. He has not, after all, protected me from Ripley in any fashion.

But I am still thinking: I can talk my way out of this. My legal training may not have benefited me much so far, but perhaps it will save me now. And Hyde is a lawyer. He will find it difficult to authorise my death without some sort of due process. I sheath my father's sword, which has been mine for less than an hour, and pass it to Ripley. He bows as if I were surrendering a whole city to him.

A clink of coins behind me reminds me that Lisette is still with us. She is sitting at the table working out her profit for the evening. It is strange that, when my mother has in the past described her as a filthy, cheating Flemish slut, I had assumed that she was employing picturesque exaggeration. But I am beginning to learn that sometimes your mother can be far more right about things than you ever knew.

Mr John Grey

It is late. I do not know the exact hour. Nor do I know the name of the place to which I have been taken. I have been hustled through the back streets of Brussels, a boy with a torch lighting the path well enough for Ripley at the front of the party but leaving me stumbling in the shadows behind. The two men holding my arms seemed to be able to keep their feet well enough, however, and to see well enough to land the occasional blow to my ears or my back as incentives not to tarry. Finally I was thrust through a doorway and up a flight of stairs. Behind me I heard a lock—a better lock than Lisette's in every respect—being turned and the key removed.

Now I sit on a stool on one side of a table. On the other is Ripley and another man who has simply been introduced as O'Neill. I wonder if this is the Daniel O'Neill that Aminta mentioned when she visited me in the Tower. I have not had a chance to ask but, if so, he clearly managed to avoid arrest. O'Neill seems pleasant enough anyway—of middle stature with light brown hair, now leaning back in his chair, his legs splayed out in front of him. He smiles at me and then belches. I think Ripley may have dragged him away from a good supper with friends. Two candles provide a little light, but I cannot make out the expressions of my inquisitors. The candles remind me of Probert's story of Manning's death. Ripley may have something of the sort in mind for me.

'Much though I hate to admit that Brodrick was right,' says Ripley, 'you really are a scurvy piece of shit, aren't you?'

Sometimes, when your opponent has made a very good point, it is better to remain silent. This seems to be one of those occasions.

'You actually thought that you could betray us, Mr…what do you want us to call you? Cardinal? Clifford? Grey?'

'As you choose,' I say. 'I have also been Mr Plautus, if you prefer that.'

'I assume Grey is your real name?'

I wonder briefly whether to claim that I was lying to Lisette for some complicated reason that I cannot quite see at present—that I had good reason to pretend to be the son of her former lover, while still being in fact John Clifford. But I think that victory may be short-lived. I shall say farewell to that alias.

'I've never claimed otherwise,' I say. 'You simply assumed I was John Clifford.'

'That may be true. And we might be forgiven for thinking that, because we did not know the truth. *You,* conversely, were well aware you were not John Clifford, and the honest thing to have done would have been to tell us, would it not? The more important fact is that you have been spying on us for Thurloe. You sought us out, offered to work for us, then went to Thurloe and sold him the information you had stolen from us.'

This is untrue, or at any rate less true than my being a scurvy piece of shit. I briefly contemplate an apology, but I'm not sure it would help. Nor am I sure that Ripley is owed one.

'You invited me to Gray's Inn,' I say. 'I did not seek you out in any way. You sent a letter to my lodgings. You promised I should come to no harm. Or you promised somebody. Who were you expecting? Sir Felix Clifford?'

'A good question, Mr Grey. To be honest with you, we were not sure who to expect. Our informant in Brussels was vague; he had overheard Hyde briefing somebody but had not seen the person concerned. And the other voice he could hear was… indistinct. Sir Felix's name was certainly mentioned several times. Our man also heard that, once in London, this person could be contacted at Mistress Reynolds's house. When you arrived— when you confirmed that you came from Clavershall West and that your family once owned the manor there, as the Cliffords did—we assumed, just as you say, that you must be Sir Felix's son. That was who you appeared to be. Our informant was clearly right in some respects but we thought he had made one stupid error. We duped ourselves, Mr Grey. A simple question to you: "in summary, are you therefore John Clifford?"—that would have saved everyone a great deal of trouble. But we live in a world in which a nod and a wink are considered better than plain words. Somehow we could not quite bring ourselves to do it. *Mea culpa*, Mr Grey. But *you* knew we had made a mistake.'

'So I did. But had I told you that I was not the man you thought I was, you would have killed me,' I say. 'Brodrick said so.'

'That may in turn be true. But—and I hate to return to this point—you did not have to go to Thurloe and inform on us.'

'Who says I informed Thurloe of anything?' I ask.

'That doesn't matter for the moment. Just believe me when I say that I know that's what you did and that there is very little point in your denying it.'

I look at him. He can't possibly be certain of that. He must be guessing. Or has Morland discovered me and informed Ripley?

'It's true,' says O'Neill, speaking for the first time. 'We know you've been working for Thurloe. Now, you may try arguing that you haven't, but we'll know it's a lie, and may not take kindly to it. On the other hand, if you tell us the truth…' He smiles as if he were my friend, or would be if I told the truth. Telling Charles Stuart the truth proved a wise move. Perhaps my luck will hold a second time.

'Going to Thurloe seemed the only way I could save myself,' I say. 'I've told you I worked for Morland before. I knew Thurloe. Brodrick was threatening to kill me. Nobody else could have offered me protection. In return, Thurloe made me report back to him. I have scarcely been working for him willingly. If the letter I brought for the King was from Thurloe, I did not know it.'

'And what did you report back to Thurloe?'

'Very little. Thurloe knows Willys is head of the Sealed Knot. I think he's known for some time.'

'That is helpful but unsurprising,' says Ripley. 'Thurloe's spies are everywhere. It would, by the way, have been polite to tell me that you were carrying with you a letter for His Majesty that you believed came from Willys. You had ample opportunity on the road to Dover and at the inns and barns in which we took shelter. It was Underhill who gave the game away, if you are interested. Lisette merely told us where you were to be found.'

So maybe Ripley does know everything. 'Underhill? Is he here in Brussels?' I say.

'He arrived recently. You have made life very difficult for him apparently. He seemed to think he had some sort of pact with you by which you would not inform on him to the State if he did not inform on you to us.'

'I made no such bargain.'

'He thinks you did. Therein lies your difficulty. He was somewhat put out to find himself arrested. He says he was not well treated by the Republic. He blames you. Once he was released, he was obliged to go to ground—not an unnatural activity for one like Underhill—until it seemed safe to make a run for the coast. He arrived here a day or two before we did, offering his services to Hyde, just as he had offered them to me earlier. He was waiting at my inn when I got there, eager to tell me that you were John Grey, an agent of Thurloe's. He was surprised to hear that you were actually in this city, since he thought such a journey would be fatal for you. Had it not been for him, when Lisette arrived to tell us that she was sheltering one John Grey and would deliver him to us for a small fee, we would have been wracking our brains where we had heard that name before. It might have been a while before we remembered your "alias" at Hampton Court. Your value would have been a shilling or two at the most. But happily, thanks to Mr Underhill, your price had by then risen to two gold sovereigns. You will be pleased to hear that Lisette would not take less for betraying you. That is loyalty of a sort. So, here we all are, Mr Grey.'

'And Underhill was working for you? He was your assassin— the person you spoke of who was willing to kill Cromwell?'

Ripley laughs. 'I am embarrassed to admit that was the case. The quality of assassins is not high. Assassins are usually men whose zeal is greater than their sanity. Underhill was the best available at the time. But we think he was working for Lambert as well as us. Why get paid once for a job when you can get paid twice? We won't be employing him again. And how many people were paying you, Mr Grey?'

'I received nothing from you,' I say.

'That is very true. And from Thurloe?'

'He arranged for me to receive my salary as a clerk to Mr Milton.'

'I hope he paid you well.'

'Not well enough since, as you know, I was fooled into carrying a forged message, to incriminate Sir Richard Willys.'

'Hyde says you think it was written by Thurloe?'

'I cannot be certain but I believe so.'

'Why do you think that?' asks Ripley. He leans forward on the desk.

'Because,' I say, 'it was brought to me by one of his agents.'

'That may be so, but how can you be certain that Willys himself has no hand in it?'

'Why should he?' I ask.

'Why indeed?' says Ripley. 'The King has honoured him and placed his trust in him. Why should he betray that? But equally you have no proof that he is not complicit?'

'No,' I say.

Ripley nods at O'Neill, who shrugs.

'So, what happens now?' I ask.

'What would you like to happen, Mr Grey?' asks O'Neill. He seems a very reasonable man. Unlike Ripley.

I swallow hard and address O'Neill. 'As you can see, this whole business is a mistake. I never bore you any ill-will. I have been duped by Thurloe. I am no danger to you. I should like to return to London and resume my studies. I shall need to pay my landlady for the room I have not been able to occupy since December, but if I can raise the necessary cash, then there is no impediment. Unless you are planning to shoot me, of course.'

'Shoot you? No, I don't think so,' says O'Neill.

'I had assumed that our conversation was a precursor to just that. That's what Sir Michael told me earlier.'

'That would be ungrateful after what you have told us.'

'So, I can leave here and steal a horse and return to London?'

O'Neill shrugs. 'Naturally. Any horse you choose. We can even show you where the best ones are to be found.'

'And there is nothing at all you want from me in return?' I ask.

'I didn't say that,' says O'Neill.

'By which you mean...'

'I think you may be able to help us. You must admit that you owe us something. I am sure that you would wish to repay that debt. I mean, for not shooting you as you deserve.'

My heart, which had briefly risen from the depths of despair, falls again. I can help them. Every time this phrase has been uttered, I have sunk deeper and deeper into the mire. I am not sure who I have to betray this time—indeed, I am not sure there is anyone left that I have not betrayed. But perhaps there is. In a moment I'll find out.

'How?' I ask.

O'Neill is silent for a long while as if trying to formulate his proposition. Eventually he leans forward, frowning.

'You will be aware from Thurloe that the Sealed Knot has long since been compromised—that he has agents within their ranks?' O'Neill raises an eyebrow.

'Yes,' I say.

'We have learned to live with that—to assume that our secrets would become common knowledge in a short time. But recently even discussions at the highest level seem to have become known to Thurloe.'

'Which is why Hyde doesn't trust the organisation any more?' I ask.

'Just so,' says Ripley. 'The lack of trust paralyses us. We no longer dare to undertake the smallest action. So, we have had to ask ourselves, who is leaking information to Thurloe?'

'I cannot help you,' I say. 'I know only you and Brodrick and Willys. You are not saying that it is one of those three?'

'It is Willys,' says O'Neill, 'though the King is reluctant to credit it.'

'The head of the Sealed Knot?'

'I did not believe it,' says Ripley. 'Brodrick still does not believe it. But an informant of ours in Thurloe's office has sent us proof—letters to Thurloe that could come only from Willys. That is why we think the letter you have brought may be genuinely from him. We think Willys is actively plotting with Thurloe against the King.'

'And your informant is Sam Morland?' I say.

Ripley smiles. 'Our informant is in a position to know. Still, he may be deceiving us. After all—a source high up in Thurloe's establishment—is that not a little too good to be true? So, Mr Grey, we need to know: is Willys Thurloe's man? You've spoken to Thurloe, as I have not. He must have let something slip.'

'Thurloe knows that Willys is head of the Sealed Knot, but at first pretended not to. When I asked him why he did not have him arrested, he said that it was inopportune.'

'*Inopportune?*' repeats O'Neill.

'And though he asked me to gather what information I could on the Sealed Knot, he told me that I should not under any circumstance visit or question Sir Richard.'

We all three look at each other.

'I think,' says Ripley, 'that our worst fears are confirmed. Willys has been turned and Thurloe has been protecting his creature in every possible way. Let us recall, moreover, that it was Willys who assured us that you were *not* working for Thurloe. He said that he had written to Brussels and was able to confirm that you were indeed John Clifford. I begin to see the hand of Thurloe everywhere I look.'

'It had seemed odd to me that Willys was so much on my side,' I say. 'But if he is working for Thurloe...'

'As indeed he is,' says O'Neill, 'then it is not so surprising. There is, you might say, a pattern to it all, but not a pretty one. I need you to come and tell Hyde exactly what you have told me. He does not trust the Sealed Knot, but until now he, like the King, has refused to believe that Willys could be false; he thinks that the letters sent to us by our contact are forgeries. Once he hears from you, I think he will change his mind.'

There is, of course, one important question to be answered before I agree to cooperate with anybody about anything.

'So, if I do all that, then I may go home?'

'Probably,' says O'Neill. 'You have deceived us, but if you have helped us root out such a traitor in our midst... Let us go and visit Sir Edward Hyde. The court keeps late hours. I am sure he will still be awake.'

I look at Ripley. I am not sure that he wouldn't prefer to shoot me.

'You should be thankful that it's Mr O'Neill's decision,' he says. 'Didn't I tell you that you were a lucky person?'

O'Neill nods at the men who had previously kicked me upstairs.

'I do not need a guard,' I say. 'I have said I will come with you'.

'It is less safe out there than you think,' says Ripley. 'I agree we do not need to treat you as a prisoner, but our swords may prove useful on a dark night.'

'I think this city is safer than London,' I say.

There is a hurried discussion. Ripley and two others will go with me. O'Neill is to go on some other mission of his own. Three will be enough to see me through the dark streets of

Brussels. I'd prefer O'Neill guarding me, but I don't think Ripley will go back on his word.

We set off, the four of us, down the dark lane. Ripley holds a torch. His companion holds my arm, as if unsure whether I may still try to escape. The last man brings up behind, looking over his shoulder from time to time. His footsteps are steady, then he stops briefly before hurrying to catch us up again. Perhaps he saw something. Ripley's enquiry as to whether there is a problem is, however, met with a laconic 'No'.

We have gone only a short distance further when I feel the grip on my elbow tighten suddenly, then relax completely. I turn to my guard. There is, in the flickering red light of Ripley's torch, a look of surprise on the man's face and the point of a sword sticking out of the front of his doublet. That is red too. Then the point is withdrawn and the man falls to the ground. From the shadows behind him somebody says: 'Stand to one side, Mr Grey. I need to deal with the last of these Royalist dogs.'

I hear rather than see Ripley draw his sword. He is holding aloft the torch, which is guttering but still throws out a dim light. For a moment Ripley stands, torch in one hand, sword in the other, squinting into the darkness to one side of me. I feel a waft of air as somebody's sword strikes home. Ripley curses, the torch falls, rolls on the cobblestones and finally goes out. Then there is another swishing in the darkness and Ripley grunts and clutches at his face. The sharp note of bright metal striking stone rings out into the warm night air.

A hand grasps my arm again. 'This way, Mr Grey. The street is uneven and we now have no torch to light our way, not that it would be a good idea to draw attention to ourselves.'

I find myself hurried along the lane by somebody who knows Brussels better than I do. We turn a corner. Somewhere behind us I hear a clatter of steel, as if Ripley is recovering his weapon, but there is no sound of pursuit. I am pulled, pushed and prodded, mainly in silence, until we reach the doorway of an inn.

As the door is pushed open, the candlelight catches the face of the man I am with.

'Mr Smithson,' I say.

'Just so,' he says. 'Let us ascend to my chamber. I have already ordered food and you must be starving.'

CHAPTER

24

Mr Smithson

'So,' says Smithson, putting down a chicken bone, 'you made things quite difficult for me. I hoped you might remember me, even though when we first met I was disguised as a beggar on Lincoln's Inn Fields. The half-crown that you gave me was generous. But clearly you have forgotten that occasion. Quite right. When thou doest alms, let not thy left hand know what thy right doeth, as St Matthew instructs us. This time, I had been tasked by Mr Thurloe to wait for you at Dover and to accompany you on the packet to Ostend, in case we failed to stop Ripley in England. I was to guard you as far as Brussels, then ensure that you were able to make your getaway after your meeting with Hyde. I discovered that Ripley had been on the boat with us; but when I later tried to speak to you in private, you evaded me.'

'I ran into Ripley,' I say. 'He offered me a place in his carriage.'

'That was not wise. Our coach was delayed an hour while we waited for your return, or I might have intercepted you on your way to Charles Stuart's court. Fortunately I knew that your father lived in Brussels and, like you, was able to discover his address. I reached the house just as Ripley and his minions were escorting you away. I followed and discovered where they planned to keep you for the time being. I was aware that, if they did not kill you there and then, they would need to take you somewhere else sooner or later. So, I waited for you all to emerge. It was easy enough, in the dark, to cut the throat of one of your captors as he tried to guard the rear of your party. The second should have realised something was amiss when I caught you all up again, but he was sadly unaware of me until he saw the point of my sword sticking through his chest. I think I have wounded Ripley, though unfortunately not killed him. He may be contemplating revenge—against both of us. But with the whole of Brussels to scour, I think they will not find us here tonight. You delivered the message, I hope?'

'Yes,' I say. 'It would have been helpful if Thurloe had told me what was in it.'

'That was not necessary. Anyway, telling people things is not Mr Thurloe's way of doing business.'

'The King did not believe it,' I say, with a certain secret satisfaction.

Smithson nods as if this was not unexpected.

'Somebody in Thurloe's office had already warned them it was a trick,' I say.

'Who?'

'Morland,' I say.

'They told you that?'

'As good as.'

Smithson nods again and wipes his fingers carefully on a napkin. He is more fastidious in his eating than Probert.

'You show no surprise?' I say.

'It was certainly Morland. You warned Mr Thurloe some time ago that he might be a risk.'

'But he did not believe me.'

'No. Not at the time. But Mr Thurloe stores things like that away. Stores them away until he has some problem that might be explained by a fact such as that. When we realised that information was leaking from our office, we wondered if you had been right. Now you have provided us with the proof. Well done, Mr Grey. Well done, indeed. Your mission could not have been more successful.'

'You mean…'

'Of course, we never expected Charles Stuart to believe that there was such a plot. He is too cautious for that. The question was whether it would be leaked. Only Cromwell, Thurloe and Morland knew of it. If word has reached Brussels that it is a trick, then it can only be Morland.'

'And that is why I was sent?'

'That is why you were sent.'

'But the Knot now knows that Willys has gone over to Thurloe. The letter implicates him.'

'It could have been done without Willys's knowledge…but I see from your face that that is not what they believe. You have an honest face, Mr Grey—has anyone ever told you that? It is, however, of no account. The Knot already suspected Willys. I think there are things that they have not been telling him for a long time—secrets that were kept from him. He was less and less use to us. Indeed, he has told us nothing of note for some months. Mr Thurloe was happy to sacrifice him while he still had a value. And we have made a good exchange of pieces—for Willys we have gained Morland. Sam Morland's fate is sealed and the State is grateful to you for uncovering such a rogue. As for Willys, the Knot will ask themselves who they can trust if they cannot trust their leader. There may be some blood-letting within their ranks, I fear. They will be even less effective than before. You have done well—very well indeed. But I am sorry, Mr Grey—you are not eating. Can I pass you a chicken leg?'

I shake my head. 'Ripley had a man named O'Neill with him. Who is he?'

'Daniel O'Neill,' he says. 'Or Infallible Subtle, as Hyde calls him—though O'Neill just refers to Hyde as the Fat Fellow. O'Neill's one of the leading Royalist agents. Maybe their very best. We almost caught him when he was in England in January, but somebody tipped him off each time. If we could eliminate him now…' He looks at me thoughtfully.

'There is nothing further I can do for you,' I say.

'But if we got a message to him, saying that you wished to speak to him…'

'We would get Ripley and twenty armed men.'

'Two or three at the most.'

'But without the advantage of surprise and a dark night,' I say.

'True. You have been lucky so far.'

'That's what Ripley thinks too. All I wish to know is when we can return to London.'

'Soon,' he says.

'Tomorrow?'

'If you wish.'

'I should like to discover my father's grave first, if possible.'

'My condolences, Mr Grey, on the loss of a parent, but such a visit would be inadvisable. Ripley may suspect that you would do that. I have no wish to be ambushed by Ripley as I ambushed him.'

'So, we leave for the coast as soon as we can?'

'I think so.'

'There are no further conditions?'

Smithson stretches and yawns. 'None. You have faithfully carried out your mission. Once we have finished eating, we must get a few hours' sleep, then we shall leave at dawn. It is a good time to go—the Knot will still be carousing in the taverns, if they have the money to do so. We shall leave inconspicuously on foot. I have horses stabled just outside the city walls. We shall ride to Dunkirk, in case Ostend is watched, then take a boat to Dover.'

I am not sure that I have faithfully carried out anything. Indeed, I feel no loyalty to Thurloe at all. I would willingly tell Ripley all I know about Thurloe or Thurloe all I know about Ripley if either would allow me to return to London and not trouble me again. I have thrown in my lot with Smithson because Smithson has (I hope) faster horses than Ripley and O'Neill. As for Morland and Willys, they both deserve whatever fate has in store for them.

'I'll take the bed closest to the door,' says Smithson. 'I'm sure we are undiscovered here, but it's best to be safe. I wouldn't want Ripley whisking you away again in the middle of the night. I think he may be less favourably inclined towards you now I have dispatched one or two of his friends. Still, it's unlikely you'll ever see him again.'

'I fear I could sleep all of tomorrow,' I say.

'I'll wake you just before dawn,' says Smithson. 'It would be as well to be on our way before daylight. The sooner I can get back to London and we can deal with Morland the better.'

I awake to find the sunlight streaming into the room. It is long after dawn. We have certainly overslept and shall need to hurry. I roll over in bed and reach across to shake Smithson's shoulder. He does not respond. Then I see that his sheets are covered in blood. I look up and there, sitting in the only chair in the room, is Ripley. His left hand is bandaged and there is a vivid red wound on his cheek. But his right hand is capable of wielding a knife, it would seem.

'Good morning, Mr Grey,' he says. 'You have slept well. I don't think your companion will be stirring today, so you may as well come with me. I am here to remind you that we have an appointment with Sir Edward Hyde.'

His Most Excellent Majesty Charles the Second, by the Grace of God King of England, Scotland, Ireland and France

It is mid-morning. The sun bathes the large room in which I met Hyde and the King yesterday. But the air is frosty for such a warm day.

Behind the table sits Hyde, leaning forwards as if to catch every traitorous word I utter, and the King, who lounges in his chair, a spaniel on his lap. These three, it would seem, are my judges. Behind them, the sunlight playing on its gold and red and forest-green threads, is a Flemish tapestry, representing some sort of allegory of justice or of enlightenment or of not getting yourself shot by first trusting your father's slut and then failing to wake up before your companion was stabbed to death. Something like that. I am reminded, but only briefly, of my samples of wool, abandoned at the inn. They will not help me now. The rest of my life could depend on what I say in the next few minutes.

To one side of me stands Ripley, the counsel for the prosecution. O'Neill sits attentively on the other side. There is no counsel for the defence.

The King yawns and stretches, almost unseating Fairfax, who growls and then settles down again.

'So,' says the King, 'it seems you are not Mr Clifford, but Mr Grey.'

'Yes, Your Majesty,' I say.

'And why were you Mr Clifford?'

'It was expedient,' I say.

The King nods. He understands expediency. 'So, as Mr Grey, did your father still fight for His late Majesty, as he did when you were Mr Clifford? Was that part of the story at least true?'

'Yes, sir. He fought for your father.'

'And he was forced to flee because Parliament declared him a traitor?'

'No, he fled with somebody else's wife.'

The King nods again, this time with greater approval. 'And he now lives with her here?'

'He left her for somebody younger,' I say.

Another nod from the King. He and my father would have got on well. 'And he is content, I hope, living here with his new companion?'

'He is not living at all, Your Majesty. He died last month.'

'My condolences,' says the King. 'But I'm sure, from what you say, that he died a happy man. Sir Michael here says that, in your capacity as Mr Grey, you have some important information for us that you did not give us yesterday as Mr Clifford. I confess that I do not entirely understand why that should be, but Sir Edward tells me that he does. That is his job.'

'There is a more important point to discuss first,' says Hyde. 'Mr Grey, whose side are you actually on?'

We look at each other. It occurs to me that not only does he know my father was a Royalist but, since he now knows my true name, he may have worked out that my mother was also a Royalist, who once corresponded with him from Essex. That might have stood in my favour. But now I think about it, my mother has, at my insistence, broken all connections with him—broken them utterly. That may not be the best advice that I ever gave her.

I think it is time to tell the truth again.

'I am on nobody's side,' I say. 'I simply wish to go home.'

The King looks upon that statement with almost as much sympathy as on my father's wish to flee the country with somebody else's wife. *I want to go home.* That is also his most fervent wish. To do so, he has allied with the Protestant Scots, he has signed the Covenant, he has resided with the Catholic French, he is negotiating with the Spanish, the enemies of both France and England. Throughout this constantly changing pattern of alliances there is one consistent policy. He wants to go home.

'What is your view, Sir Michael?' he asks.

Ripley rubs his chin with his one good hand and winces slightly when he touches the bright red wound. I doubt he feels well inclined towards me.

'Brodrick always suspected that Grey was an enemy of ours. He thought we should kill him there and then. I should have listened to him. It might have saved me a great deal of trouble. On the other hand, he has useful information for us. I think, Your Majesty, that you should hear it before we decide what to do with him. And I would ask you not to make up your mind until you have heard all of the evidence.'

That is a more generous opening submission for the prosecution than I had hoped for, but there is just a hint of menace in those final words that keeps me on my guard. Does Ripley have further accusations to make against me?

'Very well,' says Hyde. 'Let us see what Mr Grey can tell us. After that we shall decide what his fate should be. No more deception, Mr Grey. If you are to save yourself, it will be through the truth and the truth alone. Sir Michael has already explained to you the problem that we have. We have known for some time that Thurloe had a source of information high up in the Sealed Knot. One plan after another was betrayed before it could properly begin. It was as if Cromwell could read our minds. We knew that he has spies here in Brussels, but this person seemed to know everything that went on.'

'It's Willys,' says Ripley. 'As Mr Grey will now explain.'

Hyde looks at me. 'Is it?'

'Yes,' I reply.

Hyde nods slowly. 'That Willys was a traitor has been Sir Michael's fear for some time. I doubted that it could be so, but a little while ago our source in Thurloe's office provided hard evidence. He sent us a batch of papers. They were very interesting. I should like your views on them.' He passes me a document.

I read it. The letter is dated Saturday 15 November. It is signed by one Thomas Barret. He reports that an agent named Colonel Dobson has travelled to Calais, apparently to set in motion a plot to land Royalist troops near King's Lynn—reportedly six thousand men, to be led by the Duke of York. Barret asks the recipient to confirm that the letter arrived safely. He promises to write further.

'And you are saying this Thomas Barret is really Willys?' I ask.

'Exactly so,' says Hyde.

'Who is the letter to?'

'Thurloe.'

'And are the contents true? Is there any such person as Colonel Dobson?'

'It is true enough.'

'Then your plans are betrayed,' I say.

'Precisely—though they are very old plans and of no consequence now. We have other letters from the same source.'

He passes me a second. This time Barret requests a meeting with Thurloe and expresses a wish to serve him with all duty and faithfulness.

'And you say that is from Willys too?' I ask.

'Tell us what you think.'

I think I wish to get out of this alive. I apply my forensic skills as best I can.

'I believe it is the same hand,' I say.

Hyde, a fellow lawyer, nods and passes me three more, much like the first two.

I examine them more closely. Eventually I say: 'There are many inconsistencies in spelling and the method of dating. There is strangely little to them. And, in the end, they reveal no great secrets for one in such a position.'

'Could they be forgeries?' asks Hyde.

'They are strange. Take the first letter, for example. If I were Willys, I would put nothing incriminating in writing—no names, no events. I would simply contact Thurloe and say that I wished to speak to him. Why should I wish to leave a written record of my actions? And yet, if I were forging letters I would do much better than these. I would have had Mr Barret reveal things that were still current—and I would have had the letters over a much longer period than these few weeks. I would also have tried harder to ensure they all appeared to be from the same hand. In the end, it is the faults that convince me. They are too bad to be forgeries. But much also depends on your source. You say that somebody high up in Thurloe's office sent them to you? That can, as I have said to Sir Michael, only be Sam Morland. Is it?'

Hyde glances at Ripley, who shrugs. If they shoot me, it won't matter what they've told me.

'You are correct,' says Hyde. 'Morland offered some time ago to come over to us. Tell us then, can Morland be trusted? I mean, can he be trusted by us?'

'No,' I say. 'He cannot be trusted by anyone. Thurloe no longer trusts him either. Had Sir Michael not cut his throat, Smithson would have reported back to Thurloe that Morland had forewarned you that the King should not travel to England.'

'Precisely,' says the King. 'And that is why we should not believe these rumours. In spite of the other reports.'

'You have other reports?' I ask.

'Last year we sent an agent to London,' says Hyde, 'with instructions to question certain people, including Willys himself.'

'But the Sealed Knot in London was not to be told of this,' says Ripley. 'Not even I, who shared your suspicions.'

'It was necessary that it should be so, Sir Michael,' says Hyde. 'We could scarcely tell any of you of the purpose of the visit. It was better that you knew nothing at all.'

'Well, we heard anyway,' says Sir Michael. 'At least we heard that somebody was coming to London on a mission that we were not to know about.'

'So that is who you thought I was?' I say. 'This agent sent to investigate Willys.'

'Yes—until you told us that your mission was to kill Cromwell,' says Ripley. 'Then we began to doubt that the information we had received was correct.'

'That is unimportant now,' says Hyde. 'Our agent—the real one—investigated as instructed and reported back. The report was that there could be little doubt that Willys had betrayed us. He was in close contact with Thurloe and was passing information to him at every opportunity.'

'And how could your agent be so sure?' I say. 'What was the source of his information?'

'Partly what Willys said,' says Hyde. 'But also partly what a certain John Grey had reported.'

'I don't understand,' I say.

'You don't need to understand,' says O'Neill. He has been silent for some time but, now that he speaks, the room listens. 'Indeed, perhaps it is better that Mr Grey does not understand. I think, Your Majesty, that we have presented as much information as is necessary. We have long suspected Willys. We have the Barret letters, which Mr Grey believes to be genuine, as I do. We know from Mr Grey that Thurloe has been protecting Willys. We know that Willys has conspired with Thurloe to persuade the Sealed Knot that Mr Grey here was known to us—which he was not. I believe that Willys is complicit in some way in this ridiculous plot to lure you to England. And our agent, sent to investigate the matter and having spoken at length to Willys, believes he is false. I too was in England earlier this year, as you are aware. Thurloe seemed to know exactly where I was. Somebody was leaking information to him.'

'But you escaped,' said the King. 'Willys ensured that you knew when Thurloe's men were coming.'

'Then Willys is playing some sort of double game that I do not understand. He must be relieved of his command at the very least. I think he should be summoned to Brussels to account for his actions.'

The King is silent for what seems like several minutes. 'No,' he says.

'No?' asks Hyde.

'You are all deceived,' the King continues. 'Willys fought as bravely as anyone for my father and has served me well since then. This is Thurloe's plot to bring an innocent man down. Mr Grey has said very clearly that Morland is not to be trusted. These letters from Thomas Barret are Morland's work. Then Thurloe very conveniently sends us Mr Grey with a letter for me. Thurloe has previously allowed words to drop into his conversations with Mr Grey to suggest that he might be protecting Sir Richard. He forbids Mr Grey to have contact with him, causing Mr Grey to wonder why. In short, Thurloe carefully weaves a tapestry of falsehood. When Mr Grey sees the contents of the letter, his surprise is genuine and very convincing. We are led to believe, as you did, that Willys and Thurloe have colluded. Smithson then appears to whisk Mr Grey away before he can be interrogated further—before he can question him as we are questioning him now. Had you not found Smithson and cut his throat and returned Grey to us, we might just have believed the whole story. But, as it is, we know the truth. This is a clever plan by Thurloe to deprive us of our greatest asset in England. But we, gentlemen, are cleverer than he.'

O'Neill looks puzzled. 'With respect, Your Majesty, whatever you may think of the other evidence, including my own, the report from our agent is unequivocal.'

'But it is based, at least in part, on what Mr Grey had said. Hence it also originates with Thurloe.'

'There is also,' says Ripley, 'the fact of Sir Richard's having assured us that Mr Grey was vouched for in Brussels, when clearly he was not.'

'Thurloe could have falsely arranged for Sir Richard to receive the necessary assurances.'

That, of course, is also what Thurloe told me. Though I do not agree with the King, I am impressed with his reasoning.

He has talked down his most senior lawyer and left him silently fuming. That is no mean feat. And he has done so in order to leave himself the easiest path—that of doing nothing.

Ripley and O'Neill look at each other.

'But…' says Ripley.

'The matter is at an end,' says the King.

'And I am free to go?' I ask.

'Yes,' says the King. 'You have answered honestly. It is clear that you are no agent of the Republic. We have no reason to detain you.'

'I think,' says Ripley, 'that Your Majesty should hear from one further witness before we come to that conclusion.'

'Do we not already know all that we need to know?'

'Far from it, Your Majesty,' says Ripley. 'I have evidence that, contrary to what he tells us, Mr Grey was actively working for Thurloe all along; indeed, that he undertook other work for him—work that strikes at the heart of our designs. And he has chosen to reveal none of this to us so far.'

'Who says so?' asks the King.

'Esmond Underhill,' says Ripley. 'Shall I call him in?'

Mr Esmond Underhill,
His Evidence

Underhill slides into the room. On seeing the King, he wrinkles his nose as if in contempt, then makes a poor show of a bow in his direction. He is not at his ease in this company.

'You are Mr Underhill?' asks Hyde with distaste.

'Yes, Sir Edward,' says Underhill. His own loathing for Hyde is similarly not well concealed. But he does not need to conceal it. His visit here is one of mutual benefit. They need him perhaps more than he needs them. 'Formerly Corporal of Horse in the army of my Lord Lambert,' he adds, giving them a twisted smile. 'I'm also a good friend of Sir Michael's, you might say.'

'You are no Royalist, I think,' says Hyde.

'Nor no lover of Cromwell,' says Underhill.

'Tell the King what you told me this morning,' says Ripley. 'You know Mr Grey here?'

'Unfortunately,' he replies. Underhill looks in my direction. I betrayed him, as he sees it, and in a moment his revenge may be complete. 'Met him at Hampton Court, where he drank my brandy and promised friendship. But he's false, that one. He informed on me to Thurloe. Told him all sorts of lies about me. Had me arrested.'

'Mr Grey tells us that he was duped by Thurloe and that he worked for him no more than he had to in order to stay alive,' says Ripley.

'Nothing of the sort,' Underhill continues. 'He's been a willing agent of Thurloe's for months—years maybe.'

'I did work for Thurloe once,' I say, 'but I left his service. You know that already.'

'Why did you leave?' asks Hyde.

I take a deep breath. Perhaps it is best to tell the truth, or as much of it as I dare. 'I fell out with your informant Mr Morland,' I say.

'Why?' asks Hyde.

A good question from the King's Chancellor. The scene is still painfully vivid—me, Thurloe and Morland together. My accusations. Morland's suave denial. My carefully built case crumbling before me. And all I did was to convince Thurloe, quite wrongly, that the Cliffords were plotting against the State. That I was justified in accusing Morland of being a Royalist spy does not seem a good argument in this room that is full of Royalists, many of whom are spies of one sort of another.

'I had my reasons,' I say.

'Grey is full of spite and deceit,' interposes Underhill. 'Thurloe took him back on because he had a use for such a person. And Mr Grey has served Thurloe very diligently indeed.'

'These are empty accusations,' I point out. 'Let Underhill give you proof that I have willingly done anything for Thurloe. He will not be able to do so.'

'Can you do that, Mr Underhill?' asks Hyde. 'Give us proof?'

'Of course. I had the honour to serve, as I say, under my Lord Lambert. Mr Grey was sent on a mission by Thurloe to sound out my Lord on his loyalty to the State. My Lord contacted me afterwards and asked if I knew anything about Mr Grey.

I told him that Grey was a sneaking little fellow and not to be trusted. Lambert agreed. Grey was there to investigate on Thurloe's behalf. Cromwell didn't even know he'd been sent. He's Thurloe's agent, through and through.'

'Is this true?' asks Hyde.

'I did visit Lambert,' I say.

'Why?' asks Hyde.

'As Underhill says, to sound him out.'

'For Thurloe?'

'For the State. Cromwell wanted a reconciliation.'

'Why you? Why not somebody more senior?'

'I was available.'

Hyde nods. His need for agents is not unlike Thurloe's. I was available.

'That's not all, though,' says Underhill. 'Thurloe then sent him to interrogate my Lord Fairfax.'

'Did you?' asks Hyde.

'It was a similar mission,' I say.

'But hardly one for a man reluctantly doing no more than he had to,' says Ripley.

That is fair comment.

'So why the second mission?' asks Hyde.

Again, Underhill kindly supplies the answer. 'Thurloe was aware of a plot to kill Cromwell. Mr Grey was investigating it. I think you may find that that is his real reason for being in Brussels.'

They all look at me. I have to agree that it is convincing, if wholly untrue. To say that Thurloe had told me that I no longer needed to continue my investigations after Underhill's arrest will merely confirm that I had indeed been conducting enquiries into just that.

'I have told you why I am here,' I say.

The King and his dog look doubtful.

'So you see,' says Ripley, 'that is why you cannot let Mr Grey return to London. He is still working for Thurloe and we have no idea what he may have discovered.'

'But,' I say, 'there *is* no scheme to kill Cromwell, other than the feeble attempts by Mr Underhill that were so easily fore-stalled. Apart from those, there is no plot...'

Then I see the look on Hyde's face, the look on O'Neill's face, the look on Ripley's face, the look on the King's face. Only the dog gives nothing away. Of course there is another plot! They all know that there is another plot. And now I know too. And they know I know. They cannot let me return to London. Not now.

'So,' says the King, 'I agree that unfortunately changes everything. What then becomes of Mr Grey?'

'I shall deal with that problem, Your Majesty,' says Ripley. He touches the scar on his face. I remember what he told me about being unforgiving. Of course, he may have been exaggerating.

'In that case,' says the King, 'I shall probably not see you again, Mr Grey. I am sorry for it. I rather liked you. It was pleasant to talk to you about England, to which I hope to return one day. I do regret that you will not have the same opportunity.' He rises. His dog also prepares to leave.

'But,' I protest, 'am I to be condemned on so little evidence? If I am to be executed, do I not deserve a proper trial like the late King?'

But I have said the wrong thing. Here at this court nobody believes that the late King was accorded a fair trial.

'You have not been condemned, Mr Grey,' says the King. 'You are merely the victim of expediency. We cannot risk releasing you.'

'You have tried to steer a middle course,' says Hyde. 'Sometimes that works and sometimes it doesn't. In happier times it would have been commendable. Please do not blame yourself for the fact that we are going to have to shoot you. It is just that that is how things have turned out. The danger of keeping you alive outweighs any consequent benefit.'

'Wait!' I say, because if they do not wait I shall be dead very soon. 'You cannot claim I have been of no service to you. I have given you information about Willys, even if you choose not to believe it. And your agent—the man that you sent to London last year—he said that I had been helpful to him.'

'Man? I mentioned no man,' says Hyde.

The door behind us opens and I hear a familiar voice.

'I apologise for this intrusion, Your Majesty, but I came as soon as I heard that a dangerous spy had been taken.'

I turn and there is Aminta. She shakes her head sadly. 'Oh dear, Cousin John. You seem to have got yourself into a bit of a mess, haven't you?'

Aminta Pole, Her Evidence

'Will somebody please explain, to me and my dog, exactly what relevance this is supposed to have to anything?' The King looks at each of us in turn. Hyde speaks first.

'When Lady Pole was in London,' says Hyde, 'attempting to find out the truth of the accusations against Sir Richard Willys, she used some information that had been obtained from a Mr Grey—a person of whom at that time we knew very little and had no way of connecting with Mr John Clifford until now. However, Lady Pole clearly knew Mr Grey very well.'

'I therefore took the liberty of sending her a message,' says O'Neill, 'once I had worked out that this Grey was the same one that Lady Pole had spoken of in London. It seemed to me that she must know him better than anyone else and might be able to provide us with the reassurances we required as to his future conduct.'

Ripley scowls at O'Neill, but the rest of us all turn to Aminta and listen.

Aminta smiles and surveys the room. I am grateful to her for coming, but I think she may be enjoying this a little too much.

'Thank you, Mr O'Neill. I am indebted to you for calling me. As Sir Edward says, I was sent to London to investigate Sir Richard Willys. Sir Edward rightly thought that a man asking questions might arouse suspicion but that a woman asking questions would be regarded as mere tittle-tattle—a harmless feminine weakness that was of no account. Such was the case. But there were also places that a woman could not easily go. I therefore took my cousin into my confidence, knowing his impeccable sentiments and strong Royalist principles. His father fought for the late King, as you may be aware. His mother too is loyal to Your Majesty. You may remember that she corresponded with you from Essex. Indeed, it was she who recommended to me that I should seek out John in London. That is true, is it not, cousin?'

'Yes, cousin,' I reply. I dare not say more. Aminta is spinning such a delicate, sparkling web of deceit that any clumsy thing I say may break it in a moment.

'When Sir Michael's letter arrived at our lodgings,' Aminta continues, 'I knew that it would not be safe for me to accept the invitation to talk to him and his companions, but I had to find out whether the Sealed Knot suspected anything. I therefore sent John to meet them. They were, of course, surprised. They knew enough to be expecting a lady, not a gentleman...and certainly not a lawyer.'

Ripley nods. 'I admit we were expecting a lady—it was a woman's voice that our contact thought he overheard. We assumed that it might be the daughter of Sir Felix Clifford, since his name was mentioned several times. It was not surprising that we formed the view that his son had been sent instead of his daughter—that our intelligence was wrong in that one small respect.'

'Indeed,' says Aminta. 'You formed that view. John realised that you were in error but he certainly could not tell you of my true mission, so he made up a story—a slightly far-fetched one—about murdering Cromwell. It was the best he could do at the time. But you believed him and did not trouble me further. I was free to go about my business.'

Ripley is frowning, trying to tie in Aminta's story to the story that I have told him. They are, to be fair, similar in some respects. Fortunately, before he can spot any inconsistencies the King gives a laugh.

'In short, Sir Michael, the lady ran rings round you,' he says.

I think that this royal intervention has not made Ripley like me any more than he did before. Aminta, however, nods in acknowledgment of the truth of what the King has said.

'I had put Mr Grey into a very difficult position,' she says. 'Having deceived Sir Michael, for the best possible reasons, he had to persist in playing his part as an assassin while continuing to help me with my investigations. In no wise could he explain the truth. And I saw a further use for him. On my instructions, he used his old contacts in Mr Thurloe's office to gain access to Thurloe's own network of spies and to ask questions about Sir Richard there. He discovered that Thurloe knew Sir Richard well and that Thurloe was protecting him. I questioned Sir Richard myself, as you know, and his answers were most unsatisfactory. Thurloe refers to Sir Richard as his "masterpiece of corruption", by the way. He is very proud of having turned him.'

'Nevertheless,' says Hyde, 'the King believes him to be blameless. The King's view is that Sir Richard has been incriminated by a plot of Thurloe's. We have all been deliberately misled, including you. The King's word on this is final.'

'With respect, Your Majesty...' Aminta begins, but the King waves a hand wearily.

'I am grateful to you for your respect,' says the King, 'but that matter is concluded.'

Ripley fumes silently. It would seem, however, that Aminta has not finished with His Majesty.

'I cannot agree, sir. Mr Grey spoke to Thurloe himself. Moreover, when I met with Sir Richard, he was shifty and evasive. Though his lecherous gaze took in most of me, he would not look me in the eye. He is hiding something.'

The King smiles. 'As a woman you know this? You know when a man is hiding something from you?'

'Yes,' she says.

'Even if your King assures you that he is not?'

Aminta narrows her eyes. I am aware that she is making overtures to Cromwell, but she would, even so, do well not to pick a fight with the King quite so publicly in his own court. Before she can speak, however, Daniel O'Neill intervenes.

'Your Majesty's view is that Willys is innocent,' he says. 'The view of the rest of us, including my Lady Pole, is that he is guilty. The rest of us, including my Lady Pole, bow to Your Majesty's superior judgement as a matter of course. However, I would remind you that the issue before us is what to do with Mr Grey. You have heard that he has been of great service to Your Majesty. I have not heard anyone dispute it. The question is whether Grey can be trusted to keep his silence on the other great matter that Lady Pole was asked to report on—that is to say, whether the Protector Cromwell can be removed in a timely manner.'

'If we release Grey he could still report back to Thurloe,' says Ripley. 'That he has helped Lady Pole does not mean that he is on our side. And while in Brussels he has discovered too much about our plans.'

He is wrong in one sense—I am not certain that I have discovered anything new. On the other hand, he is quite right in another sense. Thurloe will undoubtedly try to get out of me anything he can.

'He already knows of the plan,' says Aminta. 'He has done so for some time. I had, of necessity, to tell him everything while I was in London. He knew and yet revealed nothing to Thurloe.'

Hyde is no fool. He can see the flaw in this as well as I can. 'Then why did Mr Grey not say that earlier?'

'Because,' says Aminta, 'he did not wish to reveal how much I had told him. He thought that he might place me at risk if he did so. He thought you would not approve my actions. But I tell you now, with due apologies if I exceeded my commission.'

She curtseys in a way that I can only describe as nicely judged. It suggests obedience and avoids any need to look the King in the eye.

'You certainly took a great risk, madam,' says Hyde.

Aminta straightens up. She's not curtseying to Hyde. 'Not at all, Sir Edward. You forget that I have known John all my life. In the village, when we were young, he was known for his honesty. He was regarded as honest almost to the point of simplicity.'

'Was I?' I say. Her father's steward knew me mainly for stealing apples from the orchard.

'You know you were, dear cousin. The village idiot was quite worried for his position. I am prepared to stand surety for my cousin. I give you my word that he will tell nobody.'

'And you are saying that we should release him and let him return to England?' asks Hyde.

'Yes,' says Aminta.

'No,' says Ripley.

'Perhaps,' says O'Neill, 'it would after all be better to keep him here. Lady Pole vouches for him. He could remain under house arrest with the Poles until such time as the information he has would be valueless.'

'Are you willing to do that, Lady Pole?' asks the King.

'My family has always served you in every way possible,' says Aminta. She curtseys again, very prettily.

'I still say that letting Grey live is too great a risk,' says Ripley. 'And as for Willys…'

The King pauses for a moment but Fairfax, impatient at the dullness of the proceedings or perhaps simply desirous of being elsewhere, jumps down from his lap and heads for the door, tail wagging. This decides the matter.

'Grey shall remain with Lady Pole,' says the King. 'He must remain within the city walls of Brussels. As long as he does so, he is under her protection and mine. I wish to hear nothing further against Sir Richard.' He rises and stretches. 'Good night, Mr Grey. I am pleased that Sir Michael will not be put to the trouble of shooting you.'

The door opens and closes. On the far side there comes a single excited bark and we all listen to the sound of receding footsteps.

Eventually Ripley breaks the silence. 'If his dog hadn't been about to shit in his lap, he might have had time to listen to what I had to say.'

'There's always somebody in his lap,' says O'Neill.

'You are fools, all of you,' says Ripley. 'I for one will not trust Willys again. And as for you, Grey, don't think that you can avoid me for ever.'

'I don't think that,' I say.

As we make our way through the moonlit streets, I say to Aminta: 'So, who is Cromwell's assassin?'

'I would hardly tell you that, my dear cousin.'

'But you told everyone that I knew.'

'But you don't, do you?'

'No,' I say.

'And that is for the best,' says Aminta.

'It is not for the best that Cromwell dies,' I say.

'True. But it may not happen,' she says. 'Indeed, after my visit to London, I think it won't.'

We walk on in silence for some way, then I say: 'Are we about to walk to Paris, if that is where you and your father now live?'

'For goodness sake,' she replies. 'I have just saved your life and you quibble about one small lie?'

'Had you said you came from Brussels, I might have worked it all out a bit sooner.'

'Which is why I told you that we were in Paris.'

'So your visit to London, assassinations apart, was only to investigate Willys? You had no real intention of compounding for Roger's ancestral lands?'

'On the contrary. In that respect I may have deceived Sir Edward just a little. I tried to reclaim them on that visit and will continue to try to reclaim them. That is why, like you, I should prefer Cromwell to live until things are a little more settled. If the King returns, he may choose to restore some property confiscated from his supporters, but he will need to placate his former opponents as well. And he will want to upset as few people as possible. Possession will still be nine-tenths of the law. So Roger and I have to continue to press Cromwell for the return of our lands now. And Cromwell must stay alive long enough to make his reply. It is important that nobody assassinates him in the meantime. I have that in hand.'

'Where is Roger?' I ask. I am not looking forward to sharing a house with him as well as with Aminta and her father.

'He has gone to England. He thinks that Fairfax, though a distant connection, may be of assistance. He will take my own representations further.'

'Is that not dangerous?'

'There is some risk of arrest still, but it must be done.'

'You would really change sides and desert the King?' I say.

Aminta stops suddenly. She looks both ways down the deserted street before she hisses back: 'You raised no objection when we were in England. Buckingham has gone over to Cromwell. Why not us? Fairfax is as likely as anyone to succeed as the next Lord Protector. Cromwell just needs to live a little longer so that Fairfax is readmitted to the inner circle. And why should you disapprove? Unless...'

'Unless what?' I ask.

'You now call him "the King", not "Charles Stuart" or "the Tyrant's son" or "the Pretender" or "the titular King of the Scots". And you did not sneer at all. Next you will be calling him "His Gracious Majesty". Your Republican principles are being eaten away, John.'

'A slip of the tongue,' I say. 'I am still loyal to His Highness the Lord Protector.'

'Whom you now seem to refer to simply as "Cromwell".'

'Another slip of the tongue.'

'You have not been charmed and won over by His Majesty?'

'No,' I say.

'The King does that.'

I say nothing and remind myself that all kingship is tyranny and the only noble form of government is a republic.

'I wish Roger well in his quest,' I say. 'I hope you recover your estates. Indeed, I have already asked Thurloe to support your request to Cromwell.'

'You mean my request to His Highness the Lord Protector?'

'I mean your request to His Highness the Lord Protector.'

She pulls me to her and gives me a kiss on the cheek. For a moment I feel the warmth of her body against mine. The happy thought occurs to me that Roger Pole may already be arrested and imprisoned by now. After all, my luck has held so far. Who knows what undeserved good fortune the future will bring?

CHAPTER 28

Sir Felix Clifford

'You are most welcome, John,' says Sir Felix, 'to our humble dwelling.'

I am sitting at Sir Felix's table, eating Sir Felix's beef, obtained on credit from some over-trusting Flemish butcher.

'Thank you, Sir Felix,' I say.

'It is my pleasure. We do not dine thus every day. We are impoverished Cavaliers, as you know. Usually a stew of beans and roots is all we have. Or perhaps a rabbit, obtained by stealth in one of the woods. Or a trout or two, netted by night—one does not ask from which stream.' He belches happily.

'Thank you,' I say again.

'Rumours of my visit to England have persuaded the tradesmen to be patient with us for a little longer,' says Aminta. 'This town is full of rumours, sometimes to our advantage. And one rumour is that the King will be restored soon and we shall all have money. I fear it may be untrue, but it is enough to put a smile on the faces of many Brussels tradesmen. When the Royalists' estates are restored, the fountains of Flanders will flow with wine.'

'Only if the Royalists waste their gold on paying their debts here,' says Sir Felix. 'Which few will do.' He cuts himself another slice of beef and examines it for a moment on the end of his fork. 'Do you know, Aminta, I think this may be horse that they have sold you. I certainly would not pay for it.'

'And you certainly will not pay for it. I obtained it on Roger's credit. Yours was used up some time ago, my dear father. If we were to live on what you could provide, we would lack even the beans and roots that you speak of so fondly.'

Sir Felix nods amiably, his mouth full of horse.

'It is excellent anyway,' I say as I chew.

'And Ripley thought that you were Aminta's brother?' he asks. 'Ha!'

'Yes. He knew you, of course. He thought that I resembled you in some way. It saved my life.'

Sir Felix looks at me, tries to swallow a piece of horse and then almost chokes. Aminta slaps him on the back and offers him beer (Roger's credit does not run to wine, it would seem).

'I am, of course, nothing like Marius,' I say, as Sir Felix coughs and splutters. 'Even if Ripley did not know that he had sadly died during the war, I am surprised at his error. How could I be him?'

Aminta is looking at me critically. 'There is perhaps a slight resemblance,' she says. 'I did not remark it at the time, when we all played together as children, but you were younger than Marius. But now...yes, I can see Marius in you.'

'A little,' says Sir Felix, having recovered his voice. 'But no more than that. You are, after all, both good-looking young men, eh, Aminta? As, of course, is your husband, I should add. Let us hope he has avoided capture in London.'

Aminta and I exchange glances. Whatever she is thinking about any of that, she is saying nothing more.

'You too took a risk in travelling to England for His Majesty,' I say to change the subject.

Aminta laughs. 'Not merely King but now *His Majesty*?'

I wonder whether to correct myself, but decide not to. He is the same Charles Stuart whatever I call him.

'I think,' says Sir Felix, prodding a fork in my direction, 'that we are sheltering a dangerous Royalist. We must be careful that Mr Thurloe does not find out.'

As I am leaving Sir Felix's modest house, I realise that I am being watched from the other side of the street. It is Underhill. I ignore him and set off towards the market. He follows me.

'Good morning, Mr Grey,' he pants, as he catches me up. 'Perhaps we could have a quiet word? Maybe in the square just ahead of us? I think that will be private enough for us. Just follow me a little way off. We do not know who may be watching us and I think we should be discreet.'

Whatever I feel about Underhill, I do not fear him. For all his claims to be an assassin, and for all his boasts of having served his Lord Lambert as Corporal of Horse, I doubt that he has much taste for cold steel in a dark alleyway. Still, I have no intention of obliging him in any way.

'You can say whatever you have to say here,' I tell him.

He looks around at the citizens of Brussels as they come and go. Nobody shows any great interest in two Englishmen conversing in the street. They have learned to despise and largely ignore the threadbare Cavaliers who have made their home here. Underhill shrugs.

'I am pleased that you are still with us, Mr Grey,' he says. 'You have no hard feelings, I trust, any more than I have hard feelings because you had me pursued and arrested by Mr Thurloe.'

'I wouldn't go that far,' I say.

'That is a pity, because I have a proposal to put to you that may be to our mutual advantage.'

'What's that?'

Underhill looks around to see if any of our countrymen might overhear him. He lowers his voice to a whisper.

'I am suggesting that in future we should work together.'

'How?'

'I think that the King may soon be restored,' says Underhill.

'I doubt it,' I say. 'So do the many others who are returning to England.'

'Maybe they don't know as much as I do, then. I repeat, *when* the King is restored, I'd like a job working for O'Neill—he's likely to be the man running the secret service.'

'I can't help you,' I say.

'O'Neill likes you,' says Underhill. 'He'll listen to you. Strangely, he doesn't like me much at all. You were at the university, weren't you?'

'Yes,' I say. 'Cambridge.'

'And your people own land?'

'They did, once. I suppose we do own land again, now my mother has remarried.'

'A lot of land?'

'Most of the village.'

'Exactly. I was never at a university, Mr Grey, and my father could never lay claim to a square yard of land until he was buried in it. O'Neill looks down his nose at me. I could walk straight past Hyde ten times a day and he'd never notice I was there.'

'He'd never notice me either.'

'But he'd not notice you in a different way. He'd not notice you as a gentleman.'

'As a practising lawyer, I am simply a man of business.'

'That's rubbish. You're still one of them. You're still gentry.'

'And what are you?'

'I'm one of the people.'

'And you think I can get you a job with O'Neill?'

'Yes, I do.'

'And what are you offering in exchange?'

'If things work out differently, as you seem to think they will, I'll put in a good word for you with General Lambert. Or Harrison. Or Fleetwood.'

'It is unlikely that I'll need that,' I say. 'Cromwell has, I hope, many years to live. If that is all you have to offer, then good day, Mr Underhill.'

'That's not quite all,' he says. 'You know there's a plot to kill Cromwell, don't you?'

'Lady Pole told me about it,' I say cautiously.

'No, she didn't. I could tell by your face you had no idea. But I think I know.'

'So, you are offering to tell me?'

'I can tell you who I think it is. I'll tell you and you put it to my Lady Pole. If I'm right, you'll see it in her face. Then you report that back to me.'

'No,' I say. 'I'll report nothing back to you.'

'You'll regret that when General Harrison comes to power.'

'He won't,' I say.

Underhill laughs. 'You're right. Whoever wins, we've already lost. You know, we almost had it within our grasp for a year or two. We might have had a democracy with all men voting for a parliament. We might have had no lords amongst us. The land could have been a common treasury for all—every man with enough to keep himself and his family and no more. Then Cromwell took control and it slipped away. The Good Old Cause slipped away.'

'It would have been different under General Lambert?'

'Of course it would. Or under Harrison or even Fleetwood. But it's Cromwell, and now he's *Lord* Protector, if you please, and wants to make himself King.'

'If you had the information—I mean, if you knew for certain who Hyde had commissioned to kill Cromwell—what good would it do you?'

'You don't need to know that, Mr Grey.'

I wonder if he plans to sell the information to Thurloe. It would, of course, be a way of getting the information to him, if that is still the right thing to do. But can I trust Underhill?

'I'm sorry,' I say. 'I can't help you.'

Lord Pole, His Plan

For a week or so I live more or less amicably with Aminta and her father. She is friendly, affectionate, but there are no further kisses after that one in the street. Not in her husband's house. There is little money but there does seem to be a great deal of credit for Cavaliers. The sentiment in the markets is clearly that the King may still be restored, for all that others may think to the contrary. Providing bread and meat and lace to the court, with payment delayed until the King enjoys his own again, is a gamble that Flemish tradesmen are now prepared to take. They seem to have news that I do not. Or perhaps they have already gambled too heavily on this card to be able to back out now.

In between meals of bread and horse, I wander the streets of Brussels because it is cheap and does not remind me how much I am beholden to the Cliffords even for the little I have. It does not remind me that Aminta and her father had to flee here because of me. Fortunately they have no idea that is the case.

Then Roger Pole returns. I find him sitting in the parlour when I come back, hot and dusty, from yet another walk. He seems at ease, as well he might be in his own house. He is wearing a pale blue silk suit, which I saw him wear in England last year. I am sure that normally he would have already abandoned it as having an inch too much or an inch too little lace or because the breeches were too wide or too narrow or because the silk was the wrong shade of blue. But he is in exile now and must wear last year's clothes. He too suffers for the cause.

'I was told you were here,' he says by way of greeting. He pours himself a glass of wine and offers me none.

'I am under house arrest,' I say. 'I may not leave Brussels. I am sorry to inconvenience you, but it is not by choice.'

'The inconvenience to me is slight, Mr Grey,' says Pole. 'I hope that intruding on my wife and her family is no great hardship for you?'

'They have been very hospitable,' I say.

Pole's pock-marked face breaks into a grin. 'I am sure they have,' he says. He holds his glass up to examine the colour of the wine that I will not be asked to drink.

'Believe me when I say that I have no more wish to be here than you wish to have me here.'

'As little as that? Surely not?' says Pole.

'I assure you, Mr Pole, that I would go tomorrow if I could.'

'You may address me as Lord Pole,' says Pole. He looks down his sharp nose at me. 'That is my title. Viscount Pole. Your Lordship, if you prefer. Or my Lord. All are equally good, if said with respect and sincerity. I in turn address you as Grey, though I hear that you prefer the name Clifford. It is certainly more distinguished than your own, rather ordinary name.'

'Your title has been restored by the King,' I say. 'But the State does not recognise it.'

'Restored by the King and about to be restored by Cromwell very soon. Lord Fairfax has spoken to Cromwell on my behalf. I hope that my own exile will soon be over. Of course, yours will continue. I doubt that Hyde will let you leave Brussels and I am certain that Ripley won't. But we shall think of you, here in this hot, dusty city, when we are at our ease on our green and pleasant estates. When I say that it is hot and dusty here, I should of course add that it is very cold and damp during the winter. And sadly you will still be here when winter comes.'

'So your new loyalties are now firmly fixed?' I ask.

'I have spoken to Fairfax and to Buckingham. We cannot afford to have anything other than a peaceful transition of power from Cromwell to one of the leading men of the country. That must be Fairfax. A group of us are working to get Fairfax named as Cromwell's heir.'

I am sure they are working. All over England people will be working to secure their positions, committing themselves as little as possible until they know which way the wind is blowing. Underhill is right. A revolution has simply put a different group of aristocrats in control of the country. A group of aristocrats untrammelled by a monarchy.

'Not working for the King?' I say.

'The King will be restored only by means of another war. Nobody wants that.'

'Nor for Richard Cromwell?'

'No. He's a good fellow, but the people will not rally to him as they will to Black Tom. I need to be in England to ensure that happens.'

Pole pauses and looks at me. He has told me a great deal. Perhaps too much. But a word from him here would still seal my fate. Or he could run me through and claim that I had attempted to escape. I matter very little. He knows I will not go to the King and say that another rat is about to desert his ship.

'I had assumed you would approve of my supporting Cromwell,' says Pole. 'Or has the King beguiled you? He has charm, even if he has little judgement. You would not be the first to throw in your lot with him simply because you liked him. His dogs adopt much the same position. Join his court and wait for him to throw you a bone. But you'll be backing the wrong runner. Fairfax is the coming man.'

'I am no Royalist,' I say. 'Nor shall I ever be.'

'How wise you are,' says Pole.

The days pass. Many weeks pass. I receive letters from my mother but no offer of financial support. I am called to see Hyde again.

'We have made further enquiries of you in England,' says Hyde. 'You have been modest about your position there.'

'I think not.'

'We think so,' says O'Neill. 'Though Ripley still urges us to the shortest way, it would seem that there are those in England who would be badly inconvenienced by your death. You are the stepson of Colonel Payne of Clavershall West, it would seem.'

'Yes,' I say.

'Your father died here in Brussels six months ago?' asks Hyde.

'So I understand.'

'Your mother has remarried quickly,' he says.

'Faster than you might have expected.'

'Clearly. You are aware that your stepfather has been talking to General Monck for us?'

'I was aware of something of the sort. I think my mother is aware of that too.'

'Your mother was formerly active on our behalf,' says Hyde.

'She remains loyal to His Majesty,' I say.

'That is as well,' says Hyde. 'Your own loyalties seem to have lain elsewhere.'

O'Neill takes up the conversation once more. 'We have made enquires of Mr Morland.'

'And he did not speak in my favour?'

'Morland confirms that you worked for Mr Thurloe but left his service after a short time.'

'That is true,' I say. 'I think he was pleased to see me go.'

'No, he regrets it. He says that he believes you are an honest man of good principles.'

'Morland says that? But we did not agree well...'

'Morland confirms that you saw through his counterfeited loyalty to the Republic and discovered his true allegiance—that is to say, to His Majesty.'

Well, Morland might say that to Hyde now. He was less impressed by my efforts when I last saw him.

'He thinks that you might be prepared to work for us,' says O'Neill.

'I simply wish to return to my studies,' I say.

'You don't know what we want you to do,' says O'Neill.

'Whatever it is, the answer is still "no",' I say.

❀ ❀ ❀

I am not permitted to leave Brussels, but I am at liberty to frequent taverns, so long as my English silver holds out. I am drinking Flemish ale at one when I am approached by Daniel O'Neill, this time alone. He smiles in a friendly way.

'Your tankard is empty, Mr Grey. Let me fill it for you.'

'That would be kind, Mr O'Neill, but I have already told you—I can do nothing in return.'

'Did I ask you to do anything?'

'No,' I say.

'Very well, then. Drink with me.'

O'Neill calls for ale for us both. 'It must be dull for an active young man like yourself, here in Brussels?' he asks.

'I am a lawyer, Mr O'Neill. I am neither active nor do I entirely dislike dullness.'

'Still, you say you'd like to return to London.'

'Working for you?'

O'Neill says nothing while ale is placed in front of us. He waits until the serving man has gone and then replies: 'Don't refuse until you know what we want. We're told that you could get employment again with Mr Thurloe.'

'Who says?'

'Morland. He says he could ensure that you get a job in Thurloe's office tomorrow. That would be very helpful to us, if you see what I mean. To have another man inside Thurloe's office.'

'You mean, would I work for you as a double agent?'

'The risk would not be great. It would be more pleasant than sitting here. We have sufficient assurance of your integrity and your principles. And when the King is restored, you would still have a place with us—regular employment. We could not pay you well until the King returns, but Mr Thurloe would very kindly look after that side of things for the moment.'

'I think,' I say, 'that I do not wish to work as a spy for anyone. I have betrayed too many confidences already. When I have been with Thurloe I have truly believed myself a Republican. When I have been with the King I feel that I might be a Royalist. This business of switching is too easy. I do not believe that it does me any credit. My career as an agent is over.'

O'Neill shakes his head. 'I think you condemn yourself too harshly,' he says. 'Your friend Marius Clifford fought and died at Worcester, did he not?'

'So we believe.'

'Many of those taken prisoner after the battle elected to join the parliamentary army. It wasn't uncommon during the war for captured men to change sides. Nobody thought badly of them.'

'Nobody?'

'Too many people have switched their allegiances of late for them to be able to criticise others who do the same. I would merely advise you to end up on the right side rather than the wrong side.'

I think of Pole, who wishes the same. But he is wrong. The people do not want to be ruled by an oligarchy of smug noblemen. It is a choice between the King and Cromwell. O'Neill's offer is generous.

'I simply wish to return to my studies at Lincoln's Inn,' I say.

'That could be arranged too. After you have helped us.'

'No, thank you,' I say.

'Perhaps you will reconsider at a later date.'

'I think not.'

'So, what will you do, Mr Grey? Will you live off Sir Felix for ever?'

'I don't think he has that much money,' I say.

O'Neill puts down his tankard carefully on the table. 'And how do matters stand between you and Lord Pole?'

'He has been absent on business,' I say. 'Now he is back, I try to see him as little as I can.'

'Business in England?'

'Just so.'

'Did he say what that business was?'

I pause, then say, 'No.' I could betray Pole, but I already have as many enemies as I need.

O'Neill nods, picks up his tankard again and drains it. 'Think about it, Mr Grey. Your position here is a delicate one and my offer is good. We'll pay for your journey home.'

He is right, of course. Sharing a house with Aminta and her father has been awkward, but Roger Pole will know how to make it utterly unbearable. And I am not sure how long I can keep his secret. I need somehow to escape.

❀ ❀ ❀

I am still pondering this when I have a second visitor to my table.

'I see you're on good terms with O'Neill,' says Ripley.

'Not as good as he would wish.'

Ripley sits down suddenly on the bench opposite me. He has been drinking. I wonder if he too wishes to make an overture of friendship.

'I can't kill you here in Brussels, but make a move outside and it will be a pleasure to ensure that you keep your promise not to leave town.'

'Then I must stay here,' I say.

'Does O'Neill want you to work for him?'

'I've told him I can't.'

'Then you're a fool. In a week or two, everyone will be flocking to the King's side again.'

'Why?' I ask.

Ripley laughs. 'Wouldn't you like to know?'

'Yes, but I doubt you're planning to tell me.'

To my surprise Ripley says: 'You're too late to stop it anyway. He'll be dead before you can get to London.'

'Who? Cromwell?'

'Cromwell. O'Neill has just been in London making the final arrangements. But it is to be done in a way that will cast no suspicion on the King, less still on Sir Edward Hyde. Because everyone knows Cromwell is sick and nobody will be at all surprised.'

'Yes,' I say. 'Bate told me His Highness is ill. I'm sure he's been telling everyone... It's Bate, isn't it? He's Hyde's assassin.'

'Of course it's Bate. He contacted Sir Edward Hyde some time ago. Your friend, Lady Pole, spoke to him in London, though she recommended we had nothing to do with it. She may have felt he lacked the nerve—or she may be playing some game of her own. Still, O'Neill seems to have made the final arrangements with him. I'll even tell you how it is being done. Arsenic. Mercury. Antimony. All good cures for one thing or another but lethal together. It will seem that Cromwell has an ague. When he dies, nobody will suspect Bate—or not very much.'

'Why are you telling me this?'

'Because it amuses me. You've been running around Europe trying to prevent this from happening. Now you know exactly what is going to take place but can't prevent it. If you try to leave Brussels—and we shall watch every coach that departs for the coast—I will have you killed. If you try to write to Thurloe, we shall certainly intercept it. You could tell one of Thurloe's agents here, if you knew who they were, but you don't. And you'd be too late anyway. All you can do is sit in the sun and drink ale and wait for the news of Cromwell's death to arrive.'

'You're drunk,' I say.

'Then don't believe me,' he says. 'It won't be my loss. Good evening, Mr Grey.'

But I do believe him.

※ ※ ※

'And you think that Bate will act soon?' asks Pole.

'It may already be too late,' I say.

We are sitting round the table—Sir Felix, Aminta, Roger Pole and I. The news that Bate was the chosen assassin has clearly not surprised any of my companions, but the timing has.

'I was certain Bate would not act,' says Aminta. 'He is a coward.'

'O'Neill's visit to London has convinced him that he will get away with it,' I say. 'Or perhaps he has reassured him that he will have a comfortable place at court once the King returns.'

'So, what now?' asks Sir Felix. 'I advised against throwing in our lot with Cromwell. It would have been better to have backed the King. Then Bate could have poisoned all the Cromwells he liked and it would have been no concern of ours.'

'All is not lost,' says Pole irritably. 'Fairfax may yet succeed him. We are already prepared.'

'What if Lambert succeeds?' asks Aminta. 'Or Harrison?'

'Harrison? Then we are all finished,' says Pole. 'But he won't.'

'Lambert may,' I say. 'He has some support still, I think.'

'Can Bate still be stopped?' Pole asks. 'Hyde could countermand it. He must realise the risks.'

'Hyde has always been in favour of assassination, as long as blame could not be traced back to him,' says Aminta.

'The King?'

'He doesn't want Cromwell's blood on his hands—another ruler executed would be a bad precedent. But his preferred course of action is simply to pretend that it isn't happening. He'll neither order Cromwell's death nor forbid it. Anyway, he's probably still in bed.'

'One of us must go to London and inform Thurloe,' says Sir Felix.

'Hardly you, my dear father,' says Aminta. 'Somebody will need to ride hard for the coast, then ride hard again from Dover.'

'It's me or Grey,' says Pole. 'I'm the better horseman.'

'But John will be listened to,' says Aminta. 'Thurloe will see him.'

They all look at me.

'Ripley has said he will kill me, if I so much as stir beyond the city walls,' I point out.

'I'll send him a message, asking him to meet me,' says Pole. 'I'll keep him drinking at some tavern. That will give Grey an hour or two to get clear of Brussels.'

'I shall need money,' I say. 'I have spent almost all I had.'

'Then you really will have to use your wits,' says Pole, 'for we have nothing to give you.'

'I think I know somebody who may be able to help,' I say.

I knock on the door of a decrepit house in a decrepit street. I hear a wooden bolt being pulled back and the door opens a crack. I shove my boot into the gap before it can close again.

'Good evening, Lisette,' I say. 'I hope you made a good profit from my last visit?'

'It was money your father owed me,' she says. 'You can't have it. It is spent.'

'I am happy to let bygones be bygones,' I say. 'I don't need your money.'

The door opens a little more. 'What do you need?' she asks.

'I should be grateful,' I say, 'if you can show me where to steal a horse. A fast one.'

I am sitting in an inn at Ostend. My horse is in the stables of another inn entirely. I have paid the innkeeper for his food for tonight and, to avoid suspicion, for mine too. Tomorrow he will find he has been gifted a horse, albeit one that will prove to be stolen if he makes enquiries. I doubt, however, that he will make enquiries, especially since the prominent white blaze can be dyed brown for as long as it takes to make a sale.

The sun is rising to the east, on the landward side. Before it sets in the west, I hope to be in Dover. There is no sign of Ripley or of anyone who wishes me ill. Pole must have detained him for more than the hour or so that he promised. I look around me for the tenth time. A merchant is sitting, reading through some bills. A couple of seamen are quietly at their tankards. When I stand, nobody shifts in their seat as if it is in their mind to follow me. Indeed, nobody even glances in my direction. I stoop and pick up my leather satchel and then, with my hat pulled down over my eyes, I stride confidently down to the quay.

'Good evening, Mr Black,' says the officer as I present my passport. 'Welcome to Dover. You have been gone some months. I hope you took plenty of orders for your wool?'

'My visit was satisfactory,' I say.

'You are lucky to have completed your crossing today. A storm is blowing up. The sea will be rough tonight and tomorrow.'

Well, that will impede Ripley if he is following in my footsteps. And yet I fear that Ripley has not followed because he does not believe he needs to follow.

'I hope I have arrived in time,' I say. 'I need to get to Westminster as fast as I can in order to report to Mr Secretary Thurloe. Do you have a horse I can borrow?'

'Of course, Mr Black. We've had one waiting for you on Mr Thurloe's instructions. Just in case you made it back alive. But you cannot travel tonight. You must hope that the storm will have blown itself out by the morning.'

Sam Morland

I had not realised, until I set out from Dover early this morning, that autumn was fast approaching. Last night's storm has stripped many leaves from the trees and they lie in green drifts across the road. Indeed, whole trees have been brought down. It was one of the roughest nights I can recall. Clouds still scud across the sky, racing east as I race west. But, though I started at dawn, it is late afternoon before I reach Westminster.

I find Thurloe in conference with Morland. They both turn to me somewhat wearily as I enter the room. You would think that they had ridden from Dover rather than I. Well, I suppose that it may be the end of a long day for them too. And what I have to say can be said to both of them. Morland's treachery, Willys's reprieve from exposure—these are matters that may need to be dealt with, but they can wait. First we must prevent Bate from killing his patient.

Morland nods in my direction. His face is as sleek, his hair as glossy as ever. I think that he may have gained a pound or two in weight since I last saw him. Whatever treachery he has indulged in, in the meantime, he is comfortable with it. But he is frowning. Thurloe too looks worried. Have they also had news of the latest plot?

'I have returned,' I say to Thurloe. 'And I have important information that touches on the safety of the Lord Protector.'

'Which Lord Protector?' asks Thurloe.

'Cromwell,' I say, confused.

'Which Cromwell?' asks Morland.

They look tired, but these questions are inexplicable. Are they both mad—or am I?

'His Highness Lord Protector Oliver Cromwell,' I say. I look from one to the other, hoping for some sign of comprehension.

'Oliver is dead,' says Thurloe. 'He died last night here in Whitehall, while the storm raged about him.'

'Cromwell is dead?'

'He has been sick for some time,' says Morland, examining his nails carefully. 'Dr Bate has been attending on him for some weeks. He has administered the strongest medicines that he dared, but sadly to no avail. The Lord Protector passed away some fifteen hours ago.'

'And the cause?' I ask.

'Ague,' says Morland.

'Bate has murdered him,' I say.

'How could you possibly know that?' asks Thurloe.

'Ripley told me in Brussels. Bate was to administer mercury, arsenic and antimony.'

'All good physic,' says Thurloe.

'In the right quantities, yes. In excess, no.'

Morland has been considering this. 'Do you bring with you any proof, other than what Ripley told you?'

'No,' I say. 'But it would seem that Bate has been in corre-spondence with Hyde.'

'Correspondence which you have?'

'No. I think that Daniel O'Neill carried the latest message. But even so—Ripley said that's what would happen and it has.'

'Will Ripley or O'Neill testify against Bate?' asks Thurloe.

'I would not imagine so.'

'No,' says Thurloe. 'I would not imagine so either—even if we could find either of them and bring him back.'

'Of course, we were warned, Mr Secretary,' says Morland, smiling.

'Possibly,' says Thurloe.

'By whom?' I ask.

'Esmond Underhill. After his arrest he was very helpful. He told us many months ago that he thought Bate was about to poison the Lord Protector. He wanted two hundred Pounds to reveal further details. And to be released, of course. But, my Lord, you thought it was not worth the money.'

'Underhill is a rogue,' says Thurloe. 'It seemed unlikely that anything he said was true.'

'Mr Secretary Thurloe thought,' says Morland, addressing me, 'that we should make further enquiries in Brussels as to whether Bate could be in contact with the Royalists there. But while we were prevaricating, it would appear that Bate has acted.'

'Underhill would have said anything to save his skin,' says Thurloe.

'Precisely,' says Morland. 'To save his skin he told us the truth. We ignored it. And now the Lord Protector is dead. Of course, Underhill's offer to us is known to very few people. Very few indeed. Perhaps that is as well. I mean, it would help nobody if it became generally known that this office had the information that would have saved Oliver but that we failed to act.'

'Where is Underhill now?' asks Thurloe.

Morland shrugs. 'Lisbon? Paris? Offering his services to the King of Spain or to the Grand Sophy of Persia? People like that are found only when they wish to be found. And I suspect he would want a lot more than two hundred Pounds to testify against Bate in court.'

'He's in Brussels,' I say. 'And I doubt he would testify against Bate either—not at any price you'd be prepared to pay. But if the Lord Protector's body is examined, it will testify. There will be evidence of poisoning.'

'Even if we could show it was poison,' says Morland slowly, 'suspicion might fall on others, not simply on Bate.'

'The only important thing now is to ensure that the Republic survives,' says Thurloe. 'Richard Cromwell must succeed to the office of Lord Protector without delay, before Lambert or Fleetwood or Fairfax can raise an army. We must move before news of the death reaches Brussels.'

'Better,' says Morland, 'that the death is announced as being the result of ague. Poison would be an unwanted complication. It opens the door to all sorts of questions.'

'Will the army accept Richard Cromwell?' I ask.

'They must be made to,' says Thurloe.

'Because,' says Morland, 'if Richard fails, then it could open the way for the Stuarts to return—which God forfend!' And Morland winks at me.

'But Bate has killed the Lord Protector...' I say. 'Is he to be allowed to escape unpunished?'

Neither appears to be listening, however. Cromwell is dead. He is part of history. There is nothing more to be done. It is more convenient for everyone that he died of ague, in spite of Bate's devoted care, than that Cromwell was murdered in a plot that Thurloe had been warned of months before and could have prevented. And Morland is not unhappy. A few months of Richard Cromwell and England will be looking across the Channel to Brussels. Why live under a Cromwellian monarchy when there is a Stuart one?

One death has changed everything. Morland, so long Thurloe's secret nemesis, is now his ally again. For the moment. All over the country, men will be re-examining their loyalties. Monck may now be ready to play his part. My stepfather will soon be writing to him again. And Willys? What is Willys doing?

'Willys,' I say. 'Did he know of this plot?'

'Willys? No, he would have told us,' says Thurloe. 'I think that the court have kept him in the dark.'

'Willys is in your pay?'

'Of course he is.'

'So Willys *is* a traitor?'

Thurloe looks puzzled. 'A traitor? No, he is on our side,' he says. 'How can he be a traitor?'

'Very well,' I say, 'what do you need me to do now?'

'Nothing,' says Thurloe. 'I am grateful to you for your work in Brussels. You are owed several months' back pay, which you can collect before you leave here. But we have no further need of you. And in any case, things have moved on. Nothing is as it was before. Nothing at all. You may return to your studies, as you wished.'

'The Republic doesn't need me further then?' I say.

Thurloe looks at me blankly. 'The Republic? No, it doesn't need you at all.'

I have one further task before I leave London. The moonlight that is assisting whatever journeys Thurloe and Morland are making is also helping me reach Gray's Inn. I know my way to Sir Richard's chambers without the assistance of any porter.

He is seated this time at his desk. The grate is empty and swept, though soon it will be time for fires again, I think.

'I bring you news,' I say. 'Cromwell is dead.'

'Dead?'

'Thurloe is, even as I speak, in Whitehall ensuring the succession of Cromwell's son. So, which side are you now on, Sir Richard?'

He looks at me. He clearly knows that I was working for Thurloe, but he also knows I have been in Brussels for some months. Whose side am *I* now on?

'Why should I tell you that?' he says.

'Because,' I say, 'your shifting allegiances have caused me many problems. The King decided you were loyal to him because you served his father well. And the King likes to think the best of people who served his father. You could not therefore have sent a letter to the King, inviting him into a trap. Except you did.'

'I knew he would not come,' says Willys.

'Why?' I ask.

'Because I had already told you that I did not have the men. And I knew you were too honest to lie to the King. I knew if you bore the letter, then all would be well.'

'You wanted the mission to fail?'

'Precisely. I intended no harm.'

'Why send the letter at all?'

'Thurloe made me send it.'

'You could not have refused? You could not be completely sure the King would not believe me.'

Willys hesitates for a moment.

'I betrayed nobody,' he says. 'You have to understand that.'

'And when O'Neill was in London? Did you tell Thurloe where he was?'

'Yes,' he says.

'And did you then warn O'Neill when Thurloe was about to arrest him?'

There is a very long pause.

'Yes,' he says.

'Why?'

'I am loyal...' he says.

'To whom?' I ask.

He looks around the room as if that person might be present. 'To...' There is another long pause. I wonder if he will ever speak again, then he says: 'You don't know how difficult it is. It is so hard to abandon your old loyalties, even when you see that the country's interests are this or that. It is difficult to betray your old friends. You must understand that?'

'And what *are* your old loyalties?' I ask. 'Which are your old ones and which are your new ones?'

Willys shakes his head. My question is too difficult. 'Does the King know everything?' he asks.

'Yes,' I say. 'But he has chosen not to believe it.'

Willys lets out a long sigh. 'My loyalty to His Majesty has never faltered,' he says. 'Never. I told Thurloe nothing that would be of use to him. I deliberately misled him. I saved O'Neill. You must tell them that.'

I wonder whether to tell Willys that Morland has betrayed him. I wonder whether to ask him about the Barret letters. He probably knows that Morland will betray him sooner or later, if it is to his advantage. Not everyone finds it difficult to abandon their old loyalties. Some find it very easy. Indeed, I think soon most people will have to do so. But there is no advantage to me in telling him what I know. Morland may, after all, be somebody I need in future. He was my enemy once, but no longer. Old betrayals need to be forgotten as well as old friendships. The world is turned upside down.

'So,' says Willys, 'all has happened as I intended. The King is well. No harm has been done.'

'If you say so.'

'Thank you,' says Willys, taking my hand. 'Thank you, Mr Grey. I am very grateful to you. Will you stay and take wine with me?'

'I am going now,' I say. 'I have to return home to Essex. My father has died recently. I have to inform my mother of the fact.'

He nods but I don't think he has heard me. He is thinking of other things.

I get up and leave the room. He does not say goodbye to me, nor I to him. After I close the door, I pause for a moment. I fancy I hear somebody sobbing. But I am not certain of that. I am not certain of anything.

I descend the stairs and go out into Theobalds Road. The sky is clear and the moon is bright. Tomorrow will be a fine day.

My Mother

My mother takes the news of her first husband's death with the stoicism that one might expect.

'Not before time,' she says. 'And the woman he was living with is left completely destitute?'

'I was able to help her earn a little money,' I say. 'But I fear it will not last long.'

'I am sure that somebody with her loose morals will think of a way of making more. She sounds as if she would stoop to most things.'

'She was recently involved in the theft of a horse.'

'A woman who will steal a husband will steal anything. If it was anything like your father, I assume that it was an old and rather useless horse?'

'No, it was the best I've had,' I say. 'I was sorry to have to part with him.'

'Did you visit your father's grave?'

'He shares a plot of ground with others. Many others. Lisette was unable to pay for a proper burial.'

'You have left your father's body in a pauper's grave?'

'Yes. I thought you would have no objection.'

'Well, he will at least be close to Lisette when she is buried. That is a comfort of sorts.'

'Mother,' I say. 'My father...'

'Who is now, as you have so often pointed out, dead...'

'Is he?'

'That is what you have just told me. You are getting more forgetful than I am.'

'No, I mean—is my father...is he actually my father? Sir Michael clearly thought I was very much like Sir Felix Clifford. When I told Sir Felix that, he almost choked and Aminta looked at me very oddly. Aminta said how much like Marius I am. Lisette said that I did not resemble the man she had been living with. We and the Cliffords have always been neighbours. And I am aware that Sir Felix has always—well, admired you.'

'You do take a long time to get to the point. You mean is Sir Felix your father? I would scarcely have encouraged you to marry Aminta if so. She would be your sister.'

'So, it cannot be true?'

My mother considers and then counts carefully on her fingers. She frowns and counts again even more slowly. For a while she holds onto her ninth finger.

'Absolutely impossible,' she says at length. 'And Aminta is married to Roger Pole now, so the question of marriage to you does not really arise.'

'Thank you,' I say. 'That is very reassuring.'

'In any case,' says my mother, 'she would only be your half-sister. And nobody would have known. Not for certain. And, when you think about it, that's the most important thing.'

'I loved her,' I say.

My mother pats my arm. 'Of course you do,' she says. 'I'd say better late than never, but I don't think that applies to love. If you have foolishly missed your chance—well, better not to know, I think. I have always believed in seizing opportunities when they arise. I hope Aminta is well?'

'Yes, when I last saw her. Fortunately she was unaware that she and her father had to leave England because of information that I had supplied to Mr Thurloe.'

'You think so?'

'Of course. She clearly bore me no ill-will. And if she had suspected, I am certain she would have paid me back in some way before now.'

'Such as ensuring that you were imprisoned on a diet of bread and water?'

'But that was necessary...'

'For as long as you were kept there? A day or two should have sufficed—a couple of weeks at the most.'

'You mean...'

'Oh, I can't be certain—but Aminta was certainly in contact with that nice Mr Morland. It is possible that she may have caused him to influence Mr Thurloe's thinking on the matter. I mean, a rumour or two may have spread to the effect that the Sealed Knot suspected you of betraying them and that it would be better that you were not released just yet.'

'I see,' I say.

'She did come to visit you to make sure that you were not suffering too much.'

'Or perhaps to make sure that I was suffering enough. She gave my cakes to the gaolers.'

'Well, that is an act of charity too. She is a kind woman. I'm sure that you bear her no ill-will,' says my mother.

'She did, of course, speak on my behalf to Sir Edward Hyde,' I say.

'Precisely. You remain very much in her debt. I hope you gave Sir Edward my best wishes, though, due to the nature of our correspondence, he would probably have remembered me as 472 rather than Mistress Grey.'

'I think Mr Morland reminded him of your past services,' I say. 'It would seem that he also told Sir Edward that my stepfather is playing an important role in the restoration of the King.'

'In his own estimation perhaps. The Colonel continues to correspond with General Monck. Cromwell's death has not stirred the General into immediate action as we hoped, but he is watching events with his usual caution. He feels, having been a Royalist and then a Parliamentarian, he can change sides only once more. If this new Cromwell does not work out any better than the old one, then I think he may finally be ready to bring his army south and support a Restoration. I do hope so. Republics are so dull. From what you tell me, the young King seems charming. He clearly charmed you.'

'He lacks seriousness.'

'I am sure that he can appoint serious ministers. Sir Edward Hyde is reputed to be very uninteresting.'

'The King is also unduly influenced by his women.'

'I am not sure what you mean by *unduly*. I think he sounds an admirable monarch—not at all like his father, who was rather cold and distant. And dead now, like your... Well, dead anyway.'

'As is Oliver Cromwell.'

'I suppose you will now return to your legal studies?'

'Perhaps. For a while. I have, however, written to a Mr Daniel O'Neill. He offered me a job. I may take it up, in due course.'

'I have met Mr O'Neill. Irish, of course, but thoroughly charming too. He will be an important man after the Restoration.'

'Yes,' I say. 'Once His Majesty returns to his rightful place.'

'I am pleased you have finally come to your senses,' my mother says, 'and that you have abandoned this Puritanism that you learned at Cambridge.'

'I was never a Puritan,' I say.

'Well, this Republicanism then,' says my mother. 'I believe you may actually become a Royalist.'

'I am beginning to think I have always been a Royalist at heart,' I say. 'And a loyal servant of His Gracious Majesty.'

My mother nods. 'As have we all. Except that some people have not been aware of it as they might have been. What an eventful year! Before we know where we are it will be Christmas again. I think this time we might find a little holly to decorate the house. And we could have a goose. With a spiced sauce. Don't you think so, John?'

'Why not?' I say. 'Why not.'

Postscript

May 1660

It is a fine day and the wind blows fair from France. The *Naseby,* hastily renamed the *Royal Charles,* is moored just off Dover beach. From the mainmast flutters the royal standard, not seen openly in this part of the world for over ten years.

A tall man with flowing black locks and blacker stubble on his chin emerges from the captain's cabin and walks unsteadily across the deck to the ship's rail. He blinks uncomfortably at the light reflected off the gleaming water. There are dark rings round his eyes. He has been up drinking all night with Sir Michael de Ripley and others, for who would waste a single moment of a day like this in mere sleep?

A flock of courtiers cluster around him, not so close as to crowd His Majesty, but close enough to bathe in the rekindled glow of kingship. Many of them have new titles, bestowed on them on board the ship. Others have had old titles restored. The Duke of Buckingham is absent, as is Sir Richard Willys, but near the centre of the group stands Viscount Pole, and a little further off Sir Samuel Morland. At the very back of the crowd, with no title at all but still content with his part in the proceedings, stands the young Mr Samuel Pepys. All seem very happy.

The King descends into a gilded barge in which he is rowed ceremoniously to the shore. Not far behind, a second boat brings many of the court—including Mr Pepys, who has used his elbows adroitly to gain a seat—and also one of the King's dogs. The dog shits in the boat. Mr Pepys laughs. Later he will write about it in his diary, but for the moment he enjoys the salt wind and the sun on his face. And, all the time, England gets closer, stroke by stroke. White cliffs tower above His Majesty for the first time in eight years.

King Charles II of France, England, Scotland and Ireland (and now recognised as such in all of those countries except France) surveys his people, clustered on the quayside. There's Monck, he thinks, with half a regiment of foot behind him. He took his time deciding which side he was on, but he's here now at least. He'll want me to make him a Duke. And that fat lump of lard must be the Mayor of Dover. He'll probably want a knighthood. They all want something from me. The pretty wench by the Mayor's side must be his wife or his daughter. Now, I wouldn't mind if *she* wanted something from me. And I'll wager the first thing the Mayor tells me as I step ashore is that he's been a Royalist all along. I can't believe the number of people who have told me they were secret Royalists the whole time. Honestly, if I'd known they were all Royalists, I'd have done this years ago. Maybe I should have even accepted Willys's offer. We might both have had a surprise.

The King places one shoe, with its bright new red heel, on the gangplank—then he pauses just for an instant, as if trying to ascertain whether this might not, in fact, be the most elaborate double-cross that Parliament has yet devised. How many times has Monck changed sides? And even if he can be trusted, do any of those men with muskets still hanker after a Republic? It would, after all, only take one. Well, there was no going back now.

He swallows hard and then raises his hat to the crowd in greeting. There is, in response, a cheer like the roar of a cannon. It both deafens and, in a strange way, soothes.

So far so good then. With his head still pounding from last night's debauch, the King proceeds slowly down the plank and enters his Kingdom.

AUTHOR'S NOTE

This book is self-evidently a work of fiction, though, equally clearly for those who know the period, many of the characters are real and many of the events actually happened.

Charles II, Cromwell, Pepys, Thurloe, Morland, Willys, Fairfax, Lambert, O'Neill, Brodrick and Bate all played a role in the real events of 1657-8. John Grey, the various members of the Clifford/Pole family, Esmond Underhill and Sir Michael de Ripley are conversely all imaginary. Especially Sir Michael de Ripley.

I have attempted to portray the real characters much as they were and to shape my fictitious ones according to the needs of the plot. I took as few liberties as possible with actual historical events. There was a plot to lure Charles II to England under circumstances not unlike those I describe—though the main source for this fact seems to be Samuel Morland, who claimed to have prevented it. He may not have been entirely truthful. Willys was certainly accused by Morland of going over to Thurloe, and the Barret letters (from which I have quoted) were cited in evidence. What Willys's motives were in doing a deal with Thurloe, how much he gave away and how much damage he did to the Sealed Knot remain a matter for debate—but Thurloe did describe him as his 'masterpiece of corruption', thus giving me a title for this book.

There were many attempts on Cromwell's life, and some were (reportedly) just as described. It is difficult to take all of the plots seriously, for the reasons I give—some were simply ludicrous and doomed to fail from the start. That, of course, did not stop the plotters from being executed. Cromwell took many of the precautions I mention in order to avoid such plots—his armour, his changes of route, his liking for rooms with more than one exit. His eventual death was announced as having been caused by ague, but it has been suggested that he was poisoned, quite possibly by his own physician, Dr Bate. It was a rumour that was current within a short time of the Protector's death, and Bate certainly never denied it. He eventually became Charles II's physician, thus serving three Heads of State.

Only very occasionally have I deliberately played around with dates or the sequence of events. One to which I must confess is the compressing of Willys's career as a double agent so that his denunciation by Morland occurs in 1658 rather than the following year. This is partly to suit the plot but also because many of the surviving facts about the case come from Morland and are not necessarily to be relied on. In any case, that Morland denounced Willys unsuccessfully in 1658 doesn't mean that he didn't successfully expose him the following year. Interestingly, there is also a story that Morland claimed that he and a 'Mrs Russell' had poisoned Cromwell and that Thurloe had 'had a lick' of the poison and been laid up by it. The source of that tale (and it is found nowhere else) is Sir Richard Willys, who may also have had a point to prove.

There is one other inaccuracy I must admit to. In the Prologue, I have Charles II sailing away from Shoreham beach under a full moon. It was in fact about ten o'clock in the morning when the boat faded from view. But this is a work of fiction and, honestly, a full moon works so much better.

ACKNOWLEDGEMENTS

Many of the books that I consulted in writing *A Masterpiece of Corruption* are listed in the acknowledgements section of my earlier book featuring John Grey, *A Cruel Necessity*. I would, however, like to repeat my indebtedness in particular to Geoffrey Smith's *The Cavaliers in Exile*, David Underdown's *Royalist Conspiracy in England*, Philip Aubrey's *Mr Secretary Thurloe* and D. L. Hobman's *Cromwell's Master Spy: A Study of John Thurloe*. Additionally, I have drawn on H. F. McMain's *The Death of Oliver Cromwell*, in which he sets out in detail the case for Cromwell having been poisoned by his doctors. For the character of Cromwell generally, books I consulted included Martyn Bennett's *Oliver Cromwell* and Christopher Hill's *God's Englishman*. Regarding the authenticity of the Barret Letters, there are two very thorough studies in the English Historical Review: David Underdown's *Sir Richard Willys and Secretary Thurloe* and Margery Hollings's *Thomas Barret: A Study in the Secret History of the Interregnum*. With regard to legal education and the status of lawyers in the seventeenth century, W. R. Preest's *The Inns of Court* provides useful information. And Lisa Picard's *Restoration London*, mentioned in previous acknowledgements, remains a joy to read.

I must also thank everyone at Constable & Robinson/Little, Brown for their help in the various stages of writing this book— especially Krystyna, Amanda, Florence and Joan (and Kate for advice on the website). My thanks are as ever due to David Headley and all at the DHH Literary Agency for their support, and last but not least to my family, including the newest member, Rachel, who shares the dedication at the front of the book.